A VERY ENGLISH CHRISTMAS

THREE LITERARY-INSPIRED NOVELLAS

CARRIE TURANSKY   MARGUERITE GRAY
CAROLE LEHR JOHNSON

FS
FLOWING
STREAM
BOOKS

A Very English Christmas ~ Three Literary-Inspired Novellas

By Carrie Turansky, Marguerite Gray, and
Carole Lehr Johnson

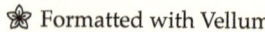

PART I
CHRISTMAS IN TETBURY
DECEMBER 2024

The streetlights in the village of Tetbury were just coming on as Emma Grace Langley towed her suitcase down Long Street, trying to avoid the deepest puddles.

Thank goodness the rain had stopped, but water still drizzled down shop windows where Christmas lights glowed on displays of holiday gifts. Evergreen wreaths with red ribbons and sprigs of holly hung from lampposts, and a few shops had small Christmas trees out front with twinkling white lights.

Seeing Tetbury decorated for Christmas reminded her of childhood holidays she'd spent with her grandparents. But as she thought of her recent losses, her spirit deflated, and the memories faded.

With a sigh, she trudged on. Up ahead, the sign for Harrison's Rare Books and Antiques swung from the wrought iron bar over Mimi's shop door. As she came closer, she glanced in the window at the display of vintage treasures—beautifully bound books, China tea sets, ivory fans, silver trays, porcelain dolls, and little figurines inspired by the characters in Beatrix Potter's books. Her throat tightened as she took in the whimsical jumble and recalled other visits. Maybe spending the next three weeks with Mimi would help her make sense of her mixed-up life and find a new path forward.

She pushed open the door, and the bell overhead jingled. Glancing around the shop, she took in the overflowing bookshelves, display cases, and tables filled with beautiful antiques.

Memories came rushing back, and she could almost see Grandpa Bill standing behind the counter wearing his navy-blue cardigan and sporting his dark framed glasses with that ever-present pencil over his ear as he greeted customers. But he'd been gone for almost two years, leaving another empty place in her heart.

"Mimi? It's Emma. Are you here?"

"Yes, dear. I'm coming." Mimi's voice floated out from her private sitting room and office at the back of the shop. The curtain slid aside, and Mimi stepped out. Her smile spread wide, and her rosy cheeks rounded. With her glowing expression and chin-length silver bob, she looked younger than her seventy-six years.

She sprang across the shop and enveloped Emma in a warm hug, bringing with her the scent of lavender and freshly washed woolens. "Oh, it's so good to see you!"

Tears stung Emma's eyes. To be wanted and welcomed was such a gift. So many others had rejected her or simply not cared enough to stay.

Mimi stepped back. "What a delight. I was thrilled when you called and said you'd like to come for a visit. I've got a pot of soup on. Let me flip the sign, and we can sit down and have dinner." She hurried across the shop, locked the door, and turned the sign to CLOSED. "So, how was the trip?"

"The train was crowded, but there was plenty of room on

the bus. It only took about three and a half hours. Not too bad for this time of year."

Mimi nodded, looking pleased. "I'm so glad you've come. It will be wonderful to have you here for Christmas. And it's especially helpful since Arleta is away. Her daughter is having a baby, and of course, she had to be there to help." She placed her arm around Emma's waist and guided her toward the back room.

A few minutes later, they sat at the small table in the sitting room. Mimi placed a bowl of chicken soup in front of Emma. The steam rose, tickled her nose, and made her mouth water.

Mimi reached across the table and took her hand. "Let's pray, and then we can enjoy our soup."

Emma nodded and closed her eyes.

"Father, thank You for bringing Emma here safely, and thank You for providing this food and all that we need every day. Please give us a good visit and time to reflect and enjoy all You have for us in this special season. We love You and pray all this in Jesus' name, amen."

Tears came to Emma's eyes as she whispered, "Amen."

Mimi met her gaze and sent her a concerned look. "What is it, dear? Why the tears?"

"It's nothing. I'm all right." Emma swiped away the moisture beneath her eyes.

Mimi tipped her head. "Emma, I've known you for twenty-seven years. I can tell when something is wrong."

Emma sipped a spoonful of the savory soup, debating her answer. Mimi had always been a kind and caring listener. She only offered advice when asked, and her words of wisdom were seasoned with love.

She pulled in a deep breath and met Mimi's questioning gaze. "I've been laid off from my job at the British Museum." Saying it aloud felt so shameful, so final.

Mimi's eyes rounded. "Oh, dear. I'm sorry to hear that. What happened?"

Emma stirred her soup, thinking of how to explain. "I took the position as assistant to the director of digital learning thinking it would be temporary and could lead to something else—something where I'd be working with artifacts and exhibits. With a master's in history from Cambridge, you'd think I could handle a simple job like that, but the director called me in last week and said they decided I'm not a good fit for the position. The door is still open for me to apply for a different position at the museum, but there's nothing open right now."

Mimi sighed. "I'm sure that's disappointing."

That wasn't the worst. The next blow had come only a few days later. "Then, last Saturday, Jason and I went out to dinner, and he informed me our relationship isn't working for him anymore."

Mimi blinked. "My goodness. What a thing to say!"

Emma shook her head. "I still can't believe it. We've been dating for almost two years. And with Christmas coming, I thought he might be ready to propose. Obviously, I was dreaming."

Sympathy shone in Mimi's eyes. "Well, if he doesn't realize what a treasure you are, then he's not worthy of you. Better to learn that now rather than later."

"I suppose you're right." She'd sensed a growing distance between them in the last few months, but she told herself it was just his heavy workload and challenging schedule with law school. She'd never imagined he was ready to break up.

Mimi laid her hand over Emma's. "Thank you for confiding in me. Now I know how to pray for you, and perhaps that's why you've come."

Emma searched Mimi's face. What did her grandmother mean?

"Not to worry, dear. Let's enjoy our soup, and then you can have a good rest. Everything always looks brighter in the morning."

∿

Emma woke to the scent of Mimi's freshly baked cinnamon rolls drifting into the guestroom. She showered and dressed, then joined Mimi in her sunny little kitchen. "Good morning."

Her grandmother looked up from her seat at the table and greeted Emma with a warm smile. Her cup of tea sat beside her open Bible. "Morning, dear. How did you sleep?"

"Very well." Which was a surprise. At her tiny flat in London, she hadn't had a good night's sleep since her dismissal from the museum. The breakup with Jason had added more distress to her restless nights. But here in Tetbury, safely tucked away from the noise of London and those painful issues, she'd finally enjoyed a peaceful night.

Mimi stood. "Let's have breakfast, then I have a new acquisition I want to show you."

Emma smiled. Mimi loved telling her about the latest items that had come into her shop—not just about the items themselves, but the stories behind them. Their shared love of history had been a bond between them for years, and the stories never failed to spark Emma's imagination.

After a hearty breakfast of scrambled eggs, cinnamon rolls, sliced oranges, and hot tea, they walked downstairs to the shop.

Mimi unlocked the front door, flipped the sign, then returned to the glass-topped display case that also served as a counter. "I have an old painting on consignment that is very unique, and if the story is true, the value will be quite high."

Emma smiled. "Tell me more."

Mimi opened the top drawer of the cabinet behind the counter. "I believe this watercolor is from the early 1800s."

Emma's eyes widened as Mimi carefully laid the painting on the counter. The woman in the portrait had a plain round face, but intelligent hazel eyes. She wore a blue dress, and a white cap covered most of her hair with only a few dark brown curls showing around her face. She sat by a sturdy tree with green and brown hills behind her.

Emma turned to Mimi. "The style of dress and cap look like they're from the Georgian or Regency era. Who is she?"

"Well . . . that is the question." Mimi's eyes twinkled. "The woman who brought it in said the artist is a distant relative who lived in Chawton and was a friend of Jane Austen."

Emma pulled in a sharp breath, and her gaze darted back to the painting. "Is this Jane?"

"She believes it is. And she has quite a story that goes with the portrait."

"If it truly is Jane Austen, you have an exceptional treasure. Who is the artist?"

"Her name was Violet Walford."

Emma thought of paintings and artists she'd studied in her art history classes. "I've never heard of her."

"Apparently, she lived a simple country life and was a busy wife and mother with a large extended family. She wasn't well known for her art."

Emma leaned closer and studied the image. It wasn't a masterful work, but it was a pleasing portrait. She looked up and met Mimi's gaze. "You say she told you the story behind the painting?"

Mimi smiled. "Yes, she did, and I think it's one you'll find especially meaningful."

A PORTRAIT OF FAITH

By Carole Lehr Johnson

"Give us a thankful sense of the blessings in which we live, of the many comforts of our lot. That we may not deserve to lose them by discontent or indifference."
Jane Austen

". . . thou anointest my head with oil; my cup runneth over."
Psalm 23:5

CHAPTER ONE

CHAWTON, OCTOBER 1816

*V*iolet Walford dragged her wet brush across the vibrant green paint block and swept it over the paper, her strokes mimicking the sway of the grass in the field before her. From the shelter of an ancient fir at the edge of a meadow, she took in the small stone barn, the next subject of her painting. The sound of the stream gurgled in the nearby woods, bringing her a sense of peace.

A cool autumn breeze tickled a tendril of her dark hair, and she pushed it behind her ear. She grabbed another brush, first dipping it into the tin cup filled with water from the stream. Raking it against the cool gray paint, she created the image of one of the tiny kittens darting through the long grass. Capturing their playful game brought joy she rarely felt except when painting.

A warm tear trickled from her cheek onto her outstretched arm, leaving a spot upon her sleeve. At four and twenty, she was officially on the shelf and unlikely to know the love of a man nor hold a child of her own in her arms. Responsibilities to her family came before all else.

A twig snapped, and Violet turned toward the sound. At the edge of the forest a woman dressed in grey stepped from the trees. Their gazes connected, and recognition flashed through Violet. The woman was Miss Jane Austen, who lived with her mother and sister down the lane.

Of course, Violet knew her, but they were not well acquainted.

"Good morning." She surveyed Violet's face, genuine sympathy in her eyes. "Are you unwell?"

Violet stood, wiping away another tear. "I am well. Thank you for your concern."

"Please excuse my impertinence, yet you do not appear so."

Disquieted by her query, as rarely did anyone ask after her well-being, Violet smiled politely. "Good day, Miss Austen."

She returned Violet's smile and dipped her chin. "Please, call me Jane."

"Very well, if you will call me Violet."

Jane's gaze came to rest on Violet's painting, and her eyes sparked with interest. "You are most talented." She linked her hands behind her back and leaned over the paper. "Such an adorable subject. I do so love to view kittens at play. Their lives appear so carefree, do they not?"

"I fear you have read my mind." Violet rarely showed her art to another, hesitant to hear their criticism.

Jane's thoughtful words eased Violet's normal reserve. As their conversation continued, something akin to fellowship settled around them, drawing them closer.

Jane asked several questions about her painting, saying her sister Cassandra was an artist. They sat and coaxed the kittens to come near and play as they trailed long pieces of grass along the ground, laughing at the antics of the furry creatures.

A clap of thunder sent the kittens scurrying across the meadow and into the barn.

Violet rose, shaking the grass from her dress. "I suppose I must be away. My mother will need my help preparing our meal." She did not mention she was solely responsible for most of the chores in their cottage, and her mother was most likely still abed.

Jane stood with her. "Yes. I as well, yet we must meet again."

Simultaneously, they said, "Indeed," making them both laugh.

"Let us do so soon," Violet said while gathering her supplies.

Jane assisted her, chatting about their chance meeting, saying God had made it so. They strolled toward the village in amiable conversation, the sound of distant thunder not hindering their pace.

Reaching Chawton Cottage first, Jane hesitated at the gate and turned to face Violet. "Forgive me for not inviting you inside. My mother frequently has headaches . . ."

"I understand. Let us meet in the meadow in a few days." Though Violet certainly did not fully comprehend Jane's reasoning for not inviting her in, she did not question her further. Word about the village said Mrs. Austen had a nervous disorder. She thought of her own mother and wondered if there were any other similarities.

"Yes. We may conspire at church. Let us devise a signal of sorts." Jane's eyes lit with mischief. She clasped her hands beneath her chin, and her gaze angled upward for a few moments. "Let us slip a note to one another should we be free to meet." She squeezed Violet's hand.

"Very well. Possibly at church?" Violet grinned. She felt like a girl again. Though their assignation was nothing of importance, it was at least a small happiness she could cling to. A new friend was not an insignificant thing.

Jane wished her well and entered Chawton Cottage, a half-smile on her lips.

A few drops of chilly rain speckled Violet's dark pelisse, but she cared not. This had been the most enjoyable day she had experienced in a very long while. After living in Chawton for seven years, she and Jane had only shared greetings at church or on the streets of Chawton, at the market, or elsewhere, but she observed that Jane was an amiable woman, always polite and agreeable.

To think after all this time, they would finally meet privately and discover they shared interests like walking, solitude, and reading.

Her thoughts wandered to earlier that year when Miss Benn requested the rector, John Papillon, attend her, saying she was surely dying. With that news, Violet's sister, Rose, rolled her eyes, saying, "She is *always* surely dying."

Jane and her family, as well as many of the villagers, were sympathetic to Miss Benn, as she was poor and, more times than not, needed assistance. The Austens often asked her to dine at Chawton Cottage, and Jane's brother invited her to Chawton House. Unfortunately, Miss Benn died shortly thereafter. Violet was glad the rector had seen her in time so he might bring her comfort. The Austens' involvement in aiding Miss Benn did them credit. Their family was most generous toward those in need.

The rain increased, pulling Violet from her memories, and she rushed home. She paused at the overhang of their thatched roof to catch her breath before going inside, gathering her thoughts to the duties awaiting her. Already late, she hoped her father had not yet arrived from his work in the Great House gardens.

When she stepped into the kitchen, he stood with hands on his hips, a glare in his eyes.

"Violet, where have you been?"

Violet shrank from his perusal, knowing she should be ashamed for her tardiness. Yet why should she not spend time with a friend—albeit a new one? Since her dearest friend, Emily, had gotten married and moved to Winchester, she had been lonely. If only her mother could pull herself from whatever plagued her.

However, for the moment, she must contend with her father. Life must have been hard for him all these years—just as it had been for her. Everyone needed grace, including her father.

"Papa, I am sorry. We will have something on the table soon. I promise." Her thoughts scrambled to discover what they may have on hand for a quick meal. Bread and onions could be found in the pantry, and the hens were laying well.

He stormed from the room, and she called after him, "We shall have the onion dish." His step faltered, and without turning, he nodded.

With a heavy exhale, she removed her pelisse and retrieved bread, onions, butter, salt, pepper, mustard, and vinegar, placing them on the long kitchen table.

"Rose, Daisy, Pansy!" Now was not the time for her sisters to be like their mother, feigning fatigue or a headache to be excused from helping. She called them again before she heard their footsteps outside the door.

"Each of you must do your part." She lowered her voice. "Papa is in a poor mood, and we must place dinner on the table quickly. Rose, slice the onions. Daisy, cut the bread, and Pansy, slice the eggs as soon as they have boiled."

Pansy nodded, setting her pale curls to dance around her face. Rose gave her a tight-lipped smile, and Daisy cocked her head and sighed.

Violet shook her head. Had they inherited their mother's failings? There was no time to ponder the situation if they were to care for their father.

Violet skittered around the room gathering plates and utensils while occasionally peering over each girl's shoulder to examine their progress. All worked quietly except Pansy. The girl could chatter away while saying nothing of consequence.

Benedict, their seven-year-old brother, bounded into the kitchen, thrusting a long stick through the air like a sword. "I have come to free the damsels!"

With a near miss of the *sword* above the bread, Violet snatched the stick from his hand and held it behind her back.

Still stinging from Papa's harsh words, she glared at her brother, using an equally sharp tone. "Ben! What have I asked you *not* to do in the house?"

He jutted his chin, no fear evident in his grey-blue eyes. "Not to bring my sword into the house."

"*And?*" Violet tossed the stick into the fire.

"Now why did you go and do that, Vi?" Benedict placed small hands on his narrow hips. "That was cruel."

Pansy halted her chattering, came to stand beside Ben, and patted his shoulder. "You can find another sword. Be kind to Violet." She nodded, wearing a somber countenance. "She is lovesick."

"Pansy! Please do not put ideas into your brother's head." Violet strode to the basin and washed her hands. "I am *not* lovesick."

Ben's expression pinched. "What does that mean?"

Violet's gaze went to Rose and Daisy, who both wore identical expressions, lips pressed tight to keep from laughing.

"Go on and laugh. You know Pansy says anything that passes through her mind without giving it any thought."

Pansy's face fell, and her chin quivered, stopping Rose and Daisy's suppressed grins.

"That was cruel too, Vi." Ben came to Pansy and put a reedy arm around her waist.

The door flew open, and their father stood on the threshold. "What goes on here? A man cannot have any peace in his own house with a wife all but dead and a brood of offspring who will not get along for ten minutes!"

He snatched his hat off the peg by the door leading to the yard. "Greyfriars will be more peaceful." He stepped outside into a thrashing rainstorm and slammed the door behind him, causing the dishes to rattle on the table.

Falling onto the bench, Violet rested her elbows on the table and buried her face in her hands. Why could she not have a normal family? She knew not what ailed her mother, yet she felt certain it was at the root of her father's distress. And his anguish flowed into the rest of the family.

She could not remember when they were an ordinary family. From the time she was a girl, before her other siblings came along, all had not been well.

Violet had taken the role of mother as soon as Rose was born. At eight, she cared for the baby, her mother, and the household duties. By the age of ten, her childhood had ended, and she had to step into adult responsibilities.

Tears spilled over her cheeks and onto the table, her shoulders quaking. Little arms encircled her neck. Ben pressed his head against her temple. Moments later, her sisters followed his gesture, and they huddled together in shared pain.

"Please do not cry, my Violet." Ben's sweet, childish voice broke her heart. She had to be strong for them. For herself. "We will heal you of being lovesick."

Violet sputtered through her tears and laughed. She

hugged Ben to her. "You certainly will, my dear. You certainly will."

The smell of burning bread and the sound of rain against the window broke the sweet moment, bringing Violet back to her reality.

CHAPTER TWO

$\mathcal{V}$iolet fed the fire in the kitchen, put the kettle on for tea, and sliced bread for their toast. The prior night's storm brought an additional chill to the air, and she glanced toward the door, a wave of relief swept through her at the sight of her father's hat hanging on the peg. He must have returned home late. She had spent the evening feeding her siblings, and while they ate, she took a tray to her mother and sat with her for a while.

After she and the girls cleaned the kitchen, she felt too weary to eat. She ushered her siblings off to sleep, then dropped onto her bed and stared at the ceiling listening for her father's return.

Once breakfast was on the table, she carried a tray up the squeaky stairs and called her father and the children to eat. The children came running, but her father did not.

Violet came down the stairs, the chatter of her siblings meeting her as she stepped into the kitchen. "Have any of you seen Papa?"

A chorus of no's and shaking heads confused her until Ben said, "He left for the Great House afore the sun."

Rose ruffled his hair. "How would you know that, sleepyhead?"

"Yeah." Pansy almost choked on her buttered bread. "You could sleep through cannon fire."

Ben opened his mouth to say something Violet well knew would be rude. "Ben—how do you know when Papa left?"

With a cheek stuffed with sausage, he said, "'Cause he told me goodbye."

Violet frowned. He had never woken her before going to work. Her gaze moved to the hat still on the peg. He would need it to shield his eyes from the sun while he toiled.

She went to the door and unhooked her pelisse, which hung next to her father's hat. "Eat your breakfast and clean the kitchen when you are finished. I will take Papa his hat. And do not be late for school."

They nodded, continuing to eat, but before she had closed the door behind her, Pansy said, "You just want to see Nate, so you can sigh over him."

Violet halted mid-step and opened her mouth to release a tart reply. Instead, she stepped out and closed the door silently, a chorus of giggles following her. She would be certain to question Pansy about her assumptions regarding Nate—yet not now.

The warm, rich scent of wood smoke brought with it the realization of the change in seasons, and Violet prayed the upcoming winter would not be harsh. Her mother may not withstand it. She appeared to grow weaker with the cold last winter, leaving her thinner.

If only Dr. White could discover the source of her ailment. Papa's behavior toward his wife held no sympathy, which baffled her all the more.

Violet felt a pang of remorse for occasionally growing short-tempered by her mother's idle behavior. Why could she not merely pick herself up and *do* something? Whenever she tried to discuss this with her father, he closed himself off and would not speak of it.

Thankfully, the walk to the Great House offered some remedy as the sun shone upon her, warming her spirit and her body. Though the distance was short, it afforded her some solitude from life's turmoil. The thought of meeting her new friend again thawed her icy mood. The sudden burning of tears brought a prayer to her lips, and her steps faltered.

"Heavenly Father, please forgive my petulance. I must count my blessings rather than my burdens."

As Violet turned onto the path leading to the Great House, something brushed against her legs, and she jumped. She looked down to see Tilly, the village cat. Her orange and cream fur glistened in the morning sun, and she bent to rub her ears.

"You are a spoiled mouser, Tilly. I must deliver Papa's hat." With one last pat, she told her, "Stay out of trouble."

The cat meowed a response and sauntered into the nearby field, taking up a position in the tall grass, eyes and ears alert.

The stone façade of St Nicholas Church stood to her right, and she wished she had time to enter and spend a moment in prayer. Perhaps on her return she could do so.

Her regard now on the Great House, she saw Mada Dacre, one of the kitchen maids, exit a side door and stride toward the stables in Violet's direction.

"Good morning, Mada. Have you seen my father?"

The girl's eyes widened, and her step faltered. "Good morning, Violet." She glanced over Violet's shoulder. "I believe he is in the walled garden."

Violet lifted the hat between them. "He forgot this."

Mada nodded but stood still as if waiting for Violet to leave.

Violet took a few tentative steps, then turned back to speak to the maid. Movement at the stable door caught her attention, and Nate stepped out pushing a wheelbarrow. Mada's face flushed, and Violet pretended she had not seen him.

"Thank you, Mada."

The girl muttered something unintelligible and rushed toward Nate. He stopped, his gaze on Violet. Mada pulled something from the pocket attached to her apron and handed it to him, which he tucked into his coat pocket, smiled, and stepped toward Violet. Mada put her hand on his sleeve, and he once again paused while she chattered on, and he listened without response.

Violet turned away and refocused her attention on her task, an odd sensation prickling her stomach. She would not look back. Nate owed her nothing since he did not know of her feelings for him, and he had never done nor said anything to make her believe he held any interest in her.

She rushed toward the garden, praying she would not have to see Nate and Mada together again.

"Violet!" Nate called after her.

The sound of her name mingled with the squeak of the wheelbarrow following behind her. She *had* to find Papa so she would not have to speak with Nate. Her tear-filled eyes would reveal her feelings, and she could not bear such humiliation.

VIOLET HELD her father's hat in both hands, extending it toward him. He leaned on the shovel's handle, the blade planted in the ground at his feet, his expression not exactly a scowl, yet his eyes held no light.

The squeal of the wheelbarrow brought his gaze to look over her shoulder. "Nate, dump the load over there." He pointed to a freshly turned bed against the far wall. Far enough that Nate could not overhear.

Violet steeled herself against the harshness in his voice. "You left this, and I know how the sun bothers you." She stretched her arms further in supplication, the hat shaking in her hands.

"Vi." Her father murmured her name. "I . . . am . . . sorry for the anger I showed." He took the offered hat and hung his head.

It had been a long time since he had used his pet name for her. She took a step closer, lowering her voice. "'Tis alright, Papa. I know it must be hard with Mamma's illness and such."

His head snapped up. "Your mother is not ill. She could control her moods if she wanted, yet she chooses not to. 'Tis all that is wrong with her." He crushed his hat onto his head and stabbed the shovel into the earth with more force than necessary.

"Papa. Please tell me what is wrong. I am no longer a child." She sniffled. "Never have I been allowed to be a child."

The shovel froze, and he looked at her, his face so full of pain Violet's breath caught.

"I know, and I am sorry for that as well. Yet your mother—"

The desire to know the truth surged through Violet.

"Why does she behave thus, Papa? Why are you angry all the time?" The tears spilled over her cheeks as quickly as the words poured from her lips. Until now she had not the courage to ask the questions that had plagued her for years. She swallowed hard, then noticed Nate across the garden watching them, expression curious and sad.

Violet backed away. "Nothing will ever change if you will

not tell me *why.*" She made to depart, and he grabbed her arm.

"Please stay." He glanced around, saw Nate, and whispered, "We will speak this evening."

The doubt she felt must have shown on her face, for he said, "I promise."

She nodded and left him, taking sluggish strides across the garden. When she reached the exit, she looked back to see Nate offering her father the bundle Mada had given to him. He opened it, broke off a piece of something, and popped it into his mouth, bringing a smile to her father's care-worn face.

Nate met her gaze and dipped his chin as if understanding their situation. She could not muster a response. A smile was all she could offer before rushing away.

Thankfully, Violet did not run into Mada again. She strode straight to the church and entered. Kneeling at the altar, she removed her handkerchief. Though tattered and sorely in need of mending, it was her favorite. Her mother had shown her how to make it when she was but five years of age. That was one of the few good memories with her mother.

Violet closed her eyes and fisted her hands together, placing them under her chin.

"Oh, dear Father in Heaven, help my mother and father. Only you know the truth and how to heal the brokenness. Please prepare my heart to hear what papa has to reveal, for it must be most dire to have caused such turmoil in our lives for so long."

The chapel door opened with a groan, and Violet shot to her feet. On the threshold stood her father, hat in hand. She choked on a sob and flew into his arms. After a slight hesitation, he hugged her tight and said into her hair, "My dear, sweet girl."

Moments later, they sat on the front pew, her head on his shoulder, cheeks damp with tears.

"It is a hard story to tell," he began. "You were too young to remember. Mayhap three."

She wanted to look into his eyes yet was afraid of what she would find there. "Yes, Papa."

"Your mother was so excited to find she was with child again. We wanted you to have a brother." His swallow vibrated, and he cleared his throat. "It was a difficult birth. The child was large, yet he came when the doctor expected. When she was lying in, there were difficulties."

"Him?" Violet muttered.

"He was to be called George after our king." His shoulders shook with the memory, and he hugged her closer to his side.

"Oh, Papa. I am sorry. No wonder Mamma was so heartbroken."

He tugged his handkerchief from his pocket and swiped his face. "Yes. As was I, yet she never considered *my* grief." He spoke the words with bitterness.

Violet did not reply, holding her breath lest he stop speaking of the past.

"It is of no importance. All that is left to say is your mother withdrew most gradually. By the time you were about eight, she took to her bed and rarely rose. I had a woman in a few times a week, and you learned much from her. It was our loss that she left Chawton to live with her daughter and help her care for her increasing brood."

He smiled to himself. "They were a lovely family. So . . . happy." He shrugged. "With shame, I must say how envious I was."

Continuing, he said, "The doctor believed another child would set things to right. For a brief time, she grew better and then Rose was born. She appeared glad for that, yet when it seemed Rose was not enough either, Daisy, then Pansy, came along, and she grew worse again. With Benedict being a boy, I felt certain he would be the cure."

Her father shook his head. "She fell further into distress. Or that is what Dr. White believed, based upon the years since George's death. For some reason he could not ascertain, he stated Benedict's birth brought back all the pain of losing George."

"I do not understand. She has a houseful of children. Why at the loss of one should she forsake the rest?"

He pulled in a long breath and released it. "She convinced herself that she was being punished because of her deep disappointment at your being a girl and then the others came —all girls."

Violet closed her eyes at the insanity of it. "But what of Ben? Did she not see him as a blessing? She had finally received a son." It was a common thing for sons to be esteemed over daughters. Unfair though it was.

"One would believe so. I asked Dr. White about it, and he had no answers. Though he said her symptoms spoke of melancholia—despondency, lack of appetite, insomnia, and irritability."

"Is there no remedy?" Violet asked.

He pursed his lips. "Dr. White said he did not ascribe to most of them, saying for his part they are inhumane—leeches or an asylum."

Violet's emotions scattered from shame to astonishment at the cruelty of it all. She thought of Dr. White and his kind ways. She silently promised to seek him out and see if a new remedy may be found. Then she prayed as she had before her father arrived. Yet this time, she understood more and prayed for her mother's healing.

CHAPTER THREE

$\mathcal{V}$iolet's dark mood hung over her like the dove grey clouds floating above as she walked to church. Dr. White was away for a time, so she could not speak with him about her mother's moods.

A redwing flew overhead, close enough for Violet to see its red underwings and black-streaked breast. Seeing one was a sure sign of winter's soon arrival.

Father trudged ahead of his family who shadowed him like a row of ducklings following their mother, Violet the last of them. She tugged her woolen cloak tighter, the wind holding a decidedly sharper chill to it than when she rose that morning.

Pansy's constant chattering flowed on the breeze toward Violet, and she winced at what the villagers thought of the girl.

"Violet," a voice whispered in her ear. She turned to peer into Jane's hazel eyes. "Good morning." Jane smiled and kept pace with Violet's stride. "I have come to church alone, so we may speak without concern. As you know, Cassandra is away to Kent, and Mother and Martha have colds." She looked around to see if anyone was nearby. "May we meet today? If so, can you bring your paints? I have a favor to ask of you."

Violet's eyebrows lifted. "Indeed?"

Jane moved closer and lowered her voice. "Yes. I have considered what Christmas gift to purchase for Cassandra and would very much like for you to do a painting for her."

The corners of Violet's mouth lifted in amusement. "Certainly, you jest."

Jane tilted her chin up. "No. I do not. You are an excellent artist, and I would be honored to purchase one of your paintings."

"No one has ever asked to possess any of my artistic endeavors." Violet slowed her steps as they turned onto the path toward St. Nicholas Church.

"Have you shared any of your paintings with others?" she asked as though she knew the answer, an undertone in her voice.

"Well . . . not precisely."

"Violet!" she said in a hushed pitch. "You have never shared your talent?"

Violet shrugged. "I have very little time to fashion much. What with the household cares, the children, and my father."

Jane cleared her throat. "What of your mother? You rarely speak of her." Curiosity as well as concern shone in her eyes.

Violet's throat tightened. Could she share her deepest fears with Jane? She longed to unburden herself to a true friend, and she sensed Jane could be trusted.

"If you are willing to hear my cheerless account, I will do so this afternoon." She gave her a polite smile, knowing it did not reach her eyes.

Jane squeezed her arm, nodded, and broke away to go into the church, striding toward her family pew.

As Violet entered behind her, she stepped toward her family pew and found her father's stern eyes upon her. He impatiently waved an arm toward her usual seat, and she slipped onto it with a miserable smile.

The sermon, Violet shamefacedly admitted, did not keep her attention. Her thoughts eddied about like the stream by the meadow, turning toward her mother, father, and Nate. More prayer was definitely needed.

Following the service, she was the last to rise from their pew. She stepped into the aisle not paying attention to her surroundings. She stumbled into the broad back of a man. "Pardon me, sir."

Nate turned and met her eyes. "No apologies are necessary, Miss Walford."

His deep voice unsettled her. Their gazes held as heat crept into her cheeks, rendering her speechless.

Nate took a step aside, lifting his hand to gesture her ahead of him.

As she passed, he leaned closer and whispered, "I adore your rose-scented hair."

Violet was certain he heard her swallow the lump in her throat. Once again, their eyes met. His gaze held no guile. If anything, those green eyes held affection. She licked her lips, and he watched the movement.

"I . . . I must go." She dipped a shallow curtsy and rushed from the church, abruptly passing Jane, who gave her a questioning stare.

Violet caught up with her family, trailing along after them as she had done on their way to the church. Her mind reeled with what she *thought* she heard Nate say. She wanted to laugh, cry, and tremble all at once. Had she imagined it?

"Violet!" Her father now walked by her side. "What was that about? You bolted from the church without greeting the rector." He hesitated, his demeanor now one of concern rather than anger. "Are you unwell?"

She gulped down her dread. "Papa, I fear I have a

headache." She pressed her fingers to her temple. "Perhaps I should lie down for a while. We have already laid out the meal. The girls can serve it easily enough and take Mamma a tray."

He placed a hand on her arm. "I am sorry, my dear. You must rest, and I shall put everything right. We can manage without you for one afternoon."

"Thank you, Papa. That is kind of you." She tried to smile —but failed. When had anyone ever been concerned about her other than doing the chores and caring for others? She reprimanded herself for the uncharitable thought, remembering to count her blessings. Perhaps their recent talk in the church had affected him as well. The tearful exchange was indeed a blessing.

Violet spent an hour in bed, forfeiting the meal she had no stomach for and looking through her small window at the soon to be leafless trees. Birds chirped their songs, the crisp scent of autumn permeating the air. The house was at rest as was the custom on Sundays, and she rose. With soundless movements, she gathered her painting supplies, put on her cloak, and slipped through the kitchen door. The air had grown more chilled, and she shivered, wishing she had remembered her gloves.

Near the stream by the meadow, Jane sat upon a thick woolen blanket, a small brown basket by her side. Jane waved her over, rising to her knees.

"I have brought fresh buns, gooseberry jam, and a jug of tea which is still hot." She removed a cup from the basket and placed it on the blanket and asked Violet to sit, pouring tea as if they sat in some lovely parlor by the fire.

"This is most thoughtful of you, Jane." She took the cup and sipped, the soothing liquid a balm to her confused emotions.

"Now, dear Violet. Tell me about your mother . . . and Nate."

Violet's hands trembled, and she nearly spilled the tea, and though warmed by it, she shivered.

"Forgive me. I did not mean to upset you. Yet it is quite clear the man has regard for you. I saw him whisper to you as you passed him in the church." One side of her mouth crept upward.

Violet studied her tea, uncertain what to say. If what she heard was true, it was most improper of him to say so. Why then did it fill her with warmth?

"Do not feel obliged to share the interaction. Your face revealed much. Do you not also hold him in regard?" Jane busied herself with placing a bun on a small plate and spreading it with jam, then placed it in front of Violet, her stomach growling at the sight.

Jane laughed. "You could not eat when you arrived home, could you?"

Violet shook her head, sighed, and took the bun. "Thank you." She ate a small bite. "This is delicious. I appreciate your thoughtfulness."

"I was concerned when you rushed away. But if I had a certain tall, sandy-haired man showing me attention, I should be quite undone. As you obviously are."

Though out of sorts, Violet grinned. "He said something to me I thought I most surely imagined."

Jane perked with anticipation. "Share all!"

Violet tilted her head back and peered at the darkening sky. "He said, 'I adore your rose-scented hair.'"

Jane straightened and clapped her hands beneath her chin. "He did not?"

"He did." Violet's spirits lifted and soared. He really had said it. It was not her imagination.

"Oh, my. Most romantic." Jane's eyes glistened, then

suddenly dimmed. "Violet, I have a confession to make. You have just shared something so wonderfully private. I fear I must do the same as we have become dear friends." Her gaze fell to the blanket. "I am a writer."

The soft murmur of the stream mingled with birdsong while Violet digested Jane's confession. "You—*write?*"

"Yes. Though it is common knowledge among my family, I want to share it with you." She nibbled on a bun. "Cassandra paints, and I write stories and plays and share them with my family. And of course, with dear Martha, and the closest of friends, which now includes you."

Jane sighed. "We have much laughter when I share my characters and their antics. Sometimes we perform small plays for entertainment."

"It sounds lovely." Violet blinked back tears. Though she and her siblings did occasionally share laughter, it was rarely enough and certainly did not include their parents. A twinge of jealousy snaked through her, and she quickly tossed it aside.

"I did not mean to cause such sad memories." Jane placed a hand on Violet's. "I now recall you wanted to speak of your mother."

It took Violet a few moments to gather her thoughts and courage, but she finally shared all her father had told her of her mother's past. By the time she finished with the dismal tale, Jane's tears flowed.

"Please do not cry. You are not to blame for my woes. Yet I thank you for allowing me to unburden myself."

They sat in companionable silence for a while until Jane said, "I believe your thought to speak with Dr. White is a good one. He is a wise man and keeps up with the most recent medical knowledge."

"As soon as he returns, I shall seek his opinion."

"And I shall keep an eye on *your* Nathaniel Byrd."

"Jane, he is not *my*—"

"Do not go against me. I have not told you how I have observed him watching you. He certainly has no interest in Mada Dacre."

Violet flinched. "How do you know of Mada and Nate?"

"I watch Nate, *and* I watch Mada. She desires him, and he desires *you*." She pinched her lips together and gave a determined nod.

Violet had no words. Did Nate truly desire her? Her heart sank. It mattered not. She was not free to be with him.

"I cannot think of him. No matter how I care to. My siblings, my father, and my mother need me. What am I to do?"

"You must love and receive love in return. Dr. White shall have an answer, and your family will heal." Jane furrowed her brow. "Tell me, for the writer within me, what is there about Nate that draws you to him?"

Surprised by the question, Violet thought carefully. "He is most handsome."

"I am aware of that truth." She laughed. "Yet what else?"

"He is polite and dignified. And good-humored." Violet's face heated. "He is also a little shy."

"Yet not shy enough to hold back his compliment of your rose-scented hair." She waggled her eyebrows.

Violet loved Jane's sense of humor and sweet nature.

"I near forgot. What about the painting for Cassandra?" Violet asked.

"Oh, yes. I hope this does not sound too vain, but would you paint a portrait of me?"

Taken aback, Violet believed she would want a painting of the kittens at play or a landscape of the meadow. "Of you?"

"And why not, pray tell?" Jane crossed her arms over her chest.

Violet shrugged. "I have never done a portrait. Only animals, cottages, and landscapes."

"You may paint anything within your sight, dear Violet."

"That is most generous of you, but I am not so certain." She fidgeted with the clasp on her paint box. "I will try."

"Thank you. Now as to payment."

"Oh, I could not accept payment. You are my friend."

"Friend or no friend, you shall accept something. Whether coin or otherwise."

Violet stared at Jane, wondering if she could achieve such a task. Knowing Nate had some regard for her bolstered her to a level she had never felt, and coupled with Jane's encouragement, perhaps she could achieve more than she had ever dreamed.

CHAPTER FOUR

The sweet scent of autumn, coupled with the recent talk with Dr. White, left her with a small measure of hope. He believed Mrs. Walford had suffered a nervous collapse when she lost her infant son years ago. At first, she lived in denial, somewhat functional as before, until Violet was about five or six.

Gradually, Violet learned by watching her mother at the daily tasks before she slipped into the collapse. Within a year or so, Violet handled most of the family's needs. She cooked, sewed, cared for the house, and catered to her mother's promptings.

The morning had been fine considering it was now November and cold yet sunny. Her mind pondered what to prepare for their evening meal. She approached the apothecary to collect the laudanum the doctor prescribed for her mother, saying there was some merit to tiny doses for her condition, and they should try it.

"Violet."

She looked up to see Nate standing outside the shop's doorway, wearing an unabashed smile. He held his hat in both hands, his sandy hair rumpled by the wind. In this state, Violet found him to be most endearing.

"Good morning." He bowed slightly.

Violet's cheeks flamed, the memory of his last words still thrumming through her mind.

"Am I so hideous as to render you speechless?" He chuckled nervously. "Shall you run from me again?" Doubt edged his words as he stepped away from the shop.

Her gaze flew to his eyes which held no humor, only questions. Did he believe her unaffected?

"No . . . I mean . . . you are far from hideous." Violet felt such a fool. Why did he cause her to flush and stammer?

He leaned closer. "I meant what I said at church."

A woman cleared her throat. "May I be allowed to pass?"

They turned to see Mrs. Deedes, the village gossip. Her feathered hat bobbed in the breeze, making Violet think of a Bantam rooster in more ways than the feathers. The birds were small of stature, with a self-assured demeanor.

"I beg your pardon, Mrs. Deedes." Nate stepped aside, allowing her to pass.

Violet did likewise. "Mr. Byrd was merely greeting me." She nodded at him, pushed past, and entered the apothecary, both relieved and regretful to break their interaction.

Mrs. Deedes huffed. "Courting on the doorstep of a shop is most unseemly and not to be borne."

Hearing the comment, Violet's already heated cheeks tingled with fire. Before the day ended, her father would hear a much-exaggerated version of the occurrence.

The apothecary gave Violet a bottle of laudanum with written instructions on how to administer the medicine, saying the doctor prescribed the smallest dose possible, and recommended the patient to take a brief walk each day.

He said the laudanum would give her mother a more restful sleep, which was something much needed for someone with her condition, affording her a little more vigor the following day.

Violet tucked the carefully wrapped bottle into her basket, and still reeling from the encounter with Nate, she made her way down the street toward home. Within a few moments, Nate walked by her side.

"Good morning again, Violet." He clasped his hands behind his back. "May I walk with you?"

Fearing he could hear her thumping heart, she nodded yet glanced around to see if anyone watched them.

He sidled closer and whispered, "Do you fear being seen with me?"

Taken aback by his question, Violet shook her head and opened her mouth to speak when Jane appeared at her other side.

"Good morning, Violet, Mr. Byrd." Her eyes held cunning, and Violet heated. What was her friend about? "Lovely day, is it not, Mr. Byrd?"

"Yes, Miss Austen." He studied Violet's face yet kept speaking to Jane. "It is exceptionally lovely, though with some *coolness*."

His enunciation of the final word caught Violet's attention. Did he suggest her attention to him was not warm enough?

Jane shot him a bewildered look, but he seemed not to notice, his eyes intent on Violet. "I merely wanted to bring you this note." She slid it into Violet's basket.

"Good day to you both." Jane gave a quick nod and rushed ahead of them, disappearing into the butcher's shop.

Violet watched her retreat, the blue satin ribbons of her bonnet trailing over her shoulder. "Jane quite surprised me. I had not expected to see her today."

"The two of you are now friends?" Nate slowed his pace, and Violet wondered if it was out of politeness or to slow their walk.

"Yes . . . well, better acquainted, since discovering we have much in common." She dared not reveal their meetings as she would not want him intruding.

He nodded. "I think it a fine thing. Everyone needs a dear friend."

"Yes. Indeed." Violet knew not what to say to the man, especially since they strolled through the center of the village with all to witness her discomfort. A sudden image of her father observing them together caused her step to falter, and Nate quickly grabbed her arm to steady her.

"Are you unwell?" True concern shone in his green eyes, his deep voice soothing.

His worried expression reminded her that beauty was in the beholder's eye, yet she thought him the most handsome man in her acquaintance. The way his sandy waves fell across his forehead when he moved quickly made her heart to flutter.

Oh! But she must take hold of herself. She could barely carry on a conversation with the man. He must think her simple-minded.

As they neared her cottage, Pansy came bursting from the door, waving something high over her head, laughing hysterically.

Violet halted abruptly and grabbed Nate's arm, tugging him off the path and into the gap in the privet hedge so Pansy could not see them.

Nate opened his mouth, and Violet shushed him with a finger to her lips. His eyes widened, and he moved closer and whispered, "Why are we hiding?"

Pansy squealed and ran past their hiding place. "You will not catch me, Ben!"

Within moments, Ben raced by. "Pansy! Stop this instant. That is mine."

Violet heaved a sigh of relief and peeked around the hedge. "They are gone. For now."

Nate's shoulders slumped, and he blinked, confusion clearly expressed in his eyes. "You did not answer my question."

Violet wanted to run from him just as Pansy ran from Ben —but for a different reason. "No, of course I do not fear being seen with you." Her voice cracked.

He stood straighter, gaze firm upon her face. "I *see* your hesitation." His lips parted, skin flushing. "Unless I have misread your intentions, I sensed you would care for my company."

"I do!" she blurted.

Pansy and Ben ran by again, this time noting Nate and Violet's presence. Pansy's eyes caught sight of them, and her mouth dropped open, but she continued running into the house.

Violet lifted her eyes heavenward. "Nate. I must apologize for my siblings' behavior . . ."

A long silence fell between them. Violet was at a loss. She wanted to become more acquainted with this man. How could she tell him her life was not her own? That her family owned her body and soul? *Oh, dear Lord, please give me strength.*

VIOLET ENTERED the kitchen and found Pansy sitting at the table nibbling a biscuit, gaze intent on the door. Her eyes gleamed with superior satisfaction.

"Good day, sister." The girl curved her lips up, more resembling a young woman of eight and ten rather than nine. "Did you and Nathaniel Byrd enjoy your journey into the privet?"

Violet breathed deeply, containing her ire. She bit the inside of her cheek, removed her cloak, and sat beside her sister, who flippantly tossed a blonde curl over her shoulder.

She clenched her teeth. "It is not wise to spy."

Pansy lazily reached for another biscuit. "I did not spy. Ben and I merely walked by and saw you."

"Running like beasts is not *walking*." Violet rose and peered down at her. "I forbid you to share what you saw with Papa."

"You shall not tell me what to do." She stood, popped the last bite of biscuit into her mouth, and stared at Violet while she chewed, eyes defiant.

Ben skipped into the kitchen and stopped when he caught sight of them staring at one another. "Papa's home. I told him about seeing you and Nate in the hedges." He snatched up a biscuit and ran like his shirttail was on fire.

Violet moaned. "To be free of this turmoil."

"What turmoil?" Mr. Walford asked from the open doorway.

The scent of burning halted the interaction. Violet grabbed a cloth and strode to the stove. "Pansy, what are you baking?"

"More biscuits." She shrugged. "Your scolding made me forget they were in the oven."

Violet jerked the pan from the oven and slammed it to the surface. "Never forget again. The entire cottage may have burned to the ground."

"Girls! What goes on here? It is unlike you to argue. Poke fun, yes, but never argue." He sat and drew the plate of biscuits toward him. "Pansy, did you bake these?"

"I did, Papa."

He took a bite. "Tasty. Just do not forget them next time. Understand?"

"Yes, Papa." Pansy patted his shoulder and shot Violet a haughty expression as she left them.

Was the girl growing up far too fast? Or was her owning secretive information making her too bold?

Mr. Walford cocked his head and met Violet's gaze. "We must speak." He waved a hand toward the bench.

Violet sat and held the basket she carried in front of her. She then recalled Jane's note inside, the signal of another afternoon meeting. She glanced at the small clock on the shelf.

"Yes, Papa." She folded her hands on the table in front of her.

"I received a visit today from Mrs. Deedes." He pursed his lips, stood, and put the kettle on. "I am in need of some tea. You?"

"I believe I shall." She made to stand, but he stopped her.

"Keep your seat. I shall do something for you this time."

Shocked, Violet nodded. He had done nothing for her since her mother took to her bed, leaving her to fend for them all, aside from the offer for her to lie down after church because of her aching head. He seemed different since their discussion at church after she had delivered his forgotten hat.

Silence settled over the kitchen until brewed tea sat before them. They sipped for a few moments in the silence.

"I know Mrs. Deedes embellishes her tales. Your mother had issues with her before you were born." The mention of her mother caused his face to flush.

Should she tell him of her visit with the doctor? Reveal what they were trying? It was unlike her to do something without asking her father's advice. She supposed desperation caused her to do so.

"Nate is a fine young man. You could do much worse than he. Should your feelings for him grow, the two of you could live here. I rely on you more than I should, Violet. Yet there is nothing I can do but insist you stay. You know I cannot do my work at the Great House and care for your brother and sisters. Not to mention your mother. She is helpless, not wanting to do anything but wallow in her self-pity. Yet she is my wife, and I must attend to her, though she wants for nothing but her own selfish needs."

Speechless, Violet twisted her fingers, head down.

"I know I ask much of you, my dear. Yet what else may I do? I need you." He placed his thick, muscular hand over hers. "Do you understand?"

In a small, timid voice she said, "Yes, Papa." A tear slipped down her cheek and landed on his hand, and he started.

"I am sorry." He released her and walked from the room.

Violet cried quietly for what seemed an age when Pansy returned. Once she met Violet's gaze, her saucy smile faded.

"Please forgive me, Violet. I was only teasing you. Nate is a very handsome man and would make you a wonderful husband." She slid her thin arm around Violet's shoulder and squeezed. "I shall stop tormenting you. And I shall tell Ben to stop."

Violet patted her hand. "Thank you. I would be most grateful."

Pansy kissed her cheek and left once again, leaving Violet to ponder what she would do. If she had a choice.

The basket caught her attention again, and she removed the note. Violet broke the wax seal, unfolded the note, and read, relieved to find she had time to make the family meal and still get to the meadow in time to see Jane. She rushed to cook a quick meal of toasted cheese sandwiches, one of her father's favorite's. Gathering eggs, mustard, butter, and bread, her mind went to the pleasant visit with Jane.

She broke the eggs into a bowl and added mustard, a chunk of soft butter, a good portion of grated cheese, and finally a bit of salt and pepper. She spooned the mixture evenly over the slices of bread and toasted them.

Making her mother's tray first, she climbed the stairs to her chamber, remembering to bring the laudanum.

Violet settled the tray on a small table near her mother's bed. "Mamma, I have a nice pot of tea for you with your meal. And Pansy made ginger biscuits. She is most proud of them. Shall you try some?"

Mrs. Walford moaned and tugged the quilt over her head. "No, thank you, my dearest. I must sleep."

Violet tried not to give in to the anger. She had heard her mother's complaints for ten and six years. How could someone feel this way for so long? Would they not die from such symptoms? She could not help but wonder if her mother had become so used to having all her work done by others, she had become accustomed to idleness. Why work when she had another to do her chores?

A heavy sigh escaped before Violet could suppress it. She put the laudanum in her pocket, left the bedside, and strode to the door, as she closed it behind her, her mother muttered as if to herself, "I cannot help myself, Violet."

Violet whispered, "So you always say, Mamma."

CHAPTER FIVE

$\mathcal{V}$iolet grabbed her well-worn, needle worked bag and slung the strap over her shoulder. The faint impressions of her grandmother teaching her how to create stitches with colorful thread still vivid in her mind.

Her father's mother treated Violet with such tender care, and she longed for her to return, yet her grandmother was in Heaven. She caressed the side of the bag with tenderness. It was her first venture into creating something she considered special.

With the children still in school, Violet felt free for a couple of hours, and her shoulders relaxed. Time to meet Jane and begin painting her portrait. Though her pace was brisk, she enjoyed being out of doors, the birds chirping around her, the breeze cooling her heated cheeks, and the earthy scent of the meadow.

Upon her arrival she spotted two women walking arm-in-arm, one of them Jane. She halted and changed course to walk along the road toward the village.

"Violet!" Jane waved her arm in the air, encouraging her to meet them.

With much trepidation, Violet strode closer and discovered Cassandra to be her companion.

She curtseyed. "It is good to see you, Miss Austen, Miss Jane."

The corner of Jane's mouth twitched with humor. "Cassy decided she must take a brief walk, leaving me at the meadow to return home. Her disposition is to never walk as far as I. Whereas I am concerned a walk cannot be long enough."

Cassandra laughed. "Miss Walford, take no mind of my little sister. She exaggerates exceedingly."

Unsure what to say, Violet remarked, "Her frequent walks on the roads and meadows suggest she enjoys long walks."

Cassandra smiled. "I see you are allies. It is good to know Jane has a friend whilst I am often away helping my brothers rear their children."

Jane nudged her sister. "You adore the children."

"As it should be," Cassandra conceded. "Though they can be more than my constitution may sometimes allow."

They chatted amiably for a brief time until Cassandra halted their exchange. "I shall leave the two of you to commence your long walk." Her look expressed false horror, and she curtsied, humming a tune as she left.

Jane laughed. "Please forgive my sister. She is a marvel at face-making and has taught the skill to the children."

"Your sister is most amiable," Violet said.

"She is a dear. I know not what I would do without her." There was a hint of sadness in Jane's voice, and she sighed deeply, taking Violet's arm. "Come. Let us take advantage of the day before we each must return to our familial duties. Me to my ever-ailing mother—and you to yours."

They released somber chuckles and walked until reaching their place by the meadow.

"Jane?" Violet hesitated. "I have shared my mother's difficulties with you, and may I ask if your mother's symptoms are much the same?"

"Not precisely the same. My mother's headaches only occur when she is avoiding some particular activity or person. She attends to her beloved gardening with gladness."

"Then she is nothing like my mamma. It is quite amazing she may even walk as her muscles receive no exercise at all." Violet considered the comparison for several minutes as she emptied her bag. "I must admit our mothers' actions are similar yet differ in severity. Mine does not function at all, while yours achieves much."

Jane's lips tightened. "It pains me to know your mother has this weakness. My prayers are with you and your family."

"Thank you." Hot tears pricked Violet's eyes, and her spirit filled with regret.

Jane pulled fabric, needle, and thread from her bag. "Will my sewing hinder your work?"

Violet welcomed the change in conversation. "Not at all." She sketched, her pencil gliding across the paper with sure strokes. "May I ask another question?"

Jane squinted as she threaded a needle. "You just did." One side of her mouth rose.

Violet looked at her, puzzled.

Jane chuckled. "I do so wish you could see your face." She placed a dainty hand over her mouth and laughed.

Violet's eyes widened. "Oh, my! I am slow headed. That is rather clever of you." It had been longer than she could recall when someone shared a jest with her.

Her laughter joined Jane's until they finally quieted.

"My question is—" She smiled. "—do you have any objection if I make a copy of your portrait for myself?"

Jane's needle hovered in mid-air, an unreadable expression on her face. "You would like *my* portrait?" She blinked. "Why?"

"Because you have become my dearest friend."

Jane's bright smile melted Violet's heart, bringing fresh tears. Of late, her emotions overcame her without warning.

"Jane, though we are not of a similar age, in my heart you have become closer than anyone I know." She sniffled. "I am ashamed to say that because I have siblings I love dearly."

"It is because your entire life has been to serve others, never thinking of yourself."

Guilt tore through Violet. "Do not make me appear so noble, for I am not. Shame fills me daily for not being more grateful for what I have."

Jane put her sewing aside. "Has no one ever praised you for your service to them?"

Violet recalled her father's recent words of appreciation and told Jane. "It was shocking to hear it from him. I do not remember him saying such before."

"Then accept it as if from God. You have finally received the appreciation you long for."

Violet blinked away the tears, contemplating Jane's wisdom. Had she been so blind as not to see the appreciation from her father in the past?

Jane resumed sewing and lifted her brow. "And do not forget your recent conquest of Nathaniel Byrd."

"My *conquest*?" Violet's hand stilled above the sketch.

"Yes. Do you not recall I discovered the two of you walking together?"

Violet's face heated. "Only because we accidentally met at the apothecary."

"One would suppose, yet I saw him waiting for you after Mrs. Deedes had her say, and you went inside." Jane pursed her lips. "He *wanted* to see you, Violet."

The declaration hit Violet forcefully. He had waited for *her*? Perhaps there may be a chance for them yet.

CHAPTER SIX

*V*iolet settled the tray on one hip, freeing a hand to open her mother's door. The shadowed room revealed Ben resting a hip against the mattress, his small hand on his mother's shoulder.

"But Mamma. Why do you not want to see me? Please come to the garden and toss the ball." His cherubic face paled, eyes wet. "I promise not to throw it hard."

"Child, can you not see how ill I am?" She rolled to her side, facing the window. "Find Pansy to play with you."

Tears streamed down his round cheeks. "Why do you hate me, Mamma!" He shouted and sprinted from the room.

Violet's fury rose, and she placed the tray roughly onto the table. "Mother! How is it possible a mother may be so cruel to her child? He barely knows who you are."

She stood over the bed, hands on hips, breathing labored. "If you have any compassion whatsoever, you shall rise, dress, and come to the garden at once." She snatched the tray from the table, sending the items crashing against one another. "You shall have your tea in the garden today, or else I shall never bring you another bite again. This must end *now!*

Henceforth, you shall come downstairs to eat. And do not coerce the girls to wait on you any longer. I shall forbid it."

Violet stormed from the room, her entire body trembling, yet by the time she reached the kitchen, remorse engulfed her. Dropping onto the bench with a moan, she rested her face in her hands.

The sound of sniffling brought her head up, and she saw Ben huddled on the floor in the corner, curled into a ball. She went to him and knelt by his side, tugging him into her arms.

"Oh, sweet boy, do not cry. Mamma does not hate you."

"She does!" He raked his sleeve across his eyes. "Mamma hates me." He choked back a sob and hiccupped. "Pansy said she did not want me when I was *borned,* so I know she hates me." He buried his face against Violet's neck, sobs jarring his slight frame.

Violet rocked him and whispered. "You are a precious, most beloved boy. Never forget that."

"By who?" he stuttered.

"You have many who love you. Me, Pansy, Rose, Daisy, Papa, your friends—and God."

He stuck a thumb into his mouth and closed his eyes, snuffling back the tears. Violet had not seen him do so for several months. It was usually when Mamma had shown no affection for him.

Violet smoothed his hair and kissed his forehead. "Let us wash your face and have a respite in the garden. We may toss the ball, and I shall bring biscuits."

He tilted his head back and peered up at her with wide eyes. "Truly?"

"Truly." She pulled him up with her and sat him on the bench, retrieved a wet cloth, and bathed his face and eyes. "Now gather the biscuits and the ball."

He stood, and his face lit with excitement. "I will fetch the ball while *you* get the biscuits."

Violet laughed. "Very well." She wrapped the biscuits into a muslin napkin and placed them in her apron pocket.

Outside in the cold air and sunshine, the boy appeared to revive, throwing the ball with more force than Violet thought possible for one so small. The kitchen door opened with a creak, and Violet glanced to see if Papa had come home from his work at the Great House.

The ball slipped from her hand.

Gardenia Walford's white-knuckled hand gripped the door frame, and she swayed on her feet. She still wore her white nightgown with a tattered blue shawl around her bony shoulders.

"Violet! Why have you dropped the ball?" Ben's gaze followed his sister's, and when he saw his mother, his mouth slackened. After a brief stare, Ben catapulted toward her and flung his arms around her waist.

"Mamma! You came!" He sobbed into her side. "You *do* want me."

She brought a shaking hand to cup his dark, curly head, ruffling it affectionately. "Yes, my boy. I have always wanted you." With a great deal of effort, Mamma slid down and knelt by his side, bringing her arms around him.

He hugged her tightly and kissed her cheeks, then her forehead, then her chin, laughing. "Are you back, Mamma? Please stay this time."

She breathed in and out deeply. "I shall try."

"You can do it. I know you can. Stay with us like this always."

Violet's eyes met her mother's, and they held as if embracing. If only her mother could live up to that declaration. Violet would do everything in her power to help her mother not only try but achieve the task.

Violet strode to them. "Let us go sit by the fire and have

tea and biscuits. Will that suit?" She forced what she hoped was a confident smile.

Ben helped his mother to stand. "Yes, please. Mamma, you must warm yourself and biscuits go nicely with tea."

Mrs. Walford laughed. "Yes, my boy, they do."

Violet marveled at the shift. Perhaps being stern held the secret all this time. They had bowed to Mamma far too long.

Ben held his mother's arm and escorted her inside, his face glowing with love.

Violet whispered, "Thank you, Father in Heaven, the Giver of all blessings. Forgive my anger. You really are the Maker of miracles."

VIOLET WATCHED THE KETTLE, willing it to boil. Two pots of tea later, her sisters arrived and gathered around their mother and Ben with shocked expressions. They gaped at her as if a stranger, eyes wide.

"Mamma!" Pansy dropped to her knees beside the chair and flung her arms around their mother's neck. "We are so happy to see you up and about."

Rose and Daisy soon followed Pansy's example, but Rose's response was not as enthusiastic, though she did hug her. Violet and Rose had felt the pain caused by their mother far longer than Daisy, Pansy, or Benedict.

Footsteps sounded, and Violet shot to her feet just as her father entered the kitchen. He froze, eyes on his wife.

Rose strode to him and took his hat to hang on the peg. "Papa, please join us for tea. Mother is feeling much better."

He opened his mouth, closed it, and pulled a chair from the table, wilting onto the seat. His dark brown eyes appeared tired and questioning.

Violet placed a cup of tea and a biscuit in front of him.

"How was your day at the Great House?" Her cracked voice attempted an even tone.

His gaze never left his wife. "It was a good day. Nate—" He shook his head. "Never mind that." He tugged a paper from his pocket and handed it to Violet. "A dance is to be held at the Great House. The entire village is invited."

The girls cheered, and Ben frowned. "Who would want to go to an old dance?" He crossed his arms over his slight chest. "I cannot imagine anything more dreadful."

For the first time in a very long while, their father laughed, and all gazes flew to him.

Violet marveled at the change as she studied his disbelieving expression, detecting something akin to doubt that his wife would truly return to normal after so many years.

Ben crawled onto his father's lap, nestling his head against his shoulder, brown curls sticking up in all directions. Within a few minutes, he slept peacefully within the one-armed embrace.

Violet's heart melted at the sights around her. The entire family sat amiably around the table, Daisy and Pansy chatting at the same time vying for both their parents' attention. Her mother's features etched with fatigue from the past few hours of activity. She had grown accustomed to lying abed. Recalling the doctor's instruction to keep the dose of laudanum small, perhaps Violet should give her a dose to help her sleep and begin anew tomorrow.

Though they had not eaten their evening meal, Violet proposed the tea might suffice in its stead as the hour had grown late, yet her father and sisters disagreed, their mood more jovial than usual.

Rose glanced at her, and Violet saw the longing laced with doubt.

Violet stood, rested her hands on the back of the wooden chair, and dipped her chin toward Ben. "Papa, shall you take

Benedict to bed and allow him to rest for a while? The girls and I shall attend to our duties, prepare the meal, and we shall have an evening of entertainments." The idea came upon her from something Jane said about their family gatherings.

Papa rose, cradling Ben against his chest. "I shall."

Daisy pressed her hands together beneath her chin. "Oh, yes, Violet. Let us please do so." She looped her arm around her mother's waist. "Mamma, would you not enjoy such an evening? It has been ever so long since you have been downstairs."

Their mother's gaze swung to Violet, a flash of fear in her gaze.

Violet shoved the chair under the table. "I am certain Mamma would enjoy it a great deal, yet I believe she may like a brief respite to renew her strength before we dine." She looked deeply into her mother's eyes and nodded slightly, attempting to send her encouragement. Violet would not allow their mother to slip into her old ways.

Mamma lifted her chin as if to show strength. "Yes, my dear. I believe that is a good idea. Then wake me when you have set the table."

She staggered a bit, and Rose took her arm. "I shall take you to bed, Mamma." She briefly focused her large, grey eyes on Violet. "And I shall awaken you when the time has come for our evening to begin."

Violet gave her a timid, thankful smile. Praise the Lord that Rose was not an immature girl at the age of six and ten. She gave instructions for Daisy and Pansy to chop vegetables for a pie, and when Rose returned, she directed her to begin the pastry. Violet retrieved the remaining ingredients and set to her own tasks.

The paper her father brought home with the details of the dance caught her eye, and she glanced over her shoulder to be certain her sisters were busy about their chores. She leaned over the invitation and studied the words. In ten days, Chawton House would hold a ball, and the invitation extended to all the villagers.

Violet swallowed hard. She would see Jane, and they would have time to converse without hiding away in the meadow. A flush crept across her cheeks. Nate would be there of a certainty.

Would they dance?

Hopeful she was until she thought of her meager wardrobe with nearly thread-worn dresses. Perhaps Jane could assist her in adorning one of her well-worn frocks. A bit of lace would not be too costly.

Her mind sorted which color best suited her dark hair. Again, Jane came to mind, solving the difficulty. A lively tune sounded from her lips, and Rose asked where she had heard it.

"I cannot recall. Humming it is all I can perform." She continued with her task, the image of she and Nate dancing to the tune played in the recesses of her mind.

CHAPTER SEVEN

*V*iolet's amazement knew no bounds when her mother asked for a bath to be brought upstairs before evening. The dress she now wore hung loosely from her thin shoulders, yet the bright pink color brought life to her ashen skin. She feared her mother would not come down after her rest, but the woman shocked them all.

Once the food was prepared and served, Violet's astonishment grew at the amiable atmosphere around the table as they shared pleasantries and jesting. The scent of roasted meat and vegetables mingled with the aroma of nutmeg and ginger from the gingerbread cakes, filling the air with the sense of a joyful Christmas.

The siblings laughed and chatted, while Violet and her parents chuckled at their childish antics, Rose joining in as often as the younger ones. They adjourned to the small parlor, and Ben insisted on sitting on a stool at the feet of his mother and father, alternately giving them looks of pure adoration.

Mamma reclined on the sofa, yet did not join in the games, watching quietly. Her nervous smile grew each time one child burst into unruly laughter and cantered about the room blindfolded while playing the game. Violet's perusal of her parents left her undecided on the possibility of their relationship being mended. Whenever their gazes met, one or the other quickly broke the contact. She silently prayed for their reconciliation. Today was but one day. She did not recall her mother's past occurrences of normalcy ever lasting more than a few moments. Perhaps this would be the beginning of a better future for them all.

Violet's mind suddenly flew to Nate. Dare she hope this would be a new beginning for her away from this place? Or were the slight attentions he recently gave her merely the fancy of a girlish imagination? *Girl.* She left that title some ten and five years past.

"Papa," Ben encouraged their father. "Please wear the blindfold and play the game." His thin arm extended, waving the strip of fabric before him. He ruffled Ben's hair and did as asked, feeling his way around the room while his prey successfully avoided pursuit. When his shin bumped into the sofa and his fingers groped about, he touched his wife's hand. The room stilled. He bent and brought her hand to his lips, whispering something Violet could not hear, then stood and said, "It must be Daisy, for her skin is much too smooth and youthful to be another's."

Father stepped back and twirled in a circle before removing the blindfold. His mirth-filled eyes roamed the room and landed on Daisy. "There you are, my dear."

Everyone laughed at the jest, and Ben sat beside his mother and took her hand. "You do have soft hands, Mamma. It must be because you do not scrub things in hot water like my sisters."

Once again, the room grew silent.

"Benedict, it is time for you to be abed." Violet cleared her throat and stood, eyes on her mother.

A single tear slid down Mrs. Walford's cheek. "You are

correct, Benedict. My hands have been unused for far too long." She eased her legs over the edge of the sofa and planted her feet on the floor. "I should like to retire, and tomorrow I shall see about putting them to use again." Her quivering voice held steely determination, and Violet grew proud of her mother's rapid progress.

Violet took her arm, helping her rise. "Come, Mamma, allow me to assist you to bed. It has been an exciting day, and you need your rest for tomorrow."

Mamma patted Violet's arm. "Thank you, Violet. That is most kind." She turned to her son. "Benedict, please take my other arm." All said good night with kisses and hugs, her father standing before the fireplace, an arm resting upon the mantle. Violet had not seen him more tranquil in a long while.

Upstairs, Violet and her mother settled Ben into bed and listened to his sweet prayers of thanking God for healing his mamma. By the time Violet escorted her mother to her bedchamber and assisted in changing into her nightclothes, the woman collapsed against the pillows.

"You are a dutiful daughter, Violet." She yawned with feeling. "Thank you for your hard words. They were the medicine I needed. Truly, they were like a lifeboat offered to a woman who did not know she was drowning."

The declaration felt as though she had been slapped in the face. "I am sorry, Mamma. My temper got the better of me. I did not intend to be cruel." Violet turned to the table and poured a small dose of laudanum into a glass and added water. "Dr. White said this shall help you sleep."

She patted Violet's cheek with trembling fingers and drank the mixture. "You were not cruel. You spoke the truth I needed to hear."

Violet kissed her forehead. "Rest. Tomorrow will not be as

taxing. We shall make certain to pace the days more slowly until you gradually gain strength."

"Wise girl." Her arm dropped to the quilt, and Violet smoothed the covers over her slender shoulders.

"Rest well. Tomorrow shall be even brighter than today."

Violet blew out the candle, and by the time she reached the door, her mother's breathing became slow and even. She prayed tomorrow would indeed prove as well as today, shoving aside the feeling that her mother may too easily slip into old habits.

VIOLET HUMMED as she prepared her family's breakfast, the sounds of shuffling footsteps above stairs as her sisters readied themselves for school. She shook her head as she thought of their names, all similar to her mother's penchant for flowers stemming from her own name. Thankfully, she had not resorted to naming Benedict in the same manner.

Benedict's daily moans of not wanting to rise for school flowed through the house as Rose persuaded him into dressing.

Boot steps entered the kitchen, and Violet lifted her head from slicing the bread. "Good morning, Father. Did you sleep well?"

His warm, yet halfhearted, smile faltered. "I did." He poured a cup of coffee, heaving a deep sigh as he sat at the table. "I would have a word with you before the children come down." He glanced over his shoulder toward the door.

She faced him, hands clasped at her waist.

"Please do not be overmuch disappointed . . ." He lowered his voice. ". . .if your mamma does not remain as she did yesterday. It was most welcome to have her return to us, yet I fear it will be short-lived."

Violet's spirit plunged like the stones she once threw into the pond as a child. Perhaps she should have considered this, yet her mother had seemed so much better than all the times before when she grew like her old self.

"Yes, Papa. I understand." She returned to her task, and they remained silent while she filled a plate with honey cake and toast for her father. He ate in silence while she continued preparing breakfast for her siblings and made her mother a tray.

Mr. Walford strode to the door and put on his hat, then shoved his muscular arms into his coat. "My girl, do not despair. We have lived through this before and shall do so again." He kissed her cheek and departed, leaving the scent of cold air behind him.

Violet released a resigned sigh as the children rushed into the room, chatting wildly.

Rose made her way to Violet's side and whispered into her ear, "Mother is up and dressing, though it is slow going." Her chocolate eyes were wide with suspicion.

Violet blinked, not believing her ears. "Truly?"

"Yes. Can you credit such a thing?" She looked toward the younger ones to be sure they had not overheard.

"It is difficult to believe." Violet dipped her chin toward the row of food-filled plates, picked up two and took them to the table, Rose following with two additional plates. "Eat up. You do not have time for a long and comfortable breakfast."

Rose made a funny face, causing much laughter. "Eat up then gather your things and let us be off so Violet may attend to Mamma and her chores."

"*Mamma* has come to wish you a good day."

All turned to face the door. Their mother stood in the opening, hands at her side, wearing a wide smile. They ran to her side, hugging and fussing over her, her eyes glistening with unshed tears. "Now, off with you. I will not have your teacher chiding you for being late."

"Yes, Mamma." They answered in unison, wearing cheerful smiles.

Violet's chest burned with shame for earlier thinking Papa may have a point about her returning to her old ways so quickly.

"Mamma, I was about to bring a tray up."

Mrs. Walford waved her frail hand in the air. "No need, my dear. Will you join me?"

"Of course. Please sit, and I shall have it ready in a moment." Violet moved with deftness around the kitchen, chatting nervously. "Tea or coffee?"

"Tea, please. And toast."

"I have some lovely marmalade of apricots given to me by Miss Austen."

"Miss Austen?"

"Yes, Mamma. Do you not remember the Austen ladies?"

"I do, vaguely. Nice enough. Yet interacted little with the villagers, as I recall."

Considering her mother's behavior, Violet found it nearly comical that she remembered the Austens, despite her husband being employed by their kinsman at the Great House.

Violet settled the plate and a cup of tea before her mother. "I am most happy to see you up and about so early. What would you care to do today, Mamma?"

Mrs. Walford lifted her eyes to Violet. "I should like to resume my knitting. The weather grows colder and certainly there is a need for gloves and such."

"That is a wonderful idea, Mamma." Violet poured herself a cup of tea and sat next to her mother. "If you are in need of more yarn, I will gladly purchase some for you."

She patted Violet's hand and gave her a warm smile. "Thank you. Allow me to go through my basket, and should I need more, I will gladly accept your offer."

They shared an hour of companionship while Mrs. Walford ate and drank her tea, then Violet settled her by the fire with her basket while she cleaned the kitchen, humming to herself. When she had completed her task, she hung her apron on its peg and stood in the doorway, watching her mother's hands working with the yarn.

"Mamma, are you in need of anything? I am going for a walk." Violet tugged her coat on, wrapping a warm scarf around her neck, then picked up her paints.

"No, my dear. I am settled quite well." Her eyes glowed with contentment. "I am happy to see you have taken up your art again."

The fire snapped and crackled cozily in the parlor, candlelight flickering an ambient glow. If not for her meeting with Jane, she would have loved to stay by her mother's side.

"Very well. I shall see you soon." Violet kissed her mother's cap-covered head and walked out into the cool morning air.

She breathed in the tranquil setting, strolling toward the meadow, humming a tune. Her thoughts returned to Nate. Would that mother could become capable again so Violet might be free to pursue a life of her own.

"Violet!" Jane stood in the distance, waving her arm over her head.

Violet rushed toward her friend, and they clasped hands, smiling at one another.

"I am so glad you have come. May I see your progress on my portrait?" Jane tapped Violet's bag with a finger, eyes gleaming with curiosity.

"Not so fast." Violet playfully swung the bag behind her back. "In good time."

"I came early and secured us a place by the water. Just as you like it."

Violet's spirit lifted, warm and thankful. "You are a good friend, Miss Jane Austen."

Jane lifted her chin. "Of course, I am. And you as well."

They laughed like schoolgirls, looped arms, and strode to the water's edge. A wool blanket lay upon the dry grass, Jane's ever-present basket in the center.

Violet sat and touched the basket. "And what have you brought us this day?" She waggled her eyebrows.

"You are a funny one." Jane lifted the lid of the basket and removed a napkin-wrapped package and placed it on Violet's lap. "An edible gift from my sister. Her biscuits are second to none."

Violet's laughter bubbled, and she reached into her bag and retrieved something from it and gave it to Jane. "And, likewise. Though my sister did not send it, yet she makes the most marvelous ginger biscuits."

"We have great minds, Violet, you, and I. For we think the same."

They nibbled on their gifts, basking in the calm, sweet day. When Jane yawned, Violet reprimanded her. "We have no time for that. I need for you to pose properly—with your eyes open, please."

Jane sighed dramatically. "Oh! The demands of the famous." She suddenly straightened her spine. "I near forgot. Nathaniel spoke with me as I saw him on my way here."

Violet's brush hovered in midair. "What?"

"Yes, he approached me and asked if I was to see you today." She lifted one eyebrow. "He wants to know if you shall attend the dance at the Great House."

Violet swallowed hard.

"I told him you would be there."

"You did?" Violet's heart skipped a beat.

"Why would I not? You *must* attend."

Violet's mind rioted with questions. Should she go? Though her thoughts had been focused on the dance and seeing Nate there, what would occur if she did go? Her heart screamed that she must attend, while her head reasoned there was no good to come of going.

CHAPTER EIGHT

*M*amma." Violet peered at her mother, quietly knitting by the fire. "Does this appear to be enough rosemary and holly?"

Mrs. Walford paused her knitting and tilted her head back, studying Violet's carefully laced sprigs of greenery across the surface of the Rumford fireplace mantle. "It is very pretty. I do so love the scent of rosemary."

"Mamma!" Benedict shouted from the kitchen. "Pansy will not let me have a ginger biscuit." Pansy's angry shout to her brother brought Violet's head around to meet her mother's gaze.

Violet's mother sent her a pointed look. "Whatever shall we do with that boy?" One side of her mouth curved upward, her eyes glinting with humor Violet had missed.

"Stay seated, Mamma. I shall see to Benedict. We cannot allow him to indulge his sweet tooth and bring on stomach pains. We have a dance to attend."

Her mother returned to knitting, avoiding Violet's eyes. "Mamma. You said you would attend with Papa, Rose, and myself. Have you changed your mind?"

"My dear," her chest rose and fell on a sigh. "I fear I am not ready to wander out yet. 'Tis too early." She hung her head, toying with the brown yarn in her lap.

Violet knelt in front of her. "Mamma, I understand, yet you must leave the house eventually. Others are asking about you, wishing you well." She lay a hand on her mother's forearm. "Please."

Violet's heart skipped at the weak smile that met her. She was proud of her mother's progress the past few weeks, her body strengthening more each day.

"I do not think your father is over fond of attending the dance. We shall stay home and spend time with Daisy, Pansy, and Benedict. They will like that."

"I am certain they shall." Violet would not distress her mother any further. There would be other dances. She and Rose would attend the upcoming festivities.

"If you are certain."

The clock chimed the hour, and Violet shot to her feet. "I have lost the time." She kissed her mother's cheek and rushed to the kitchen. "Rose, we must dress for the dance. I fear we shall be late."

A small squeal rent the air, and Rose ran to Violet and grabbed her hand, pulling her toward the stairs. "Hurry!" Violet grumbled about keeping Ben from eating more biscuits before she and Pansy could stop him.

"Do not give it another thought. Allow Daisy and Pansy to care for our little brother. They are more than capable." Rose's grip tightened as she pulled Violet at a faster pace up the stairs.

Rose's laughter rang throughout the house, blending with the bickering children in the kitchen. Violet hoped the noise did not upset Mamma overmuch. Papa would soon be home and could calm her lively siblings. Perhaps Mamma would not suffer much before he arrived.

"Violet!" Rose pressed her fists on her hips. "You are not listening. Please help me dress. We shall *not* be late for the dance."

Violet released an unsteady breath. "Dear Rose, I can assure you no one would be offended by our delayed arrival. We are not royalty."

Rose turned her back to Violet. "Please do not make my stays too tight as I want to eat as much as possible."

Violet chuckled, thinking of something Jane had told her. *"'To my high amusement, stays now are not made to force the bosom up at all as it was a very unbecoming, unnatural fashion.'"*

"What makes you laugh?" Rose threw a scornful expression over her shoulder.

"Nothing of consequence." Violet shook her head. "There! All done. Now you must attend to mine."

They exchanged places and Rose repeated the process, circling Violet to assess her work. "You look lovely. Nathaniel will be unable to keep his eyes from you."

Violet stilled, her stomach tightening. "Why would you say such a thing?"

"Because it is true. I have seen how he looks at you—*and* how you look at him when he is not aware."

Something sparked inside her. Violet opened her mouth to lash out at her sister when Jane's words slammed into her. *"He wanted to see you, Violet."*

Could there be a slight chance for her and Nate? Just as her heart calmed, her father's words returned. *"I rely on you more than I should, Violet. Yet there is nothing I can do but insist you stay."*

Hot, angry tears stung her eyes. No. She would never have a home of her own. Why had she ever thought otherwise?

CHAPTER NINE

$\mathcal{F}$lickering torches lined the pebbled drive leading to Chawton House, sending tiny sparks of light into the leaden sky. Though not yet evening, the sullen, overcast heavens near mimicked that of the inky darkness of night. Sad thoughts from her father's earlier words sprang into Violet's mind, and she attempted to shove them aside. Not wanting to break Rose's heart, she had only come as an escort for her sister.

Violet smoothed the worn fabric of her grey wool gown against her middle, now covered with an equally well-worn pelisse. Although the added crimson velvet ribbon made the garment appear more stylish, she hoped the candlelit room would hide some imperfections. Though it was merely a country dance, she wanted to look her best.

She shivered inside her brown silk pelisse, though it held enough warmth to ward off the early evening chill. Rose's gaze swung to meet hers.

"Are you cold?" Rose gave her a side-hug, then looped her arm through Violet's. "I am much too excited to feel the night air. Can you not wait to dance? How exciting it shall be!"

Though her heart was not in attending the dance, Violet sent her sister an encouraging smile. "Yes. Very exciting, indeed."

A voice called out from behind, and they turned to find Jane and Cassandra rushing to meet them.

As they exchanged pleasantries, Jane took Violet's arm and tugged her to a slower pace. Cassandra complimented Rose's gown, admiring the heavy detail around the hem, and they walked on ahead.

"Well, are you eager to see Nathaniel?" Jane whispered into Violet's ear as they dropped behind their sisters.

Embarrassment heated Violet's cheeks, and she averted her gaze toward Chawton House's heraldic stained-glass windows. The candlelight from inside created an aura of shifting, multi-colored light, creating a bright display.

"Jane, there is no need for me to dwell on Nathaniel. He and I . . . shall never be."

"Do not be so downcast. Both of you are in God's hands. Try to take pleasure in this evening. If it is within His will, you and Nate shall be together. Allow Him to work."

She patted Violet's hand and increased her steps. "Come. We shall eat, dance, and sing our way through this Christmas entertainment. I am certain the festivities Edward has approved shall be wonderful to contemplate."

Violet could not deny the truth in her words. Jane's brother had been a most kind and generous squire to the village. Her spirits lifted at Jane's encouragement, and her disposition lightened as they entered the Great House. Music and laughter met them, and they exchanged wide smiles.

Once servants collected their outerwear, they made their way to the great hall, where a lively quadrille had commenced among scores of candles and crystal candelabras sprinkled throughout the massive room.

"I am uncertain the atmosphere is quite festive enough for me." Jane waved a hand to encompass the liveliness of the great hall, and her wry tone brought a chuckle from Violet.

Violet said, "I cannot say, as this is the first time I have attended in a long while. I must admit I had forgotten what a pleasure it is to attend."

The dark, polished paneled walls gleamed, and the agreeable scent of beeswax candles surrounded them. Violet wished her parents had attended. It would have raised her mother's spirits, even if she could but sit on the side and watch as she listened to the music.

The musicians changed to a Scotch reel. A young man approached and asked Jane to dance. A quick glance of apology at Violet for departing, and she was away, leaving Violet to stand alone and watch them dance the Boulangeries.

Violet took in the dancers for a few moments, then her attention drew to the holly and ivy adorning the mantle, while rosemary lay atop the gold framed paintings. Mistletoe garnished the chandeliers hanging from the ceiling, and she flushed, thinking of what it must be like to kiss Nate. Laughter bubbled up inside her. She had never been kissed.

The music changed again, and long lines of couples started and performed figures and progressed up and down the set.

Violet's gaze found a row of tapestry-covered chairs near a corner of the room and slowly crossed toward them and sat. A servant carrying a silver tray approached and offered her a cup of Negus. She gladly took the ornate glass cup and demurely sipped the warm liquid while she watched the dancers. The flash of a yellow gown gathered her attention, and she found the wearer to be Mada Dacre. She caught her breath when she saw Mada's partner—Nate. Her stomach roiled, and she gulped the drink and placed the cup on a nearby table. Why had she looked forward to seeing him again? He obviously held an affection for Mada—not her.

Rising to her feet too quickly, Violet's head spun, and she staggered for a moment, then righted herself and hastily retreated to the door, dodging guests as she made her way to fresh, cold air. Unfamiliar with the layout of the Great House, she faltered until locating the way to the garden. The chilled air hit her heated face with force.

Jane was wrong. Nate held no regard for her.

VIOLET HUDDLED in the walled garden where she had so often been to visit her father at his work there. Today it held no pleasure. Situated on a bench underneath a leafless beech tree, Violet's shoulders trembled. Hot tears trickled down her cheeks, sprinkling her wool gown.

The heavy, somber clouds threatening rain mocked her. Would they soon pour out their wrath upon her? She sniffled, and the sound of footsteps on the graveled path made her rise and hide behind the vast tree trunk.

When the steps soon faded, she slanted her head to peek around the tree. A man's tall form disappeared beyond the torches lining the path that led further into the garden away from the house. His hands clasped behind his back as he walked stirred a memory in Violet. Nate walked in that manner. He had done so the day they met at the apothecary.

Violet watched his retreating back and released a shaky sigh. Should he return in this direction, she did not want to be found. She ambled along the path in no hurry to return to the house, often glancing over her shoulder to be certain she did not encounter Nate.

Bracing herself to enter the Great House, she gave one last

glance backward. One more step and she slammed into someone.

"Oh! Please forgive—"

Strong hands gripped her upper arms, securing her balance. "Violet . . . are you unwell? I saw you fly from the great hall. You appeared ill, so I came looking for you."

Violet blinked, not understanding. "I . . ." Unable to complete her sentence, she paused. "You came for me?" The tangy lemon scent of Nate's skin unsettled her senses.

He nodded, green eyes glowing with concern.

"But you danced with Mada." She frowned in confusion. "I mean—you left while dancing with her?" Why would he leave Mada so he could come after her?

His hands still held her arms, and he took one step toward her, closing the space between them. "You arrived after the dancing commenced." He was close enough for her to see his throat convulse on a hard swallow. His voice lowered. "I only danced with Mada because she asked me, and I did not want to embarrass her by declining."

Nate's gaze held hers while releasing a long, deep sigh. "Violet, I—"

The door to the Great House flew open, shooting a bright spear of light across the path.

"Violet!" Jane rushed to her side. "Are you ill? I could not find you until Rose said she saw you leave."

Jane's eyes roamed their near embrace, and Nate dropped his hands and quickly stepped away from Violet. He bowed. "I shall leave you ladies to discuss . . ." He smiled and left them.

Following Nate's departure with her eyes, Jane then faced Violet and placed her palms against her cheeks. "I am sorry to have interrupted." She whispered, "Did he kiss you?" Her eyebrows shot upward, an inquisitive smile gracing her lips.

Violet's emotions scattered about her like the fallen leaves from the beech tree she had hidden behind.

The answer to Jane's question came slowly, her mind aflutter. "No, he did not."

"Yet I believe he was about to. I begin to hate myself for disturbing you." Jane took Violet's hand in hers. "Please forgive me. My concern over your well-being overtook whatever senses I have remaining." Her enigmatic smile spoke much to Violet.

"Dear Jane. Do not reproach yourself overmuch. You could not have known what I was about." Nate's words of why he danced with Mada sounded in her heart. What was he trying to say when Jane interrupted?

The door opened again. Rose and Cassandra trailed into the garden.

Rose halted in front of them, fisting her hands against her hips. "What do you have to say for yourself? You frightened us beyond belief. We did not know what had become of you."

Violet strode to her sister and put her arms around her. "Thank you for caring for me, my dear Rose."

Cassandra smiled at her sister. "Just as I would have worried after you, Jane, had you skittered from the dance as Violet did."

"You are all so very thoughtful. Thank you." Violet gave a shallow curtsy and laughed. "You have lightened my temper quite nicely."

Jane huffed with a smile. "So let us return to the merriments. 'Tis time to see what delicacies Edward has approved for the gathering. My stomach has designs upon small sandwiches, biscuits, fruits, cold meats, pies, and pastries, should there be some such." She laughed. "As I know my brother, there shall probably be all and much more."

Violet joined in the laughter, and they entered the jolly

party with renewed joy, the great hall active with dancing. They stood on the side watching for a time when a long-time friend of Edward's came and asked Jane to dance.

Once again Violet stood alone, yet she bolstered herself by recalling Nate's earnest attentions in the garden. A country dance ended, and the musicians paused for a brief respite. Violet's gaze searched for Rose and discovered her speaking with an unknown young man across the room. While others surrounded them, Violet thought it desirable to traverse the press to meet her sister's suitor.

She set the punch cup on a nearby table and straightened when a hand lightly touched her shoulder.

"May I have the next dance?"

Violet's eyes met Nate's scrutiny, and her heart skipped a beat. His gaze traveled to her lips, then returned to her eyes.

He held his hand out.

She took it. "There is no music."

After a brief silence, they laughed. Nate shook his head. "I suppose I got ahead of myself." He kept hold of her hand. "It should begin soon."

The musicians played, and Violet's heart thudded again, anticipating her first dance with Nate. He led her to begin and then stopped.

As if on cue, the sounds of a Christmas carol rang out, and the guests began singing.

While shepherds watched their flocks by night,
all seated on the ground,
an angel of the Lord came down,
and glory shone around.

For but a second, her disposition darkened, disappointed their dance was not to be. Regret replaced the sentiment, as she had much to be thankful for. They celebrated their risen Saviour. They could have a dance anytime.

Thank You, Father, for this night. You bless me far beyond what I deserve.

It mattered not that she and Nate must delay their dance. Again, Violet's heart pounded against her chest. The music for Nate had been playing in her heart since their interaction in the garden.

CHAPTER TEN

*M*oonlight replaced the ominous sky while Violet strolled, her arm hooked through Nate's. Jane, Cassandra, and Rose walked in front of them as their escorts.

The night had been magical—nay, was still so. Their dance became a blur in Violet's mind, their gazes constantly holding one another's throughout. Jane's insight about them brought a restrained smile to Violet's lips.

Nate's tender touch atop her hand squeezed. "I have long admired you, Violet. You are not only a lovely young woman, you also have a generous and caring heart. The many times you have visited your father at the Great House reveals such." He paused, a mischievous glint in his eyes. "May I ask the cause of your smile?"

She slanted her head to peer into his eyes, which reflected the moon's golden radiance. "Nathaniel Byrd, I trust you know the answer to your impertinent question."

His teeth flashed in a wide smile. "Most likely. Yet I would hear it from your charming, soft lips."

Violet's breath caught, lips parting.

His step faltered, his expression now somber. "That was much too bold."

She tugged his arm, and they resumed a slow pace, keeping her gaze averted. She whispered, "How would you know they are soft?"

Nate's questioning countenance clouded for a moment, then was replaced by a gentle look. He leaned close enough for their shoulders to touch. "If I may have your permission to taste them, I shall see for myself."

Violet stared, unable to take her gaze from his. The mere thought of the sensation of his lips touching hers caused an intense longing.

The bright moon revealed his blush. "I humbly ask your pardon."

A long silence lay between them until they reached Chawton Cottage. Jane leaned close to Violet with a hug and whispered, "Let us meet tomorrow. I want all the scandalous particulars."

Violet pulled back with a quivering smile. "Yes, we shall take care of that soon."

All chorused a good night and a happy Christmas. Rose skipped ahead of Violet and Nate, giving them some semblance of privacy, though the excited girl tossed questions over her shoulder all the way back to their cottage.

Violet became exasperated at her sister's incessant chattering by the time they arrived. Nate hung back, his jaw tense.

"Rose, why do you not go in and put the kettle on? We shall need a hot drink to revive us from the frosty night."

Her sister's eyes bored into Violet, then wandered to Nate. When she next looked at Violet, her mouth hung open, her head nodding. "Oh. Yes. Of course." She turned without another word and slipped into the cottage, closing the door quietly behind her.

The sweet trill of a song thrush sounded in the night, creating a moonlit serenade. Violet licked her lips then regretted the motion, having been told since childhood not to do so in the winter. Now her lips would dry and split. Her thoughts raced back to Nate's statement about asking permission to . . .

The thoughts became words and spilled from her mouth. "I give my permission."

Nate blinked rapidly, his eyes narrowing.

Violet glanced at the door, expecting it to open at any moment, her father perched on the threshold. She turned back to Nate, too embarrassed to repeat the statement. Her fingers lifted to touch her lips, believing she would never know the sensation of a kiss.

He cleared his throat, moving closer. "I now understand. Please forgive my simple mind. Thank you for your permission."

Nate's palm cupped her cheek, and he bent his head near hers. He scanned her face as though memorizing her features before placing his lips gently on hers. The sensation coursed through Violet like a burst of sunlight on a dark day.

When they parted, their sighs mingled in the air between them. A titter of laughter shoved them apart. Pansy stood in the now opened doorway, hands crossed over her chest. "Papa wants to know when you are coming in."

Violet coughed, angry at being interrupted, nearly overriding the pleasure of the kiss. She shyly looked at Nate, who wore what she believed to be a similar expression.

Pansy huffed. "Papa said to bring Nate in for a cup of tea." She ground out the words with irritation.

Fear swept through Violet. Would her father rebuke Nate for keeping Violet alone in the dark?

Nate's fearful expression matched Violet's thoughts, yet she entered the cottage, Nate on her heels. Suddenly, siblings surrounded them.

He politely greeted her mother, then her father, and last, the others. Benedict, excited to have another man in the cottage, claimed Nate and revealed his sword.

Violet stared at the offending weapon. "Benedict, where did you get that?" She pointed in his direction. "I distinctly recall burning it not so long ago." She crossed her arms over her chest and glared at her little brother, feeling like a scolding parent.

The boy paled and held the toy behind his back, sending a pleading glance toward his father.

Mr. Walford, sitting beside his wife on the sofa, looked at his wife, then at Violet.

"Vi, he means no harm 'Tis but a toy."

Ben's shoulders squared, and the mutinous look he sent to Violet caused a shift in her good temper.

"Papa, I had to take the other one from him because he flailed it around inside, to the harm of all in his path."

Mr. Walford brought his regard to his son. "Is this true, Benedict?" He cocked his head, lips pursed. "If so, this deserves punishment for not obeying your sister." He shook his head from side to side in disappointment. "Where did you get this one?"

Benedict hung his head in defeat. "William's elder brother made a sword for him and asked if I would care for one."

Their father's brow wrinkled. "Did he now?"

Heavy silence filled the small parlour, and Rose entered carrying a large tray holding mugs of steaming tea. Her gaze swept the room. "What have I missed? You all appear as if someone has died."

Pansy burst into laughter. "Ben has done it again—gotten himself into trouble."

Rose sniffed. "And what is so unusual about that?"

The not-so-well-meant statement brought a chorus of laughter, including Nate's. His hearty laugh caused Violet's chest to tighten with joy, the picture of her and Nate in a cottage full of children scurrying about, bickering playfully. The return of her father's words about how he could not allow her to leave them replaced her joy with a sob. She slapped a hand over her mouth and rushed to the kitchen door, but a firm hand held her in place.

"Vi, please stop. We must speak." She turned to meet her father's gaze. His hesitation caused fresh tears to spring forth.

"Forgive an old man for his selfishness. Nate is a good man, and I would be honored to have him marry my daughter."

Violet blinked as her father's image distorted through watery eyes. "You would? But—"

"I would. Though I have not told him." He winked.

She flung her arms around his neck and hugged him with fierceness, whispering into his ear, "Yet he has not asked me to marry him."

"I feel certain that is next, my girl." His rough laughter rang in her ear, and when she opened her eyes, Nate stood across the kitchen watching them, a confused expression marring his handsome features.

Mr. Walford released her, and when he turned and strode by Nate, he slapped him on the back. "Have a care for her or I shall bury you in the Great House garden at night. No one would be the wiser."

Violet noticed Nate's throat bob in a hard swallow as he made his way to her.

"Was he serious, or was that another of his jests?"

She took his hand in hers. "He did not jest."

A slow smile lifted his lips. He glanced over his shoulder

and when he found no one watching them, he gave her a quick kiss.

"Sir," Violet said in a derisive tone, "I did not give you permission to do that."

"So, I must ask permission for every kiss?" He lifted his brow.

This time Violet looked over his shoulder toward her family, then quickly returned the kiss. "For every kiss you steal without asking, I'll steal one in return."

The pleasing smile he wore melted her heart, and she sent a silent prayer of thanksgiving for this fine man.

THOUGH THE DAY WORE A DARK, heavy cloak, Violet's heart soared with radiance. She rushed to the meadow to spend time with Jane and tell her of all that had transpired after the dance the previous night.

Disappointment met her when Jane was not in their usual spot. She had but a few finishing touches remaining on Jane's portrait, though they were simple things she could do without Jane's presence. Yet more than painting occupied her mind, and she wanted to share the news with her friend.

She waited for no small time, and when Jane did not appear, she trudged home to prepare the evening meal. Entering the kitchen, her mother sat at the table chopping vegetables and her gaze lifted to Violet. "Did you have a pleasant walk, my dear?" Mrs. Walford smiled, her face aglow with the promise of new health.

Distracted, Violet hung her woolen cloak on a peg by the door. "Hm? . . . Oh, yes."

"What ails you, child? You do not appear to be yourself." She paused in her chopping and studied Violet.

"I do not ail, Mamma. I was to meet Jane, and she was not there."

Her mamma pointed with the tip of the knife to a letter on the opposite end of the table. "That came for you just after you departed."

Violet glanced at the table and snatched the paper up, sitting as she broke the seal and read.

My dear Violet,

I am downtrodden to tell you I am ill and unable to keep our meeting. My dear, please know that I am the sicker for it in not being able to join you today. Please know I shall contact you as soon as I am able to be of good company for you. Whether from fatigue or anguish of mind, the pain in my back does usually right itself in short order.

Yours affectionately,

J.A.

Violet lifted her gaze. "Oh, Mamma, Jane is most ill and could not meet with me today. How very sad is that?"

Mrs. Walford wore a sympathetic smile, her eyes moist. "As cold as it is, 'tis best she remains indoors."

The letter floated to the tabletop, Violet's mind working to discern how serious Jane's ailment may be. A sudden reminder leaped into her mind—she must finish Jane's portrait and deliver it to her in time for Christmas. She could complete her own copy at any time.

"Mamma, are you well enough to complete the soup?" She stood, clenching the note in one hand. "There is something I must do for Jane."

"Yes, dear. Carry on with your commitment."

Violet gave her mother a kiss on the cheek and flew up the stairs to her room. She retrieved her paint box and began creating the final touches to Jane's image.

Time passed quickly and once the work was complete, she set it aside to dry and packed her paints away. As she descended the stairs, sounds of a happy family wafted with the aroma of rich soup, and her stomach rumbled. While the painting dried, she would have a bowl, then take Jane the gift before the hour grew too late.

At her entrance, Ben's head popped up from his soup. "Where have you been, Vi?" His sweet little face tugged at her heart.

She ruffled his hair as she went to the sideboard and retrieved a bowl. "I shall tell you another time, my sweet."

Pansy's tongue set off on another one of her long tales of her day, all nodding or chiming in with a laugh or comment.

How long had Violet ached for such a pleasing time with her family? She silently prayed this would not be a temporary time, and that her mother was truly mending, though she knew it would take time to renew all her strength.

After they ate and enjoyed a hot cup of tea to stave off the cold evening, she slipped out and returned to her room to wrap the portrait, pondering on how to leave the house without being questioned. By the time the family settled in the parlour, she stood ready to leave, the muslin-swathed gift under her arm.

Easing down the stairs, she hugged the wall so as not to walk in the center of each step, making them creak. She had no time to hear a lecture about being in the night alone. She left by the kitchen door, closing it gently, not bothering to put on her cloak or pelisse.

The first step into the garden, she bumped into Ben.

"Where are you going, Vi?" His little face upturned to meet her eyes in the moonlit night. He did not wait for an answer, saying. "I am now ready for tea and biscuits." He shoved past her and entered the kitchen.

Violet laughed as she sprinted toward the garden gate, seeing Nate coming toward her.

"Nate. Please forgive me. I must take something to Jane.

My failure to deliver this tonight will vex her." She held the package out for him to see.

He nodded, eyes searching her lack of outer wear. "I shall fetch your cloak." He made to step around her, and she placed a hand on his arm.

"Nay. Please—I do not wish to be questioned why I must go. It shall only take a few minutes. Will you wait for me here until I return?"

He cocked his head, lips pursed. "I shall accompany you. Your father would be displeased if I let you go alone."

Violet's thoughts ran riotous. There was no time to argue. What if Jane and her family were abed early? She *must* depart now.

Without another thought, she grabbed Nate's arm and pulled him toward the gate. "Let us hurry and return quickly.

Eyes wide, Nate followed without protest as she practically ran down the lane and arrived at the door of the Austen's cottage. Violet's breathing came in gasps as she pounded on the door.

Martha, the Austen's friend, answered, her eyes wide. "Miss Walford. How may I help you?"

Violet addressed the woman between gasps. "I am quite sorry to disturb you so late, yet I must see that Miss Jane receives this immediately." She pulled in a deep breath. "*Please.*"

Martha blinked rapidly and hesitantly reached for the outstretched package. "I shall see she does."

Violet's shoulders relaxed at once. "Oh, thank you so very much. God bless you and merry Christmas!"

"And a merry Christmas to you, Miss Walford." With a skeptical look, Martha shut the door, and the clank of the bolt rang out. Violet and Nate stood facing the door—alone.

∼

A NOTE from Jane arrived Christmas morning. Violet sat at the kitchen table, mince pie, plum pudding, and other holiday treats lay before her covered with a linen tablecloth. The aromas of Christmas surrounded her, the laughter of her parents and siblings filling the cottage. She broke the seal and unfolded the message.

My dearest Violet,

It was with great happiness I received the gift. Though I was very tired, and glad to get to bed early, I was not sleeping when Martha came to my chamber. I confess my back does pain me at present, though not enough to keep me from tomorrow's festivities.

Cassy slept, so I shall present her with the gift tomorrow before we depart for church.

I shall see you there, my dear friend.

Yours most truly,

J.A.

Violet's worries vanished when she read Jane's kind letter. The delayed delivery had not caused her any disappointment at all. Christmas was a time of rejoicing for the delivery of their Saviour and was no time for fears to burden them. All was well.

"*Violet!*" Her mother's musical voice came from the parlour. "We are ready to depart. Gather your cloak and let us leave."

Violet rose, snatched her cloak and gloves from the peg, and met her family at the door. "My, but do you all not look cheery and festive this morning?"

Benedict hugged closer to his mother's side. "But Mamma, I am sleepy."

Papa bent to Ben's level and wrapped his arms around him. "Allow me to carry you. You may have a short sleep while we walk."

Ben put his arms around his father's neck and lay his

brown, curly head on his shoulder and whispered, "Thank you, Papa. It is surely needed."

Chuckles sounded all around as they made their way down the lane to the church, small flakes of snow drifting around them like white goose down. Violet slowed her pace following her family, the warmth of their companionship filling her with a sense she was uncertain she had ever felt before meeting Jane.

They met villagers as they walked, sharing Christmas greetings and good wishes. Violet noticed the windows of Chawton cottage held no lit candles in the early pre-dawn. Violet prayed Jane was well enough to attend today's service.

Showers of wispy snowflakes veiled the reddish-brown stone. The image of her and Nate exiting the church on their future wedding engulfed her. She tittered. He had yet to ask her the important question. A sudden surge of panic gripped her, but it disappeared as quickly as it had come.

When he asked, she was certain that a spring wedding would be her choice—among the fresh growth and the scent of blooming flowers in the air.

"Violet?"

Her hand flew to her chest, and she whipped around to find Nate smiling behind her.

"May I walk to church with you?" He lifted his bent arm.

"Nate. You gave me a fright!" She took his arm and thought of the day she would do so as his wife. He *would* ask her to marry him—would he not?

"You appear lost in thought. Will you share what takes you from this place?"

The glint in his jade eyes captured her. It was as if the two of them alone existed in this moment, strolling arm-in-arm toward the church, a fairyland of white flecks in the air, gathering to cover the surrounding landscape.

Nate drew her closer against his side, their heat intermingling. His warm breath fanned her cheek. "I spoke with your father."

Violet's breath caught, and Nate slowed his steps, bringing her pace to match his own. Tiny snowflakes gathered briefly on his eyelashes before dissipating, mirroring her warming heart. If possible, the affection she felt for him grew.

"Though this is not the most private of settings, I would have you answer a question before we reach the church." He glanced around, then settled his gaze upon her once again.

She swallowed the lump in her throat and nodded, unable to speak.

He brought his head nearer and whispered, "Will you become my wife? I fear I cannot end this day without knowing your heart."

She blinked, eyes widening. Was this truly happening? The snow increased, each flake growing in size, collecting on the branches of the giant yew in the churchyard.

Her hoarse reply brought the reality of the moment to settle around her like a perfect spring day, absent of the cold. "Becoming your wife shall make me the happiest woman in all of England."

He laughed and squeezed her hand. "We shall seal the occasion with a kiss once we are alone." He lifted his brow.

Violet's lips quivered, struggling to keep the laughter from spilling forth. "How am I to sit still through the service? You ask too much, sir."

They entered the church, and the scent of rosemary, laurel, and beeswax candles greeted them. Garlands and sprigs of greenery adorned the windows with twigs of red-berried holly, marking the festive atmosphere.

Violet searched the pews for Jane, and when their eyes met Jane sent her a knowing smile. Her pale face did not alter the happiness she expressed on Violet's behalf.

A sense of peace overcame Violet, and she tightened her

grip on Nate's arm. His penetrating gaze reassured her he, too, felt God's grace surrounding them, and their blessings were immeasurable.

The decorations created a sea of remembrance of the greatest gift of all time—God's own son. The added blessing of Violet's newfound friendship with Jane—a loving, encouraging friend who gave her hope. And now Nate.

God's gifts . . . my cup overflows with blessings.

PART II
CHRISTMAS IN TETBURY
DECEMBER 2024

That evening, as they sat by the fireplace and enjoyed cups of hot chocolate, Mimi finished telling Violet's story. With a smile, she turned to Emma. "So, what do you think?"

"It's a sweet story." Emma gazed into the dancing flames in the fireplace. "You often hear about Jane's close relationship with her sister Cassandra, but it's touching to know she had a friend like Violet."

Mimi nodded. "It might have taken much longer for Violet and Nate to come together without Jane's support and encouragement."

"I'd say their friendship filled a void in both their lives."

"Yes. That's how the Lord designed us. We need each other and gain strength and direction through friendship and community."

Emma pondered the ideas of friendship and community. Since she'd left Cambridge, she'd lost contact with most of the friends she'd known there. Moving to London, taking the job at the museum, and dating Jason had limited her desire to make new connections. What had she missed by not maintaining those longtime friendships or building new ones? If she had introduced Jason to her friends, would they have helped her see what was missing in their relationship? Would they have been there to support her through the breakup?

"I remember you mentioning your friend, Heidi," Mimi said. "Are you two still in touch?"

Emma glanced toward the window to avoid Mimi's direct gaze. "We text once in a while, but I haven't seen her since last summer."

"Why is that?"

Emma gave a slight shrug, but she knew the truth. "I spent most of my free time with Jason. I wanted him to know I was committed to our relationship. But look where that's taken me." She clicked her tongue and blew out a breath. "I should have seen this coming. Why am I such a failure at relationships?"

"Don't be hard on yourself, Emma. It makes sense you wanted to spend most of your time with Jason. Still, it's important not to let your other friendships fade away."

Emma sighed. "I probably hurt Heidi. I'm sure she's moved on and doesn't want to hear from me."

"You won't know unless you try. Why don't you reach out to her? Be honest and tell her what happened. I have a feeling she's more loyal and forgiving than you expect."

Emma took a sip of her hot chocolate. Was Mimi right? If she told Heidi what happened, was there a chance to renew their friendship?

She looked up and met Mimi's gaze. "I suppose it would be foolish not to try. Heidi and I have been friends for a long time. I don't want to lose our connection. I'll call her tomorrow."

Mimi gave an approving nod. "Maintaining friendships and building community are important for everyone who wants a happy and healthy life."

"Thanks, Mimi." Emma reached over and squeezed her grandmother's hand. Mimi's kindness and wisdom were good reminders that she did not have to face life alone. The Lord had designed her to connect with others, to give and receive strength. That was what she needed, and that was what she intended to pursue.

~

Two days later, Emma spent the morning doing a few errands for Mimi and a little Christmas shopping. She wanted to find a small gift for Heidi to follow up on yesterday's phone call. Heidi had been understanding, eager to catch up, and sympathetic about the breakup. Emma hoped the gift would show Heidi how much she appreciated her.

As Emma walked up Long Street, she glanced at the thick gray clouds gathered overhead and slipped her hands into her pockets. She should have worn gloves. The temperature had dropped several degrees, and snow was predicted overnight.

When she reached the shop, she pushed open the door and found Mimi dusting a display of China teacups and humming a Christmas carol.

"Hello, dear. How was the shopping?"

"I found the perfect gift for Heidi." Emma opened the bag and removed the small box containing the sapphire pendant necklace. "Heidi's birthstone is sapphire."

"That's very pretty. I'm sure she'll be pleased." Mimi set down the feather duster. "I'm glad you called her."

Emma slipped the box back into the bag. "I'm glad you told me that story."

They exchanged a smile, and Mimi motioned toward the glass display case. "I have a new item I'd like to show you."

"Something came in this morning?"

"Yes. It's very rare and probably one of the most valuable items I have in the shop." She pulled her keys from her pocket, stepped behind the counter, and unlocked the glass case containing rare books. She took out a slim volume with a faded cinnamon-colored cover. "This is a first edition of *A Christmas Carol* by Charles Dickens."

Emma's eyes widened, and she stepped closer. "A first edition?"

Mimi's eyes glowed as she nodded. "That's right. It has some water damage to the back cover, but other than that, it's in good condition. I believe the value is between twenty-five to thirty thousand pounds."

Emma pulled in a sharp breath. "Mimi, that's a huge sum."

"I won't receive it all, but there will be a nice commission when it's sold."

"Who brought it in?"

"A man named Daniel Richards. He said it's been passed down in his family for many years. He's reluctant to sell it, but he recently retired and wants to buy a home in the country. The proceeds will help with the down-payment."

"I love Dickens' stories." Emma motioned toward the book. "I've listened to the audio version and seen several films based on *A Christmas Carol*."

Mimi opened the book and turned it so Emma could see the first color plate. "Mr. Richards told me a very interesting story about this particular copy."

Emma met Mimi's gaze. "Really?"

Mimi nodded. "It changed the course of one young couple's lives."

A tremor of delight coursed through Emma. "Oh, I can't wait to hear their story."

A VICTORIAN CHRISTMAS TALE

By Carrie Turansky

"I believe that virtue shows quite as well in rags and patches
as she does in purple and fine linen."
Charles Dickens, Essay in *Household Words*

The LORD does not look at the things people look at. People
look at the outward appearance, but the LORD looks at the
heart."
1 Samuel 16:7 NIV

CHAPTER ONE

LONDON, OCTOBER 1843

*C*lara Raymond's stomach tensed as she reached for the driver's hand and stepped down from her family's carriage. Without warning, her left leg gave way. She gasped and stumbled.

The driver's hand shot out to steady her. "Are you all right, miss?"

She straightened. "Yes. I'm fine. Thank you." But her face flamed, and her leg throbbed. She should've been more careful. Stepping down was always a challenge. After twenty-four years of dealing with a weak leg that was several inches shorter than the other, she ought to have mastered that movement, but obviously, she hadn't.

Her mother, Mary Raymond, studied Clara as she waited beside the coach. Her perpetual frown deepened. "For goodness' sake, Clara, you must be more careful."

Clara clenched her jaw, holding back a retort. Why couldn't Mother be more understanding? The answer rushed in with a painful stab to her heart. Mother never liked to be reminded of Clara's defects, especially in public. They were an embarrassment and needed to be hidden—*she* was an embarrassment. Tears burned her eyes, but she quickly blinked them away.

Her older sister, Emily, stepped down beside her. She slipped her arm through Clara's and sent her a reassuring smile. "Don't let Mother upset you," she whispered.

Clara blew out a breath. Emily was right. She must not allow Mother to ruin this outing. She'd been looking forward to visiting the Foundling Hospital for several months. Emily had been volunteering there while her husband was away, working in Scotland. Clara longed to join her, but first, they had to convince Mother it was acceptable for a young unmarried woman to take on that role.

Mother instructed the driver to wait for them, then strode through the open wrought iron gate and up the walkway toward the main entrance to the Foundling Hospital. Clara and Emily followed at a slower pace. The scent of burning leaves hung in the air, although all evidence of autumn leaves had been cleared from the large open courtyard.

Mother glanced over her shoulder. "Now remember, I must be home by two o'clock. We have eight guests joining us for dinner, and there's much to be done."

Clara sighed. Mother needn't be in such a hurry. They had a large staff of servants to prepare the house and meal. She lifted her gaze and scanned the façade of the large U-shaped brick building. Emily had told her it housed almost two hundred young children whose mothers had given them into care at the Foundling Hospital when they were infants. Shortly after a baby arrived, they were sent out to the country to stay with a family until they were five years old. Then they returned to begin their schooling and training. Most would leave before they turned twelve to work as apprentices or domestics. Clara's heart clenched at the thought, wishing she might do something to brighten their days.

Emily came once a week, reading to the girls and helping them learn sewing skills. Her sister found it very rewarding, and the stories she relayed had touched Clara's heart and made her long to accompany her.

They reached the front door, and Mother pressed the bell. The door opened, and a girl who looked about twelve led them down a dim hallway. The strong scent of some type of cleaning solution hung in the air and stung Clara's nose.

They reached the matron's office where five well-dressed women and two men waited in the hall.

Mother took Clara's arm and guided her toward the group. "Mrs. Worthington, what a pleasure to see you. You remember my daughters, Clara and Emily."

Mrs. Worthington, a well-dressed middle-aged woman, smiled and nodded. "Of course. It's nice to see you again. I didn't realize you were a supporter of the Foundling Hospital."

Mother's eyes widened. "Oh, well, my daughter Emily volunteers here, so naturally we're interested to learn more."

"My husband, Gordon, and I have been supporters for several years." Mrs. Worthington nodded to her adult son who stood beside her. "And Archibald is eager to join us." She turned to Clara. "You remember Archibald, don't you?"

Clara's shoulders tensed. She'd met Archibald a few months earlier at a dinner party, and they had shared an uncomfortable exchange. After dinner, he'd asked her to dance, and she'd declined. He'd insisted, and she'd felt she had to explain why she could not. His stunned response had made it clear he would not ask her again.

She nodded to him. "Mr. Worthington."

He returned a polite nod. "Miss Raymond." But the tilt of his chin and dismissive look in his eyes made it clear he remembered her deformity.

A sinking feeling hit her stomach. Would she ever meet a man who would not look down on her for her defects?

The matron's office door opened, and a tall, thin woman dressed in black stepped out. She wore a white cap covering her hair, and wire-rimmed spectacles sat atop her pointed nose. "Good morning, and welcome to the Foundling Hospital. My name is Martha Langtree. I am the matron, and I'll be escorting you on your tour today." She scanned the group and frowned slightly. "We're expecting two more guests to join us."

No sooner had she spoken, then the bell rang. The girl who had greeted them hurried down the hall and opened the front door. Two gentlemen stepped in and started toward them. Both men were well dressed and looked to be in their late twenties or early thirties.

Recognition flashed through Clara, and she froze. She'd met the taller man with brown hair and deep blue eyes, at the same party where she'd met Archibald. He'd introduced himself as John Stafford, and his kindness and the conversation that followed had stirred her heart. It had all gone so well . . . until his fiancé arrived and whisked him away.

"What is it?" Emily whispered.

She gave a slight nod toward John. "I recognize that man."

Emily kept her voice low. "Of course. That's Charles Dickens."

"What?" Clara's gaze darted to the shorter man with darker hair who walked beside John. "You mean the famous author?"

"Yes. Paul and I met him and his wife Katherine at an event last year. I'm sure that's him."

There was no time to say anything more, as John and Charles joined the group.

The matron stepped forward. "Welcome, Mr. Dickens. It's an honor to have you with us today."

Mr. Dickens nodded. "Thank you. We're glad to be here. This is my associate, John Stafford." Then he glanced around the hallway, as though he were taking mental notes of all the details.

Was he going to write a new story that would include the Foundling Hospital? Was that why he'd come?

Several people stepped forward to shake hands with Mr. Dickens and compliment him on his writing. Clara held her breath as she watched John. Would he remember her? A second later, their gazes connected. His eyes lit up, and he smiled.

Her cheeks warmed as she returned a smile then looked down. The thrill faded as she remembered he was engaged to be married, and she must guard her actions toward him.

Mother shifted impatiently and pursed her lips, looking as though she had no intention of speaking to Mr. Dickens, but Mrs. Worthington ushered him closer, and John followed.

Mrs. Worthington motioned toward Mother. "Mr. Dickens this is Mrs. Mary Raymond and her daughters, Emily Wright and Clara Raymond."

Mr. Dickens made a slight bow. "It's a pleasure to meet you, ladies."

Emily smiled. "Thank you. Clara and I love your books. I come here each week as a volunteer, and I've been reading *Oliver Twist* to the girls."

Charles's eyebrows rose. "Well, that's wonderful to hear. I hope they enjoy it."

"Oh, they do, very much."

John stepped forward and offered Clara a slight bow. "Miss Raymond, it's good to see you again."

Clara swallowed and nodded. "Mr. Stafford, it's a pleasure to see you as well." She wished she could say more, but her face was flaming, and her throat felt dry as a bone. She pressed her lips tight and silently scolded herself for reacting like a silly schoolgirl.

"Ladies and gentlemen," the matron called. "If you'll follow me, we shall begin our tour."

JOHN CLASPED his hands behind his back as members of the tour group thanked the matron and shook hands with Charles. A few of them offered John a polite nod as they passed, but many walked by without acknowledging him. John was used to his friend's notoriety and didn't mind standing in his shadow. He and Charles had been good friends for many years. Their love for literature had drawn them together long before Charles became famous.

As their friendship grew, Charles confided in John and often asked him to read his writing before it was published. John gave his honest review and offered much needed encouragement. He also accompanied Charles when he met with his publisher and helped negotiate contracts and payments, duties that Charles found distasteful. And with Charles's artistic and sometimes volatile nature, he often needed a buffer between himself and his publisher.

John smiled as he watched Charles say goodbye to a few more guests. This visit to the Foundling Hospital had been a good idea. John had suggested it, hoping it might spark a new story idea for Charles. His last two projects had not been well received, and that put Charles under tremendous financial pressure. And when Charles struggled, John felt it as well. Charles was more than a friend. He'd become like a brother to John.

He straightened as Clara, her mother, and sister approached. Mrs. Raymond offered a few brief words to

Charles, then turned and started down the hall without speaking to John.

Clara slowed and looked his way. "I hope you enjoyed the tour, Mr. Stafford." Even though she only spoke a few words, he sensed her warmth and sincerity.

His chest expanded. "Thank you, Miss Raymond. I did enjoy it. The Foundling Hospital is an important charity. These children will have a chance for a meaningful life—something they might never experience if their mothers had not had the courage to bring them here." His throat tightened, and he looked down, embarrassed by his unexpected emotion.

It was the truth behind his statement that struck a chord. He'd spent most of his childhood at the Foundling Hospital, having been left there when he was only a few days old. It was a fact he rarely revealed. Even Charles didn't know that portion of his history.

Clara's brown eyes glowed. "Yes, they do wonderful work here. I'm very impressed."

He wished he could continue their conversation, but her mother stood a few feet away, watching them with an impatient look. He focused on Clara. "I hope I'll see you again soon."

A flicker of surprise crossed her features, then her cheeks turned pink, and she offered another sweet smile. "I hope so as well. Good day, Mr. Stafford."

"Good day, Miss Raymond." His gaze followed her down the hall, and he pulled in a slow deep breath. She was a lovely young woman with a kind and sensitive heart. He noticed her limp, and it reminded him of the conversation they'd shared the night they'd first met. His thoughts returned to that evening.

It was unusually warm that twenty-first of June. He

remembered the date clearly because it had been an important turning point in his life.

He'd slipped away to a side room after dinner, hoping for a cool breeze and a few moments alone to consider the disturbing rumor he'd been told about his fiancé. The accusations were humiliating. He would have to confront her. If they were true, he would have no choice but to break off their engagement. He could never marry a woman who was unfaithful.

He crossed the dimly lit room toward the open door to the balcony. A slight gasp sounded to his left, and his steps stalled.

A young woman looked up at him from where she sat in an overstuffed chair facing the balcony.

He took a step back. "I'm sorry. I didn't realize anyone was in here."

Moonlight shone on her face highlighting her softly rounded cheeks, wide brown eyes, and glossy brown hair. She sent him a slight smile. "It's all right. I don't mind. I was just hoping to find an out of the way spot to wait until my parents and sister are ready to leave."

He studied her a moment more. How intriguing—an attractive young woman who would rather avoid the company of others than take advantage of the connections she could make at a dinner party like this.

His fiancé had left his side a few minutes after they'd arrived to make the circuit of the room, speaking to everyone she knew and becoming acquainted with those she hadn't met before. Her actions added more weight to the rumor. He frowned and pushed down the hurt. Why wasn't she content to stay by his side and enjoy his company? Why wasn't he enough?

The sound of the quartet playing a lively tune rose in the adjoining room, and they both turned toward the music.

"It sounds as though the dancing has begun." He looked her way again. "Will you rejoin the party?"

Her smile faded. "No, I don't dance."

He sent her a quizzical look. "I'm sure there are many men who would enjoy partnering with you."

She lowered her gaze. "It's not that I don't want to dance . . . I can't."

He cocked his head. "Come now, a pretty young woman like you is surely brave enough to join in the dancing." He'd hoped the compliment and light tone would please her.

Some unnamed emotion flickered in her eyes. "My decision not to dance has nothing to do with a lack of bravery."

He grinned. "Are you sure about that?"

She rose from the chair. "Excuse me."

He'd done it now—offended her and stolen her hiding place. "I meant no offense."

"None taken." Yet hurt was evident in her voice.

She stepped to the left, then teetered and gasped. He reached out, but not quick enough. She fell against the small table next to the chair and cried out.

His heart jerked, and he grabbed hold of her arm, righting her. "Are you hurt?"

She winced as she sucked in a breath. "No. I'm fine." Her skirt had fallen to the side exposing one shoe with a sole several inches thick.

Understanding struck, and he froze. She didn't dance because it would be difficult for her, if not impossible. Regret swamped him, and he clamped his jaw. "I beg your pardon. I should not have teased you as I did."

Their gazes connected, and silent understanding passed between them. She knew he'd seen her shoe and was embarrassed by it.

His chest tightened as he searched for words to fill the silence. "I should have introduced myself," he hurried on, hoping to soothe her discomfort. "My name is John Stafford. I write articles and books about history and government. Not very exciting topics, but they've opened the door to publishing for me. I'm also a literary and dramatic critic for the *London Daily News*." He was rambling, but he had to say something. He had embarrassed her and had to make it right.

She sent him a skeptical look as though she debated if she would answer.

He softened his tone. "I truly did not mean to offend you."

She released a deep breath and faced him once more. "Very well. Let's begin again." She held out her hand. "My name is Clara Raymond. I'm the daughter of George and Mary Raymond."

Relief rushed through him, and he took her hand and bowed slightly, relieved she'd abandoned her plan to dash away. How could he make up for his thoughtless comments? Continuing the conversation seemed the best path.

"And what do you do, Miss Raymond?"

She laughed softly. "I do what all young women of my station do. I pay calls, I receive calls. I attend church and help with charitable causes. On occasion, I'm obliged to attend dinner parties as I did tonight. But I prefer reading, playing the piano, and arranging flowers, rather than attending balls and large parties."

"I'm very fond of reading myself." He was about to say more when the door opened.

Letitia strode in. "John, there you are. I've been looking—" Her gaze connected with Clara. Her steps stalled, and her eyes widened. She shot John a look filled with accusations.

Heat rushed up his neck, and his cravat suddenly felt too tight. He'd done nothing wrong, but he could imagine how it appeared. He stepped forward. "Letitia, this is Miss Clara Raymond." He turned to Clara. "This is . . . Letitia Farthington."

"His fiancé," Letitia quickly added with a lift of her chin and a look meant to put Miss Raymond in her place.

Clara blinked, then offered a slight smile. "I'm pleased to meet you. I wish you a happy engagement and an even happier marriage."

Letitia nodded. "I'm sure we'll be very happy." She slipped her arm through John's. "Come, John. The dancing has started, and we don't want to miss that."

The scene faded in his mind, but his stomach clenched as he recalled the conversation that followed that dance and Letitia's unwillingness to acknowledge or deny the rumor.

"John, did you hear what I said?" Charles's voice pulled him back to the moment.

John shifted and focused on his friend. "Sorry, I was miles away."

Charles grinned and put his hand on John's shoulder. "And I can guess where you were. I saw the way you spoke to Miss Raymond."

John grimaced as he started down the hall toward the front door. "I won't deny it was good to see her again."

"So, this wasn't your first meeting? Even better! She's a very pretty, young woman, though her mother was a bit disagreeable."

That was true, but John kept that thought to himself.

"So, when will you call on her?

John shook his head. "I've no plans to call on Miss Raymond."

"Then make plans! You've suffered in silence long enough because of what happened with Letitia. Let it go, man! Make a fresh start! A world of happiness awaits you, if only you'll take hold of it."

John clenched his jaw. Charles was always so enthusiastic. He never saw an obstacle that couldn't be overcome. John, on the other hand, had experienced the harder side of life and was more cautious and practical. His broken engagement with Letitia had wounded his pride and made him skeptical of ever finding a woman worth pursuing.

The image of Clara rose in his mind, but he quickly doused it. As attractive as he found Miss Clara Raymond, he wasn't ready to risk his heart and reputation . . . or another betrayal.

CHAPTER TWO

*C*lara tucked a golden chrysanthemum into the flower arrangement and stood back to check the design. With a smile and a nod, she lifted the heavy vase from the sideboard. Hopefully, Mother would be pleased. She carried the arrangement into the dining room and placed it in the center of the table.

Mother was hosting another dinner party that evening, and she'd asked Clara to make an autumn-colored arrangement that would complement the China and linens she had chosen.

Flower arranging was a task she always enjoyed, and she'd gladly agreed. The flowers had been delivered an hour earlier, and she'd quickly set to work. Delighted with the beautiful array of colors and heady scents, she'd soon lost herself in the process.

Footsteps sounded in the hall, and Clara looked up. Emily walked into the room. Her sister's cheeks were rosy from the cold. "Hello, my dear. How are you?" She crossed the room and kissed Clara's cheek.

"I'm well."

"I have wonderful news!" Emily pulled off her gloves.

"What is it?"

Emily glanced over her shoulder and lowered her voice. "Is Mother here?"

"No, she's calling on Mrs. Downing, but I expect her back soon."

"Good. That gives us time."

"Time for what?"

"To make a plan."

Clara laughed. "What are we planning?"

Emily slipped off her coat. "Has Mother agreed you may volunteer at the Foundling Hospital?"

"Not yet." Clara bit her lip, embarrassed that she hadn't pressed the issue with Mother.

"Well, I have an idea that may help persuade her."

Clara's heartbeat quickened. "Tell me more."

"Mr. Dickens is speaking tomorrow night at an event that's planned to raise funds for the Foundling Hospital. If we convince Mother and Father to attend and they see how many of their friends are supporters, I think they'll be convinced it's a respected charity and let you volunteer." Emily grinned, and her eyes twinkled. "And I believe *your* Mr. Stafford will also attend."

Heat rushed into Clara's cheeks. "He's not *my* Mr. Stafford."

"Well, the way he was speaking to you when we were at the Foundling Hospital, makes me think he might like to be."

Clara shook her head. "I told you, he's engaged."

Emily tipped her head and searched Clara's face. "Are you certain?"

"Yes. The night I met him last summer, his fiancé made sure I knew she was his intended."

"Even so, I think we should still go. I want to hear Mr.

Dickens speak, and since Paul is away, I can't go alone. Please say you'll come with me."

Clara smoothed a slight wrinkle in the tablecloth. She would enjoy hearing Mr. Dickens. And the thought of seeing Mr. Stafford again made her sister's invitation even more appealing. But convincing her parents to go with them or allow her to attend with Emily would not be easy. Neither were fans of Mr. Dickens. Her spirit deflated. She hated conflict, especially with her parents.

She looked up and met Emily's gaze. "I'm not sure Mother and Father will approve."

"Goodness, Clara! You're twenty-four. Don't you think it's time you started making your own decisions and living your own life?"

"That's easy for you to say. You're married to Paul and have a home of your own. I must live here and keep the peace with Mother and Father. You know how difficult they can be when you cross them."

"Yes, but you are a grown woman. You have thoughts and interests of your own. Mother and Father need to accept that. This is an entirely proper event. I think we should plan to attend with or without them."

John's image rose in her mind, and with it, the longing to see him again. Was it wrong to hope that he might be there and speak to her as he had last summer and at the Foundling Hospital? What if he was already married? The thought pained her and reminded her she should not be thinking about John Stafford in any way except as a pleasant acquaintance.

Courage stirred her heart, and she straightened her shoulders. She loved Mr. Dickens' novels, and she wanted to support the work of the Foundling Hospital. It was time she stood up for herself and risked her parents' disapproval. That was the only way she would ever gain a life of her own, and with it, her freedom.

～

THE LOW HUM of the audience drifted past the closed curtain of the Wainwright Music Hall. John and Charles stood backstage, waiting in the wings, while the thrum of the crowd vibrated the stage floorboards. John glanced at Charles and noted his stiff shoulders and flushed face. Concern shot through him. He had better offer some words of encouragement or his friend was going to bolt.

John pulled his pocket watch from his waistcoat. "Don't worry. Not much longer now."

Charles turned to John. "Do I look all right?"

John scanned Charles from head to toe. "You look like a well-dressed and much-admired author of award-winning novels, although your cravat is a bit crooked."

Charles groaned and lifted his chin. "Katherine left early to meet her parents. Will you fix it?"

"Of course." John adjusted his friend's cravat, then he stepped to the side and looked around the edge of the red velvet curtain. Every seat in the cavernous hall seemed to be filled, and a buzz of excitement hung in the air.

Charles frowned and tugged his waistcoat straight. "Do you see Katherine?"

"Yes, she's seated in the front row with her parents."

Charles nodded, but the news didn't seem to soothe his agitation.

John looked out again. As his gaze swept the audience, he spotted a familiar face, and his heartbeat surged. In the third row, Clara Raymond sat with her mother, sister, and a distinguished man in white tie with impressive muttonchop sideburns. He had to be her father.

His gaze returned to Clara. She wore a light blue dress that highlighted her attractive figure. Around her creamy neck hung a double strand of pearls. She was a vision. He blinked and swallowed.

He'd thought of her often since they'd spoken at the Foundling Hospital last week, and he'd wondered if he might see her again. With this massive crowd would he be able to find her and speak to her after? If she knew his background, would she even want to speak to him? His spirit deflated, and he turned away from the curtain.

Charles looked his way and frowned. "What is it, John?"

"It's nothing. I just saw someone I recognized."

Charles gripped John's sleeve and leaned closer. "Don't tell me Hillmont is out there."

Daniel Hillmont's scorching literary reviews had damaged Charles's reputation with countless readers. No matter what Charles wrote, the man always found something to criticize. John believed he was simply jealous that Charles had such a large following. But Charles took his critical words to heart and dreaded seeing Hillmont or reading his reviews.

John shook his head. "No need to worry. It's not Hillmont."

"Thank heavens!" Charles paced a few steps, then swung around and faced John. "Why did I ever agree to do this? I could be at home working on my book!"

John's eyebrows rose. "You have a new idea for a story?"

Charles broke eye contact. "Not exactly, but I'll never find one if I have to spend all my time preparing to speak to crowds like this." He lifted his hand and rubbed his eyes. "Oh, why do I put myself through this torture?"

John put a firm hand on Charles's shoulder. "You do it for your readers. They want to see you and hear from you."

"They can *hear* from me by reading my novels."

"Yes, and if we want them to keep reading your novels,

then they must see you in person from time to time." He wouldn't remind Charles that his last two projects had been flops. These personal appearances were key to holding on to his readership until he could give them a new story, hopefully one that would capture their imagination and hearts as *Oliver Twist* had.

The stage manager approached. "Are you ready, Mr. Dickens?"

Charles straightened, looking grim but determined. "Yes, I'm ready."

John squeezed his shoulder. "You'll do fine, Charles. Just go out there and give them what they came for."

Charles rolled his eyes, but he appeared to accept his fate.

The stage manager signaled Mr. Ridley, President of the Foundling Hospital Committee.

Mr. Ridley stepped out in front of the curtain. "Ladies and gentlemen, thank you for coming this evening. It is my pleasure to welcome you to tonight's program in support of the Foundling Hospital and their work to care for children in need." Polite applause rose from the audience. "And now I present to you one of Britan's most beloved literary figures, the author of *Nicholas Nickleby, Oliver Twist,* and many other fine stories . . . the one, the only, Mr. Charles Dickens!"

APPLAUSE ROSE and filled the auditorium, and Clara joined in with the others. A few audience members added boisterous cheers and loud whistles as Mr. Dickens walked to center stage and bowed.

Father's eyebrows dipped, and he turned toward Clara. "This crowd sounds more like rowdy fans at a cricket match than respectable members of society."

Clara smiled and continued clapping. "Everyone admires Charles Dickens, Father."

"Not everyone," Father added with a sour look.

Mr. Dickens nodded and mouthed the words, *thank you*, several times while he waited for the applause to die down and for the audience to settle in their seats.

At the right side of the stage, the curtain shifted slightly. Clara glanced in that direction, and her breath caught. John Stafford stood in the wings, watching Mr. Dickens with a steady gaze and a slightly creased forehead.

He looked quite handsome, dressed in a deep blue suit with a brocade waistcoat and an ivory cravat. But even more appealing than his appearance was his obvious concern for his friend. She had noticed the way he stood with Mr. Dickens the day they'd toured the Foundling Hospital, waiting patiently while everyone in their group wanted to speak to the famous author and mostly ignored him. He seemed to be a humble and loyal friend. Those were fine qualities that increased her admiration.

But reality rushed in. She closed her eyes and pressed her lips tight. No matter how much she admired John Stafford, he was committed to another. She must guard her thoughts about him, or she would risk embarrassment and heartache. She swallowed past her tight throat and trained her gaze on Mr. Dickens.

The beloved author held the audience in the palm of his hand as he regaled them with tales of his recent tour of the United States and his impression of the people and their customs as well as scenic sights he had enjoyed. He was a master storyteller, and Clara found herself lost in those stories.

An hour and a half later, she scanned the crowd lingering in the lobby following Mr. Dicken's presentation. Was there still a chance she might see John? She released a deep breath and looked down. Why did she keep thinking of him?

Emily leaned closer. "Have you seen him?"

Clara's face warmed. "Who?"

"You know very well who I'm speaking of."

Clara sighed. There was no use pretending. Her sister often seemed to read her private thoughts. "I saw him at the side of the stage when the program began, but not since." She glanced toward the auditorium door. Mr. Dickens had not passed through the lobby yet. Would he and John make an appearance before she and her family had to depart?

Mother and Father continued speaking to Mr. and Mrs. Worthington. Clara clasped her hands, resisting the urge to fidget.

"Clara, Mrs. Worthington asked what you thought of Mr. Dicken's speech." Mother arched her eyebrows and sent Clara a pointed look—a silent reprimand for not paying attention to the conversation.

Clara turned to Mrs. Worthington and forced a smile. "I enjoyed it very much, especially his humorous stories about his travels in America."

Mrs. Worthington returned Clara's smile. "Yes, it sounds as though he received a very warm welcome on his tour. And I appreciated his appeal tonight. It was very heartfelt. I'm sure it will increase donations for the Foundling Hospital."

Clara nodded, recalling Mr. Dicken's comments about the children. His thoughtful plea had been very moving, and she wished there was more she might do to help. The thought of volunteering rose in her mind again, and her stomach tightened. Pressing the matter with Mother would be difficult, but it was certainly a worthy cause.

Emily tugged Clara's sleeve and shot a glance toward the auditorium door.

Mr. Dickens stepped into the lobby, walking arm-in-arm

with his wife. An older couple followed them, and John brought up the rear.

Clara's heart lifted. John's fiancé was not on his arm tonight.

Murmurs of approval moved through the crowd. Mr. Dickens smiled and nodded to those who greeted him. Soon he and his wife were encircled by well-wishers eager to shake his hand and offer words of praise for his presentation.

Father frowned and shook his head. "Such a fuss! You'd think the man was the prime minister."

Emily smiled. "People love his stories, Father. He receives this kind of welcome wherever he goes."

"I don't understand it," Father continued. "Why does he always write about orphans, pickpockets, and poverty? Why not feature upstanding characters who deserve our admiration?"

Clara straightened. Father had never read a Dickens novel. His opinions were formed by reading reviews, which were sometimes critical and unfair. "Mr. Dickens stories highlight the struggles of those who are less fortunate. I believe he wants to stir readers' hearts with compassion and understanding."

Father huffed. "What those people need to do is work hard and support themselves. If not, there are workhouses and prisons."

Clara was about to reply, when John's gaze connected with hers. A smile broke across his face, and he wove through the crowd toward her.

Clara reached for Emily's hand. Before she could explain, John stopped in front of her.

"Miss Raymond, it's a pleasure to see you again."

Clara's heart leaped, but her words seemed frozen in her mouth.

He shifted his gaze to her parents and offered a confident smile. "How do you do, Mrs. Raymond?"

Mother gave a slight nod, but she did not return his smile. "Mr. Stafford."

Clara found her voice and motioned to her left. "May I introduce my father, Mr. George Raymond."

John extended his hand. "I'm pleased to meet you, sir.

Father looked him over, then slowly reached out and shook his hand.

Clara looked from John to Father. "Mr. Stafford is an author and literary critic for the *London Daily News*. He's also a good friend of Mr. Dickens."

John sent her a warm smile, looking pleased that she recalled what she'd learned about him.

Father frowned. "An associate of Mr. Dickens, are you? I can't say that's the best recommendation. I don't approve of Mr. Dickens' novels and his focus on the dregs of society. Isn't there enough trouble in the newspaper each morning? Why waste readers' time with topics such as those?"

Clara's face flushed. "Father, there's no need to quiz Mr. Stafford about Mr. Dickens' choice of topics."

An awkward silence followed until Mrs. Worthington said, "Mr. Stafford, I remember meeting you when we toured the Foundling Hospital."

"Yes, I was pleased to see the good work they're doing. It's very impressive, especially when you realize many of those children might have died if they'd not been taken in by the Foundling Hospital." John sent a serious look around the group. "They deserve our generous support."

Mrs. Worthington's eyes lit up. "Yes, how true! It's good to hear you're such a strong advocate for the Foundling Hospital. Perhaps you'd like to join our committee."

"What committee is that?" John asked.

"I've contacted a few people about planning a Christmas party for the children."

Clara's heartbeat quickened. "A Christmas party?"

Mrs. Worthington turned to her. "Yes, we're gathering at my home next Tuesday afternoon at two to discuss our ideas and begin making plans. Would you like to join us?"

Clara blinked. Could she step out on her own for a cause like that? Mother might not approve, but the answer flooded her heart. "Yes, I'd love to help."

Mother sent her a sharp look. "I'm not sure Clara is free that day."

Clara met Mother's gaze, accepting the challenge. "I don't recall I have any commitments on Tuesday."

John turned to Mrs. Worthington. "A Christmas party sounds like a wonderful idea. I'd be glad to join the committee and do whatever I can.

Emily grinned. "I'd be happy to help as well."

Mrs. Worthington clasped her hands to her heart. "Wonderful! The more the merrier!"

John sent Clara a smile, and her heart surged. She would see John on Tuesday, and they would put their efforts toward giving the children a Christmas party to remember.

CHAPTER THREE

*J*ohn glanced out the window of the hansom cab as it rolled past rows of wealthy homes on Saint James Street in Mayfair. His home in the Bloomsbury section of London wasn't nearly as elegant as these, but he had come a long way from his humble beginnings at the Foundling Hospital.

Pushing aside the comparison, he lowered his gaze and read Mrs. Worthington's note once more. She was ill and unable to host the committee meeting to plan the children's Christmas party. Rather than postponing, they had moved the meeting to Clara Raymond's home.

His smile widened as memories of Clara filled his mind. Last Saturday evening, she'd looked lovely in that sky-blue gown with pearls around her neck and a few more tucked into her chestnut brown hair. She seemed pleased to see him, and her welcoming expression and kind words had stirred his hope.

Her father's critical comments about Charles's writing had struck a nerve, but Clara's announcement that she wanted to help plan the children's Christmas party prompted him to join the committee as well.

Moving the meeting to Clara's home seemed like a wonderful stroke of luck. But then, he remembered his prayer that morning, asking for guidance concerning the future. Perhaps the change of venue was an answer to that prayer. He intended to take the opportunity to get to know Clara and see if her character matched her open spirit and outward beauty.

The chance to spend time with Clara at her home was the second bit of good news he'd received that day. He'd visited Charles earlier, and his friend told him he'd finally found an idea for the next story. He planned to write about a miserly man who was visited by three ghosts on Christmas Eve, and they would teach him lessons that would stir his heart.

His friend outlined the opening scenes in his usual dramatic fashion, then turned to John. "Well? How do you like it?"

John stifled a grimace. "I'm not sure about the ghosts. Don't you think that's a bit gloomy for a Christmas tale?"

Charles blinked, looking surprised and a bit hurt by John's question.

John quickly added, "But if anyone can carry it off, I'm sure you're the man."

Those words seemed to bolster Charles, and John left his friend feverishly scribbling away in his study, lost in the world of ghosts and graveyards.

The driver pulled the cab to a stop in front of an elegant three-story house with marble steps and four tall white columns across the front. John spotted the number seventy-eight by the front door, confirming this was the Raymond's residence. The style and location reminded him once again of their wealth and position in society.

He swallowed, recalling his prayer, then stepped down

and paid the driver. He turned and scanned the house's impressive façade. Clara's family might be wealthy, but she never acted superior or self-important as many of the upper-class women he'd met. Certainly, she was nothing like Letitia.

He quickly mounted the steps and knocked on the door. A tall, thin butler with silver hair answered. John gave his name and asked to see Miss Clara Raymond.

The butler led him through the entry hall to the door of a large sitting room. "Mr. John Stafford to see you, miss."

Clara rose and crossed toward him. She offered a sweet smile and extended her hand. "Mr. Stafford, I'm so glad you could come. I was afraid you might not have received Mrs. Worthington's message in time." Her warm welcome boosted his confidence.

He took her hand and returned a smile. "Thank you. I was out this morning, but I returned home about noon and found the message waiting for me."

"Please come in and sit down." She motioned toward the chairs and sofa grouped near the fireplace.

Before they could be seated, Clara's sister ,Emily, walked in and greeted Clara with a kiss on the cheek. She turned to John. "Hello, Mr. Stafford. I hope you're well."

"I am. Thank you." He turned to Clara. "And I'm eager to begin making plans for the Christmas party. Are the others going to join us?"

Clara sent him a worried look. "Everyone else sent their regrets."

Emily's eyebrows rose. "No one else is coming?"

"I'm afraid not." She turned to John. "I'm sorry you came all this way. We can set a new date to meet when Mrs. Worthington is well."

"We don't need to wait for Mrs. Worthington and the others," he said. "The three of us can begin the discussion."

Clara's expression brightened. "I have given it some

thought, and I'd love to hear your ideas." She motioned toward the sofa and chairs.

John waited for the women to be seated, then he joined Clara on the sofa.

"Mrs. Worthington sent her notes." Clara opened a leather folder and removed a few sheets of paper. "She spoke to the matron at the Foundling Hospital, and they've given us Saturday, the 20th of December from 2:00 until 5:00. We have full use of the dining hall and may come as early as 12:30 to prepare for the party."

John smiled and nodded, envisioning the dining hall with the long rows of tables and benches that could be easily moved aside to make room for the party. "Excellent. That's a large area with plenty of space for the children to play games. Since it's just off the kitchen, that will be helpful when we serve refreshments."

Clara sent him a questioning look.

John realized he'd spoken with unexpected familiarity about the dining hall and kitchen. They had looked through the doorway on the tour, but the children were eating, and they hadn't entered.

He cleared his throat, hoping she wouldn't guess why he knew those details. "What decorations do you have in mind?"

They spent the next half hour discussing how they might make the dining hall look festive, what type of parlor games would be appropriate for the different ages, and what special treats the children would enjoy.

"I know it will be a challenge with two hundred children, but I'd like each one to receive a gift," Clara added. "Perhaps something practical like new mittens, a hat, or scarf as well as a sweet or two."

Emily's expression brightened. "Why don't I ask the ladies of the women's guild at church if they could knit some gifts for the children? And perhaps you could ask the ladies at Saint John's."

Clara smiled. "That's a wonderful idea. I know several women who are very skilled knitters. I think they'd be willing to help. And let's ask them to use bright colors. The children would like that."

John's spirit rose. How pleased the children would be to receive those gifts. The Foundling Hospital could be cold in the winter, and those practical gifts would meet a need as well as brighten their holiday.

Emily glanced at Clara's list. "These all sound like good ideas. But how will we raise the funds to pay for the food and decorations?"

John rubbed his jaw. "Do you think the churches will cover the cost of yarn for the gifts?"

"We've done other projects like this before," Emily added, "and the church was happy to purchase the yarn."

"That would be helpful," John said. "We'll need to seek donations to cover the other expenses."

Clara looked from Emily to John. "Where do we start?"

"I suppose we can approach those on the committee first. Then we can visit business owners and ask them for contributions."

"It sounds daunting," Emily added. "But I'm sure when we tell them what we want to do for the children, some will help."

Clara sat up straighter. "I'll speak to Father."

Emily sent Clara a doubtful look. "Father doesn't usually give to charity."

"Well, he heard Mr. Dicken's appeal last Saturday, and we're both on the committee. That should motivate him to contribute something."

Emily glanced toward the fireplace for a moment then looked back at them. "What if we printed a program and listed the patrons? That could inspire him to make a donation."

Clara grinned. "Yes, that might help. We could print it as a Christmas card with a list of all the donors and give those to the volunteers, staff, and children at the party."

"That's an excellent idea." John thought of Albert Patterson, the man he'd worked for as an apprentice when he was young. "I know a printer who might be willing to make those for us."

A door opened in the entrance hall, and footsteps sounded. Mrs. Raymond walked into the sitting room, wearing a brown wool coat with a fur collar and a matching hat with a large silk ribbon tied under her chin. Her gaze darted from her daughters to John, and her eyebrows rose. "Clara, I wasn't aware you were receiving callers this afternoon."

John stood and turned toward her. "Mrs. Raymond. It's a pleasure to see you again."

She pursed her lips as she looked him over. "Mr. Stafford."

Clara rose. "Hello, Mother. Mrs. Worthington was unwell, so I offered to host the committee meeting here."

Her mother glanced around the room. "This looks like a rather *small* committee. Where are the others?"

"They sent their regrets."

"You should have postponed the meeting."

"Mr. Stafford came all this way, and we had Mrs. Worthington's notes."

Mrs. Raymond sent Clara a sharp look.

Irritation coursed through John. Why was this woman so disagreeable, especially toward her own daughter? He met Mrs. Worthington's gaze. "We may be small in number, but we've come up with some fine ideas that are sure to cheer the children this Christmas."

Emily stood next to Clara. "Yes. Wait until you hear what

we've planned. It's going to bring so much joy to the children."

John would not be put off by Mrs. Raymond sour mood. He turned to Clara. "We have only eight weeks to prepare for the party. I suggest we begin collecting donations as soon as possible."

"I agree," Emily added. "And I like your idea of speaking to businesses and shop owners. We might even visit some bakeries and sweet shops. Perhaps they'd be willing to provide the refreshments."

John nodded, pleased with her suggestion. "I have time on Thursday afternoon. Would that be convenient for you?" He glanced from Emily to Clara.

Clara smiled and nodded. "Thursday would be fine."

"I am free after one," he added.

"I'm available then as well," Emily said. "Shall we meet here and use our family's carriage?"

Mrs. Raymond stiffened. "You'll have to speak to your father about the use of the carriage."

Clara nodded. "I'll ask him."

Mrs. Raymond gave one more critical look at each of them before she turned and strode through the doorway.

Clara waited until her mother's footsteps faded, then turned to John. "I'm sorry. Mother seems a bit out of sorts."

He sent her an understanding smile. "It's all right. The important thing is—we have a plan that will delight the children and make their Christmas holiday special."

Clara's smile returned and hopeful light glowed in her eyes. "Yes. That's what matters most—the children."

ON THURSDAY AFTERNOON, Mother paced across the foyer then turned and faced Clara. "I do not approve of this outing. You are a young unmarried woman, and you should not be parading around town with a man like John Stafford."

Clara clenched her jaw, slipped on one glove, then reached for the other. She would not let her mother's harsh words stop her. "John Stafford is a respected author and literary critic, and we won't be parading around town. We'll be in our family's carriage."

"It's not proper! What will people think?"

"Emily will be with us. She can act as a chaperone. And if anyone hears that we're collecting donations for the Foundling Hospital Christmas party, it will raise their opinion of me, not damage it."

Mother sighed and lifted her hand to her forehead. "I don't understand. You've never acted like this before. Why now? Why with *that* man?"

"Mother, please try to understand." Emily's words rose in her mind. "I'm twenty-four years old. I must start making my own decisions and living my own life."

"But why must you associate with John Stafford? Who is he? Who is his family?"

Irritation coursed through Clara. Was a man's family the most important matter when judging his suitability? What about character, manners, and compassion? "Mr. Stafford is a gentleman. He hasn't mentioned his family, but I'm sure if they're anything like him, they are perfectly respectable."

Mother shook her head. "I know why he joined this *committee*! He knows your father has wealth and standing, and he wants to take advantage of the connection."

"That has nothing to do with it." She tugged on her other glove.

Mother's eyes widened. "Oh, yes it does. He's set his cap for you!"

Clara's face flamed. If only that were true. "You needn't

worry, Mother. Mr. Stafford has given no indication he's interested in calling on me as a suitor."

"Oh, Clara, you are so naïve. It's going to be your downfall!"

Clara pulled in a deep breath and forced her voice to remain even. "I appreciate your concern, but I'm going with Emily and Mr. Stafford to seek donations for the children's Christmas party. I'll be home in time for dinner. Please don't worry."

Mother raised her hand and covered her mouth, tears shimmering in her eyes.

Clara's heart clenched, and she almost gave in. Why was Mother so afraid to let her go? Did she doubt Clara had enough common sense to protect herself? Or was she more concerned about the family's reputation? That last thought sealed her decision.

A knock sounded, and they turned toward the front door.

Clara crossed the foyer, but Simmons, their butler, strode past at a quicker pace. Clara's face flamed. Simmons must have heard every word of the argument with her mother. He reached the door first and pulled it open.

Mr. Stafford looked in and met her gaze with a smile. "Good day, Miss Raymond."

"Good day, Mr. Stafford." Clara walked past the butler and out the door. "I sent our driver to collect Emily. They should be here soon. Let's wait outside."

Questions flashed in John's eyes, but he followed her down the steps. "Is everything all right?"

Clara slowed and looked up at him. "My mother can be . . . overly protective. She's not in favor of this outing, and she made that quite clear."

His brows dipped. "I'm sorry. I didn't mean to cause a disagreement between you and your mother."

Clara shook her head. "Please, don't worry. You're not to

blame. Emily has been encouraging me to speak up for myself. I'm afraid that's not been my habit, but I see the wisdom in her advice now."

He nodded with a look of approval in his eyes.

The family carriage rolled to a stop in front of the house. Emily looked out the side window and lifted her hand in greeting.

Mr. Stafford stepped forward and opened the door, then turned to help Clara.

She took hold of his hand, praying her leg would not fail her, then she stepped up into the carriage and took a seat beside her sister.

Mr. Stafford spoke to the driver then joined them in the carriage, sitting on the opposite bench. "I asked your driver to take us to Creston Street in Bloomsbury. I know a few business owners there who might donate to the cause, and there are also several shops we can visit."

Clara nodded, pleased he had planned ahead. As they rode across town, they discussed more ideas for the party.

"I remember a game we used to play when I was young called Ball of Wool." Mr. Stafford looked from Emily to Clara. "Have you played it?"

They shook their heads, and Clara said, "Tell us how it's played."

"You sit around a table and place a ball of wool in the center. I suppose at the Foundling Hospital we'd need to use the long tables in the dining hall, but I think that would still work. Everyone blows on the ball and tries to keep it away from themselves. If the ball rolls past a person on his right and off the table, then he or she must sit out the next round. You keep playing until only one person remains, and he or she is declared the winner."

Clara grinned, imagining the children enjoying the game. "Do you think all ages could play?"

He nodded. "I believe so." He pulled a small notebook from his pocket and thumbed through the pages. "They could also play The Minister's Cat, Charades, Pass the Slipper, or the Sculptor." Mr. Stafford lifted his eyebrows, and his gaze darted from Emily to Clara.

Her faced warmed. She'd heard of Charades, but not the other games.

Emily leaned forward. "Those games sound wonderful. Clara and I didn't play many games when we were young, so it's a good thing you're on the committee."

"Speaking of the committee, have you heard from Mrs. Worthington? I hope she has recovered from her illness."

"I sent her a letter with a summary of our discussion on Tuesday," Clara said. "But I haven't received a reply yet."

"We should forge ahead." Mr. Stafford glanced out the carriage window, then looked back at Clara. "I think she'll be pleased we've started seeking donations."

"Yes, I believe she will."

The carriage slowed to a stop. Mr. Stafford opened the door and helped Emily down. He looked up and offered his hand to Clara.

She hesitated, and concern flashed in his eyes. He took a step closer, sending her a silent message of understanding.

She took hold and carefully stepped down. His warm firm grip kept her steady and sent tingles up her arm. When both feet were firmly on the ground, she looked up and met his gaze. "Thank you."

John gave her a warm smile. "I'm glad to be of assistance." He released her hand and motioned down the street. "I suggest we start with a visit to Mr. Thaddeus Finch. He's the owner of Finch's Apothecary. After that, we can work our way down the street."

He spoke to the driver and asked him to return for them in one hour. The driver nodded, and the carriage rolled away.

Mr. Stafford stepped forward and opened the door to the apothecary, causing the bell to jingle as they stepped inside.

Clara glanced around the small shop. Shelves lined the back wall filled with various size bottles and jars. The scent of herbs, camphor, and drying lavender drifted toward her. A wiry man with grey, thinning hair stood behind a long wooden counter, weighing a bundle of dried chamomile. He glanced their way with a wary expression.

Mr. Stafford stepped forward with a polite smile. "Good afternoon, Mr. Finch."

The shopkeeper tucked some of the chamomile in a brown paper packet. "Afternoon. How may I help you?"

Mr. Stafford glanced at Clara, and she gave a slight nod, thankful he would speak for them. "We're here on behalf of the children of the Foundling Hospital. On the twentieth of December we'll be holding a Christmas party. We hope to bring them some joy during the holiday season and are seeking donations from kind-hearted businessmen."

"You're seeking donations?" Mr. Finch sniffed and folded the paper packet with sharp creases. "I run a business, not a charity."

Clara swallowed and stepped up next to Mr. Stafford. "We want to purchase a few decorations and treats for the children. Even a small donation would be a blessing."

Mr. Finch glared at her. "Do you know how many people come in here asking for charity? If I gave to every one of them, I'd end up in the workhouse." He tapped the counter with a bony finger. "People rarely consider what it costs to run a shop like this." He waved his hand toward the shelves behind him. "These medicines and herbs are expensive, then there are the licensing fees!" He shook his head. "I can't give to every do-gooder who walks through my door."

Mr. Stafford's jaw tightened. "Of course, Mr. Finch. We understand—"

"No, I don't think you do!" Mr. Finch narrowed his eyes. "Winter is coming and with it come coughs, chills, and fevers. I'll have no time to spare, and certainly no money to throw away."

Clara's throat burned, but she tamped down her anger and sent him her most earnest look. "Please, Mr. Finch. Think of the children."

He returned a haughty glare. "They have food to eat and a roof over their head. They ought to be grateful and not expect a holiday party. No, you'll not talk me into giving you any money."

Clara's smile faltered, and she dipped her head. "I see. Well, thank you for your time."

Mr. Finch grunted and returned to his work.

Mr. Stafford tipped his head toward the door, and Clara and Emily followed him out.

When Mr. Stafford closed the door, Emily huffed and pulled her cloak tighter. "What an odious man. He has no heart at all."

Clara couldn't agree more, but she held her tongue.

Mr. Stafford released a deep breath and glanced down the street. "Not everyone will refuse us. Let's try the next shop."

Clara lifted her chin. "Yes. I'm sure the next shop owner will be more agreeable."

CHAPTER FOUR

*T*he following Tuesday, Clara, Emily, and John met again for a second round of visiting businesses and soliciting donations for the Christmas party. Clara had been eager to see John again, but after two hours walking, her leg throbbed. She bit her lip and pressed on, unwilling to mention her discomfort to Emily or John.

Emily stopped at the corner and glanced in the clock shop window. "Oh, look at the time. Paul's train arrives at four. I promised I'd meet him at the railway station." Her sister's eyes glowed at the mention of reuniting with her husband who had been away in Scotland for almost three months.

John glanced down the street. "Shall I hail a cab?"

Father had needed the family carriage that afternoon, so they'd come to this area of town in a hansom cab.

"Thank you, Mr. Stafford." Emily shifted her gaze to Clara. A hint of concern lit her eyes. "I'm sorry to leave you."

A wave of uneasiness passed through Clara. Mother would not approve of Clara spending time alone with John. But Emily and Paul's house was on the opposite side of town. It wouldn't make sense for them to go with Emily to the station and then back across town to return Clara to her home.

She stifled a sigh. She must stop weighing every decision based on her expectation of Mother's approval or disapproval. "Please don't worry. I know you're eager to meet Paul, and you must not be late."

"There's a cab." John stepped toward the street and lifted his hand. The cab slowed to a stop. He opened the door for Emily, and she climbed in.

"Give my greetings to Paul," Clara called as her sister settled in the cab.

"I will." Emily returned a warm smile.

John closed the door, gave the driver Emily's destination, and the cab rolled away.

He turned to Clara, his blue eyes reflecting the afternoon sunshine. "We've accomplished quite a bit today. Would you like to stop for some refreshment before I escort you home? The Beresford Hotel is just down the street. They have an excellent dining room."

Pleasing warmth flushed Clara's face. John wanted to spend more time with her. But another thought rushed in and deflated her spirit. What if someone saw them entering the hotel without a chaperone? She silently debated a moment more, then lifted her chin. Her conscience was clear. It was time to stop worrying about what others thought.

She looked up at him. "I'd like that. Thank you."

He returned a pleased smile and escorted her down the street. When they reached the Beresford Hotel, the doorman, clad in rich livery with gleaming brass buttons, opened the heavy oak and glass door. Clara and John stepped inside and were greeted by a rush of warm air that carried the scent of beeswax polish and fresh flowers.

She looked up, and her breath caught. The foyer's high ceiling was covered with intricate plasterwork and fresco paintings. A sparkling crystal chandelier hung in the center, casting a soft glow over the walls, furnishings, and polished marble floor. Two footmen dressed in livery stood at the ready near the bottom of the staircase, while gentlemen in fine suits and ladies in silks and feathers crossed the hotel's grand foyer.

"Everything is so elegant," she whispered.

John's eyebrows arched. "You've not been here before?"

"No, I haven't." Her parents didn't frequent hotels, and she'd only been in one other that was not nearly as beautifully decorated as the Beresford.

"The dining room is this way." John nodded to the right and offered his arm. Clara slipped her hand through, and a delightful thrill raced up her back. How thoughtful he was to offer his arm.

The maître d' greeted them at the entrance to the dining room, and John requested a table for two.

"Right this way." The maître d' led them past tables covered with crisp white linen and glistening China and silver. Another large crystal chandelier bathed the room in soft light, reflecting off the mirrored walls.

He seated Clara, and John took the seat opposite. He gave them menus and stepped away.

Clara glanced at the menu, then looked around the room. A few gentlemen, who were seated alone, scanned newspapers, while a family with two young children enjoyed a late luncheon.

Her focus returned to John as he studied the menu. His high forehead, straight nose, cleft chin, and wavy brown hair gave him a very pleasing appearance. She recalled his polite manners and the way he handled the shop owners and businessmen they'd spoken to. He remained calm, even when they were turned away. And he showed sincere gratitude when one of them agreed to help fund the Christmas party. Her admiration for him grew each time they were together.

Why didn't he ever mention his fiancé—or was she now his wife? Her stomach clenched. Would he even suggest they stop here if he were married?

He looked up and met her gaze. A slow smile widened his mouth, and a hint of amusement lit his eyes at catching her studying him. "Shall we order tea and cake?"

Her cheeks warmed, and she lowered her gaze to the menu. "Yes. Tea and cake would be lovely."

The waiter appeared, took their order, and soon returned with a silver tray and tea service. He placed a selection of small cakes on the table and poured their tea.

Clara added milk and sugar to hers. "It's very kind of you to give so much time to help raise funds for the children's party."

"I'm happy to do it."

"You've mentioned spending time with Mr. Dickens. Do you have other close friends . . . or family in London?"

His hand stilled, and he studied her face. Slight lines creased his forehead, and he looked down. "There are a few writers at the *Times* I consider friends, and others at church, but no family to speak of."

There was no more putting it off. She would have to be direct and settle the matter. She fixed her gaze on him. "When we first met last summer, you introduced me to your fiancé. Will she be joining us for the Christmas party?"

His face turned ruddy, and a muscle flickered in his jaw. "Letitia and I are no longer engaged."

Clara pulled in a sharp breath. "You're . . . not engaged?"

"No, I am not."

She blinked, still trying to take it in. "I'm sorry."

"It's been almost five months now, and I see the wisdom in my decision."

Clara's eyebrows rose. He'd been the one to break it off. "So, you have no regrets?"

A thoughtful look crossed his face. "Strong marriages require a foundation of common beliefs, respect, and trust. Letitia and I . . . were not well-suited."

This news put a new light on John's attention toward her, and hope rose in her heart. "Common beliefs are an important foundation. And of course, marriage partners must fully trust each other."

"I'm pleased to hear you agree, Miss Raymond."

"Please, call me Clara."

Delight shone in his eyes. "Thank you, Clara. And you must call me John." He slid his hand across the table and covered her hand. "I've enjoyed our time together. Would you consider—"

"Miss Raymond?" Archibald Worthington approached their table.

Her stomach plunged, and she slipped her hand from beneath John's.

His gaze darted from her to John, and his brows dipped.

"Mr. Worthington." She forced out the greeting.

His expression hardened and seemed to demand an explanation.

John rose. "Mr. Worthington, I'm John Stafford. I believe we met at the Foundling Hospital." He held out his hand.

Archibald hesitated, then accepted the handshake. "Yes. You were with Mr. Dickens."

"That's right. And you were with your mother."

The men exchanged challenging looks.

Clara swallowed, knowing she must clarify the situation. "Mr. Stafford and I are members of the committee planning the Christmas party for the children at the Foundling Hospital. My sister Emily is also helping. We've been out seeking donations today. I'm sure your mother will be pleased when she hears how much we've collected."

He cocked his eyebrow. "You've been soliciting donations?" His tone and look conveyed his doubt.

John remained standing. "Yes. We met with several shop owners and businessmen who have agreed to help fund the party. I believe we have collected almost all the donations needed."

Archibald sniffed and turned to Clara. "Are your parents aware you're here with Mr. Stafford?"

Clara stiffened. Who was he to ask such a question? She opened her mouth to reply, but John spoke first.

"Miss Raymond's sister, Emily, was with us until a short time ago. She needed to leave for another appointment. We saw no harm in stopping for refreshments before I escort Miss Raymond home."

"A gentleman should always guard a lady's reputation and not put her in a position that could call it into question."

John's gaze drilled into Archibald's. "A gentleman should also believe the best about people and not cast aspersions against their character."

Archibald's eyes flashed, and his face reddened. "I simply want to protect Miss Raymond from being the focus of unpleasant gossip."

John's expression hardened. "If anyone does spread gossip, we will know the source."

Clara stifled a gasp and wanted to cheer. How brave and clever of John to put Archibald in his place.

Archibald shifted his haughty gaze to Clara. "Good day, Miss Raymond." He turned and sauntered away.

John returned to his chair. "I'm sorry. I hope I didn't overstep with my remarks to him."

"You've no need to apologize. I appreciated how you handled it." She released a deep breath. "He'll probably report the conversation to his mother who will no doubt speak to mine."

Concern filled John's eyes. "I didn't intend to put you in a difficult position. I'm so used to my bachelor ways, it didn't occur to me we ought not to stop here without your sister. Shall we leave?"

"No, let's finish our tea and put his interruption out of our minds." She tried to infuse confidence in her voice, but her stomach twisted. How would she explain this to her mother and father? Would it be a black mark against John?

JOHN PACED across Charles's study, glaring at the floor as he silently replayed Archibald Worthington's rude interruption that afternoon at the Beresford Hotel.

Charles put down his pen. "You're going to wear out the carpet. What's wrong?"

John shook his head. Charles had just summarized the next section of his Christmas ghost story and asked for John's input, but it was hard to concentrate with the events of the afternoon still running through his mind.

"Come now, I can see something is bothering you."

"We're speaking about your writing."

Charles waved away John's words. "You always listen to my troubles without complaint. It's high time I listened to yours."

John pulled in a deep breath. Perhaps Charles could give him some advice. "I've just spent three hours with Miss Clara Raymond."

Charles's face lit up. "Wonderful! I'm glad Leticia is no longer clouding your thoughts. She was not worthy of you. Miss Raymond seems like a much better choice."

Charles was about to say more, but John lifted his hand to stop him.

"What's wrong? Surely, Miss Raymond returns your feelings, doesn't she?"

John slowed his pacing as he considered the question. Clara always greeted him warmly, and she seemed pleased when he suggested they stop at the hotel for tea. When he'd offered his arm, she'd taken it and sent him a bright smile. And there was that time he'd caught her studying him and then blushed in the most pleasant way. Surely those were signs she'd welcome him as a suitor.

John glanced at Charles. "I believe she does. But just as our conversation was moving toward matters of the heart, Archibald Worthington interrupted us."

Charles cocked his head. "Who?"

John huffed. "We met him when we toured the Foundling Hospital. He was that tall, blond man, dressed like a dandy, and accompanied by his mother." He couldn't keep the disdain from his voice. The man was pompous—not someone he would ever call a friend.

"Oh yes, I remember. He seemed a rather proud, self-absorbed fellow."

"That's him."

"Where were you when he interrupted your conversation?"

John sighed. "Having tea in the dining room of the Beresford Hotel."

"Does he have intentions toward Miss Raymond? Is that the problem?"

John's steps stalled. Was Worthington hoping to win Clara's affection? Was that why he'd been so obnoxious? How did Clara feel about him? He recalled her response and shook his head. "He might have his sights set on her, but she did not seem pleased to see him. Of course, that might be because he pointed out she was there without a chaperone."

Charles sent John a surprised look. "No chaperone?"

"Her sister, Emily, was with us all afternoon while we visited shops and businesses, seeking donations for the Foundling Hospital Christmas party. But she had to leave before Clara and I stopped at the hotel for tea."

Charles grinned. "That was convenient, giving you time alone with Clara, but it put her in an awkward position to be seen there with you."

John huffed. "Blast those silly rules. How is a man to make his intentions known if he doesn't have a moment alone with a woman?"

Charles sent him an indulgent smile. "So, you'd hoped to make your intentions known?"

John's face heated. "At least I wanted to test the water."

"Well, I'm sure there's no real harm done. Why not speak to her father directly and ask to call on her? Surely, that would be the proper next step."

John rubbed his chin. Leticia was an independent woman without family ties in London. He hadn't needed to approach anyone about courting her or asking for her hand in marriage. But it was different with Clara. She came from a respected, well-to-do family. If he wanted to pursue her, he'd have to seek permission from her father.

He swallowed. No doubt her father would want to know if he was worthy of his daughter's affection. What standards would he apply? Would his character and accomplishments be enough, or would questions about his family—or lack of family—make courting Clara impossible?

CHAPTER FIVE

*C*lara tiptoed across the entrance hall and cocked her head to listen. Distant voices drifted toward her, but she couldn't distinguish the words. John had been in her father's study for at least ten minutes. How long could it take for him to explain his hope to call on Clara?

The door opened, and John stepped out. He walked toward her, head bowed, shielding his face from her view.

His slow pace and the slope of his shoulders made her stomach plunge. "John?"

He looked up. Hurt and regret shimmered in his eyes. "I'm sorry, Clara."

Her throat tightened, and panic surged through her. This couldn't be happening. John was a good man, a kind man who truly cared for her. Why would her father turn him away? "I don't understand. What did he say?"

John's jaw firmed. "I'm sure he'll make the reason for his decision clear." He started past her.

"John, please don't go." Desperation filled her voice. "I'll speak to him."

He shook his head and turned toward the door. "It won't help. I must leave you now."

Clara lifted her hand and covered her mouth to stifle a cry.

The butler stepped from the sitting room, crossed the entrance hall, and pulled open the front door. John strode out without looking back.

She spun and almost lost her balance. "Father!" She righted herself, hurried down the hall, and pulled open his study door. "Why did you send him away?"

He looked up with a frown. "Lower your voice, Clara. Come in and close the door."

She did as he asked and crossed to his desk, her heart pounding.

He straightened in his chair. "John Stafford is not the right man for you."

"How can you say that? You barely had ten minutes with him!"

"That was long enough to learn his background disqualifies him as a suitor."

"I don't understand. What about his background is so offensive?"

Father arched an eyebrow. "He didn't tell you?"

She swallowed hard, and her mind spun with questions.

"John Stafford doesn't even know who his parents are. He was given over to the Foundling Hospital as an infant and has no family to speak of. He is probably illegitimate, and that makes him unacceptable."

She blinked, trying to make sense of her father's words. John was a foundling who had grown up in an institution? Even if that were true, he had gained an education and become a respected author. That proved he was a man of character and courage.

She pulled in a deep breath. "John Stafford is a kind, intelligent, and successful man. It doesn't matter to me he spent his early years in the Foundling Hospital. He has overcome those obstacles and worked hard to build a good life for himself. And he is the trusted friend to one of England's most celebrated literary figures."

Her father shook his head. "He may have befriended Dickens and have a stable occupation, but that doesn't erase his questionable birth and lack of social standing."

"Those make no difference to me! He is the only man who has seen past my defects and shown genuine interest. Please, Father, you must reconsider!"

His eyes flashed. "I am not in the habit of being told what to do by my daughter!"

She closed her eyes and tried to get a grip on her emotions. She could not let Father separate her from John, but what choice did she have? She was a dependent daughter.

"In time, you'll see I am right." The lack of caring in his voice cut her to the heart.

Her throat burned as she opened her eyes. "No, Father. You are wrong. Time will not change my mind about John or dampen my affection for him." She turned and strode out of the room. As soon as she reached the hallway, tears flooded her eyes, and she could barely see to climb the stairs to her room.

FATHER's harsh words replayed through Clara's mind as she lay on the bed with her face buried in her pillow. She pulled in a shuddering breath and tried to slow her tears.

Emily touched her back with a gentle hand. "I'm sorry, my dear. I know this is terribly upsetting."

"John is not like the other men. They saw me as a cripple and only called on me because of my future inheritance. They weren't truly interested in winning my affection." Clara turned and looked up at Emily. "How can Father be so hard-hearted? Doesn't he want me to be loved, to marry, and have a family? Why would he turn John away simply because of the circumstances of his birth?"

"John never told you about his time at the Foundling Hospital?"

Clara bit her lip, wishing he had. Would it have made a difference if she could have prepared Father for that news? She released a deep sigh. "No, but I don't think he intended to be deceptive. We've had very little time alone together."

"What about when he took you to the hotel for tea?"

"He told me he was no longer engaged, and I could tell he was about to say more, when Archibald Worthington came to our table and was so unpleasant."

"Mother said Mrs. Worthington called and relayed Archibald's story." Emily pulled in a deep breath. "That was a most unfortunate encounter."

Clara huffed. "I thought Mrs. Worthington was a sympathetic friend, but now I see she's more interested in passing along gossip than maintaining my friendship."

"Will you continue with the committee for the children's party?"

Clara silently debated her decision. "It may be uncomfortable, but I joined the committee to help the children. It wouldn't be right to bow out now."

"Do you think John will continue?"

Clara's breath caught. Would he step away because her father had refused to let him call? "I hope so . . . with all my heart."

Emily sat at Clara's dressing table. "Remember the way John spoke about the Foundling Hospital dining hall and kitchen when we were planning the party?"

Clara nodded, recalling that conversation.

"He probably knew those details because of his time there." Sympathy filled Emily's expression. "It's sad to think he grew up without the care of a mother and father, or the security of an extended family."

Clara's throat tightened, and conviction rose in her heart. "Knowing he was a foundling makes me even more certain I want to continue on the committee and see this through—for John's sake and for all the children who have no family to give them a special Christmas celebration."

"If you're continuing, I will as well." Yet, a look of caution rose in Emily's eyes. "It's certainly not John's fault that he's a foundling, but I can see how it might make Father see him in a negative light."

Clara sat up and wiped her cheeks. "But you like John, don't you?"

Emily nodded. "He's well-spoken, and he's always treated us with kindness."

"Yes! He's generous, polite, and respectable—a very worthy suitor. Oh, there's got to be some way to make Father see John as I do!"

Clara rose from the bed, crossed to her dressing table, and glanced in the mirror. A red-eyed blotchy face stared back at her. She huffed out a breath. This had to stop. She was a grown woman, not a child. John deserved her devotion and commitment. She would find a way through this problem.

Emily met her gaze in the mirror, and hopeful light reflected in her eyes. "Remember when Paul spoke to Father and asked for my hand?"

Clara had been visiting her grandmother in the Peak District that summer when Emily had written with the news. "Yes, you said Father refused because he didn't believe Paul could provide for you."

Emily nodded. "I was heartbroken and sure I'd never see Paul again. But he sent me a note with the promise he'd look for a new position, remain faithful to me, and pray for God's direction. He encouraged me to do the same." Her gaze softened. "It took time, but he found a new, better-paying position. We continued praying and trusting the Lord to work out what was best. Nine months later, he asked again, and Father finally consented."

Clara sighed. "I'm glad it worked out so well for you and Paul, but our situation is different. There's nothing John can do to change the circumstances of his birth."

"True, but the Lord is still able to make a way. I believe He used our prayers and patience to soften Father's heart." Emily looked up at Clara. "Don't give up hope. Do what you can, then pray and trust the Lord for your future."

Clara wanted to believe her prayers could make a difference, but she'd never stepped out in faith with such an important matter. She lifted her hand and rubbed her eyes as a prayer rose from her heart. *Lord, do You see me? Are you listening? Can You break through my father's resistance and help him see John for who he truly is? Show me the right path forward. Help me want what You want for me.*

JOHN HUSTLED down Whitmore Street in central London. "Charles, wait! Where are you going?"

Charles marched on without slowing. "I'll show them! I'll publish the book myself!"

A chilly wind rushed past, and panic shot through John. If Charles published this story on his own, it would take a huge financial investment—money his friend did not have. John increased his speed and caught up with Charles. "I know that meeting did not go well, but there's no need to make a rash decision. I can go back and try to renegotiate the contract."

Charles spun around, his eyes wide. "They don't believe I

can finish in time. You heard them." He muttered an oath under his breath, then turned and started down the street again. "I'm going to find my own illustrator, my own printer. I'll show them! This story will be out in time for Christmas!"

John strode after him and caught hold of Charles's arm. "I understand what you're saying. But let's slow down and think this through."

Charles's gaze darted to the right and left then focused on John. "Yes, yes. You're right. We must make a plan."

John blew out a deep breath, lifting a silent prayer of thanks. Charles disliked being crossed or questioned about his writing ability or the timing of his projects. He needed support and encouragement to be productive. Those were truths his publisher, Richard Bentley, did not seem to grasp. "Simmons' Coffee Shop is just ahead. Let's stop there."

Charles agreed, and they slowed to a more reasonable pace. Soon, they reached the shop and found a seat at a small table near the front window.

After removing his hat, Charles settled in his chair, across from John. "How can Bently be so shortsighted? Why doesn't he see the potential for this story? It will make readers see Christmas in a new light!"

John tipped his head. "Well, it is November fifteenth."

Charles frowned. "I'm nearly done! They could get it out in time if they believed in the story, but that's the problem. They don't believe in me or my stories anymore."

A young woman in a white apron and cap approached their table and took their order. She had brown hair and eyes that looked very much like Clara's. The reminder of losing her pierced John's heart again. It had been two days since he'd spoken to her father and been turned away. The pain of that decision still burned in his mind and had made sleeping and eating nearly impossible.

"John, did you hear what I said?"

John's head snapped up. "What? I'm sorry."

"What's bothering you? You've been in the dumps all day."

He didn't want to burden Charles, but it might bring some relief to explain the situation. He leaned forward and lowered his voice. "I followed your advice and spoke to Clara's father."

Charles's eyes widened. "And . . . what did he say?"

"He seemed amiable at first, but then he questioned me about my family." John's throat tightened.

"And?"

He straightened and met Charles's gaze. "I had no answer. I know nothing about them."

Charles frowned. "I don't understand"

John swallowed. It was time to tell his friend the truth. "I was given into the care of the Foundling Hospital as an infant, renamed, and raised there until I was ten when I went out as a printer's apprentice."

Charles blinked. "You spent your childhood at the Foundling Hospital?"

John nodded. "The people there don't tell you anything—not your parents' names or why they gave you up." His face heated, and his stomach clenched. "I'm most likely illegitimate."

Charles's eyes clouded. "I'm sorry, John. I had no idea. Why didn't you tell me this before?"

"It's not the kind of thing I want to make known." He kept his voice low and glanced at those seated around them. Thankfully, no one looked their way or seemed to be listening.

Charles sat back. "Well . . . I suppose we all have elements of our past we'd rather keep to ourselves."

John searched his friend's face. Did Charles have secrets in his past?

Charles cleared his throat and shifted in his chair, looking uncomfortable.

The young woman returned with two cups of steaming coffee, and they thanked her.

Charles stirred cream and sugar into his coffee. "So, what will you do now?"

"What can I do? Her father refuses to let me call. There seems no way forward." The pain of that decision swirled through his midsection, carving a hollow, hopeless feeling in his gut.

Charles clicked his tongue. "Well . . . maybe it's for the best."

John looked up. "How can you say that? My hope of building a future with Clara has been destroyed—all because of the choices my parents made twenty-eight years ago—choices in which I had no part."

Charles nodded. "I'm sorry. That was a thoughtless comment."

John released a sigh and shook his head. "It's all right. I know you didn't mean to rub salt in my wounds."

"No, definitely not." Charles frowned and tapped his chin. "So, the principal objection is the unknown circum-stances of your birth."

John grimaced. "Yes. That's what her father said."

Charles thought for a moment, then lifted his finger. "Why not return to the Foundling Hospital and find out the truth? Maybe your situation is not as bad as it seems."

"The records are sealed. I don't' believe they'll give me the information."

Charles's mouth quirked up on one side. "They might not tell you, but perhaps they'll tell me."

CHAPTER SIX

*J*ohn and Charles followed the young girl down the main hall of the Foundling Hospital. She wore the same simple brown dress with a white apron and cap all the girls had worn eighteen years ago, when he had been a resident. Nothing seemed to have changed, and for a moment he felt like he had stepped back in time. A shiver raced down his back, and he willed it away. He was no longer a child trapped in here with no escape. He was an adult, free to make his own decisions and choose his own path.

Charles sent John a meaningful look. "I think it's best if I lead the conversation."

John nodded and blew out a breath. He wasn't sure what tactic Charles had in mind to convince the matron to give him the information they were seeking, but he was glad to have his friend speak for him. Charles could be quite persuasive when he put his mind to it, and his notoriety might also help.

The girl knocked on the matron's partially open door. "Miss Langtree, there are two gentlemen here to see you."

"You may show them in."

John straightened his shoulders and followed Charles into the matron's office.

Her eyes widened as she rose from the chair behind her desk. "Mr. Dickens, what a pleasure to see you again. Please come in."

Charles smiled and nodded. "Thank you, Miss Langtree." He motioned to John. "I'm sure you remember my friend, Mr. John Stafford. Your tour last month impressed us both. You are obviously deeply devoted to the children and manage your responsibilities here very well."

Her thin face flushed. "Thank you." She nodded to John. "Mr. Stafford." Her gaze shifted back to Charles. "Now, how may I help you?"

Charles expression turned more serious. "We have an important matter we'd like to discuss."

"Of course. Please, be seated." She motioned to the two chairs facing her desk, and they all took seats.

"I know your time is valuable, so I'll come right to the point." Charles motioned to John. "Mr. Stafford was a resident here from 1815 until 1826. At age ten, he went out as an apprentice to a printer. Through hard work in that position, and in his schooling, he has become a very successful author and literary critic. He is also a generous supporter of the Foundling Hospital. In fact, he is a leading member of the committee planning the Christmas party for the children."

John's face warmed. His friend often seemed distracted and lost in his story world. But it seemed he had been paying attention and filed away many things John had told him.

Charles sent him an approving smile, then turned back to Miss Langtree. "And now, it has become important that he learn the names of his parents and the circumstances of his birth."

She blinked a few times. "Oh, I'm sorry. We don't release that information."

Charles tipped his head. "Come now, Miss Langtree. Surely, after all these years it wouldn't hurt to tell Mr. Stafford his parents' names."

She pursed her lips and glanced to the left. Rows of leather-bound ledgers filled the wooden bookshelves with dates inscribed on the spines. She returned her gaze to Charles. "We assure those leaving children here that we will maintain confidentiality of their circumstances and identities."

"I understand you want to protect the parents," Charles added. "That makes perfect sense."

A look of relief crossed her face.

"But Mr. Stafford would like to court a young lady, and as you can imagine, he needs to tell her family the truth about his birth. I'm afraid, if he can't provide that information, it will destroy his hope to pursue her."

Miss Langtree lifted her hand to her heart and sent John a sympathetic look. "Oh my, that is unfortunate."

John sat forward. "If I give you my word the information would only be shared with this young woman and her parents, would that be agreeable?"

Her brows dipped. "The rules for privacy are set by the governors. I could be dismissed if I break them."

"We certainly wouldn't want that to happen." Charles added in a soothing tone.

"I should hope not." She shifted in her seat and adjusted her glasses.

"Miss Langtree," Charles sent her an indulgent smile. "I was so pleased to help raise support for the Foundling Hospital when I gave my presentation last month. Were you able to attend?"

"Yes. I heard you speak."

"I understand my appeal brought in several generous donations."

"Yes. We're very grateful."

"I was happy to lend my name and support to such a worthy cause." Charles clasped his hands in his lap. "As you can imagine, I am a very busy man, but I might be willing to find time to make another presentation in the new year . . . if you were willing to fulfill our request."

She glanced away, warring emotions evident on her face.

John held his breath. Would Charles's offer sway her?

Her expression eased, and she turned back to them. "I suppose under the circumstances I might make an exception to the rule."

John's chest expanded. "Thank you."

"You are very kind," Charles added.

She rose from her desk and ran her finger down the row of ledgers. "You were born in 1815?"

"Yes, on the fifteenth of July."

She pulled a ledger from the shelf, placed it on her desk, and took a seat. Opening the ledger, she flipped through several pages and stopped near the middle of the book. Her eyes scanned down the page. "Here it is. Your parent's names were Dwight and Ethel Woodbury, ages twenty-seven and twenty-two."

John pulled in a sharp breath. His parents were married!

"He was a shipwright, and she was a homemaker. You have no siblings. Your father was killed in an accident at the docks before you were born. Your mother passed away the day after your birth from complications."

John's throat tightened. How tragic. They were so young.

"Your grandfather, Chester Woodbury, took you in. He was eighty-two and a widower, but he was unable to care for you. He brought you here on the second of August. Your name at birth was Peter Dwight Woodbury." She looked up and met his gaze. "You were baptized when you were one month old and given the name John Alfred Stafford."

John's eyes stung, and he blinked away the moisture. His parents must have loved each other and looked forward to his birth until that terrible series of events had changed everything for them and for him.

Charles sent him a triumphant look. "Why don't you make a note of what we've learned?"

"Yes, I want to remember it all." John pulled his small notebook and pencil from his pocket and quickly jotted down the names and details. When he finished, he closed his notebook and met the matron's gaze. "I appreciate this very much. Thank you."

She sent him a serious look. "I hope you'll only divulge this information as you said and not mention my name as the source."

John gave a solemn nod. "You have my word."

She closed the ledger, rose, and placed it back on the shelf, then turned to Charles. "I believe May or June would be a good time for our next fundraising event. Please let me know what day you'll be available to give the presentation."

Charles stood. "I'll be in touch."

John rose, and he and Charles walked out of the office. He lifted his hand to his pocket and felt the outline of the small notebook. Knowing his parents' names and a little about the circumstances that had sent him to the Foundling Hospital was a great comfort. But would the truths he had learned be enough to change Mr. Reynold's mind and open the door for him to court Clara?

CLARA WALKED through the back entrance to the Foundling Hospital. Their driver, Stevens, carried a large wooden crate filled with knitted hats, mittens, and scarves for the children.

She looked over her shoulder "Thank you, Stevens. It's right this way."

He nodded and smiled. "Glad to help, Miss. I'm sure these gifts will give the children a happy Christmas."

She smiled, imagining the boys and girls receiving the colorful handknitted items at the party. They continued down the hall, and she motioned up the steps. "The matron said we can store the crates in a room next to the dining hall."

"Very good, Miss." He hefted the crate higher.

She stood back and let him pass, then climbed the steps after him at a slower pace. Some days her shorter leg was such a bother. She huffed and dismissed that thought. She had two legs, and she could walk. That was enough to carry out what the Lord had planned for her to do that day.

Stevens waited for her at the top of the stairs, holding the door open.

"Thank you. It's down the hall, this way." She motioned to the right. Footsteps sounded, and she looked up.

Two men rounded the corner and started toward them. The taller man lifted his head and met her gaze. Recognition flashed through Clara, and her breath caught.

John's eyes widened. "Clara."

"Hello, John." She swallowed and motioned to the driver. "Stevens and I are bringing in gifts for the children's party."

Charles nudged John and looked her way. "Are there more crates?"

"Yes, there are two others."

"Why don't you take this one, John." Charles motioned to the crate." Then I can go with this man and help bring in the others."

Clara's cheeks warmed. Was Charles suggesting this to give John and her time alone?

"Yes, of course." John stepped forward and accepted the crate. Then he turned to her with a questioning look.

"The matron said we could store them in the room next to the dining hall." Her heartbeat throbbed in her chest as she started down the hall with John walking at her side.

"I'm glad to see you, Clara." His voice softened. "I've missed you."

Her heart melted, and she met his gaze. "I've missed you as well."

He adjusted his hold on the crate. "Did your father tell you why he declined to let me call?"

She hesitated, sorry the conversation had turned that way so quickly. "Yes. And it's so unfair. A man ought not be judged by things he cannot change."

"I'm glad to hear you say that."

"I'm certain what you experienced as a child has made you a better and more compassionate man. That's something to be proud of, not something that should disqualify you."

Hope lit in his eyes. "Has your father changed his mind?"

She hesitated. "Not yet, but I'm praying he will."

A shadow passed across his face, and he nodded. "I understand."

"I haven't given up, and I hope you won't either."

He glanced away, looking torn. She imagined he didn't want to come between her and her parents and wouldn't force the issue.

They passed the dining hall and reached the room where they were storing items for the party. She pushed open the door, and he stepped through. "You can stack the crate against the wall with the others."

He lowered the crate to the floor and glanced at those lining the wall.

"Those contain all the knitted items made by the women at Emily's church. The crates we're bringing in today are from my church. We have enough for all the children now." She reached in the top crate, pulled out a pair of bright green mittens and held them out to him "Aren't these sweet?"

He accepted the small set of mittens with a nod. "Nicely done. I'm sure the child who receives these will be very grateful." Their gazes met, and approval glowed in his eyes.

Her heart warmed, knowing he was pleased with what she had done to organize the women and collect the gifts. "We missed you at the last planning meeting."

His expression sobered. "I wasn't sure if I'd be welcome. And I didn't want to make it awkward for you."

"Oh, you must continue with the committee. We need your insight and help with collecting the donations. And you mentioned a printer who might print the cards listing the donors."

He nodded. "I can speak to him and continue with the committee if you're sure it won't be a problem."

"I'm sure." She wished she could say how much she longed to spend more time with him and couldn't imagine hosting the party without him, but that seemed too bold.

He stepped closer. "I've learned something about my family—something that might make your father more inclined to consider me as a suitor."

She pulled in a quick breath. "What is it?"

"I've learned my parents were Dwight and Ethel Woodbury, a young married couple who lived here in London." He sent her a meaningful look.

Hope flooded her heart. "That's wonderful news. Did you learn anything else?"

"My father was a shipwright. Unfortunately, he died before I was born, and my mother died shortly after my birth. I was their only child, so I have no siblings. My grandfather cared for me for a short time, but he was an elderly widower and gave me into the care of the Foundling Hospital when I was a few days old. My mother named me Paul Dwight

Woodbury, but of course, they rename you when you're baptized here." He released a slow deep breath.

Wonder filled her along with a rush of gladness. "How did you discover all this?"

He glanced toward the door and lowered his voice. "Charles convinced someone on the staff to tell us. I had to promise to only reveal those facts to you and your family." John reached for her hand. "Do you think this news might change your father's opinion of me?"

"I . . . I don't know. He's very traditional and concerned about rank and social standing."

A look of determination crossed his face. "I'll speak to him and make my case."

"I'll pray he'll listen and see you for the fine man you are."

New hope flickered in his eyes. "Yes, we must both pray and ask God to intercede for us. He sees our hearts and knows the truth of the situation."

CHAPTER SEVEN

*C*lara clutched the envelope to her heart and climbed the stairs to her room as quickly as she could. The unexpected message from John had arrived moments before, and she did not want to risk opening it downstairs where her mother might appear at any moment.

She slipped into her bedroom and quietly closed the door. With trembling hands, she opened the envelope and pulled out the sheet of ivory paper. John's clear, masculine script filled the page.

DEAR CLARA, I'm writing to let you know the outcome of my conversation with your father. I'm sure he will tell you about our meeting, but I wanted to give you my thoughts on the matter.

I told him the truth about my parents and the events that led to me being given into the care of the Foundling Hospital. I appealed to him in a calm and respectful manner, and he listened to all I had to say. But in the end, he was not persuaded. He said my lack of family and the stigma of being an abandoned orphan are obstacles that cannot be overcome. He will not allow me to call on you or hope for anything more between us.

Of course, I was deeply disappointed, and I must confess, angry that he would not change his mind. I'm confident my parents were honorably married, loved each other, and looked forward to my birth. Their deaths and my grandfather's inability to care for me are facts I cannot change. I am not ashamed of my family or those circumstances. God allowed them, and my grandfather made the choice he thought best for me. I received a good basic education at the Foundling Hospital and was then given an apprenticeship with a wise and kind man who opened many doors for me. I've made every effort to live a life worthy of my faith and develop the gifts and talents I've been given.

My only regret is that the circumstances of my birth will separate me from you and the hope I had of building a future with you. Clara, you are intelligent, kind, and tenderhearted, and I have come to care for you in a deep and abiding way. But I will not come between you and your parents.

I will fulfill my commitment to help with the children's Christmas party and see you then, but after that, I must honor your father's request and not attempt to see you again.

Even then, I promise to remain your faithful friend,
John Stafford.

TEARS COURSED down Clara's cheeks, and she shook her head. She'd been so hopeful her father would accept the new information about John's background and finally see him as a worthy suitor. Instead, her father's decision would separate them forever.

It wasn't fair or right. How could this be the answer to her prayers?

≈

JOHN REREAD the last paragraph of Charles's *A Christmas Carol* and swallowed hard. He looked up and met his friend's worried gaze. "It's good, Charles, very good—maybe the best you've ever written."

Charles's face lit up. "You really think so?"

"Yes. It's not a long story, but it touches the soul in a powerful way. The focus on celebrating with family and sharing generously with those in need will remind readers of the true meaning of Christmas. I'm sure it will be well received."

Charles sprang from his chair. "Then we must take it to the printer!" He gathered the pages of his manuscript. "What is his name?"

"Mr. Albert Patterson on Chestnut Street." John rose and followed Charles out of his sitting room.

"Katherine, Katherine!" Charles spun around in the foyer as though searching for something.

His wife hurried down the stairs. "Charles? What's wrong?"

"Where is my hat?"

She quickly scanned the room. "On the side table, dear."

"Oh yes, there it is!" Charles snatched up his hat and plopped it on his head. "There's still time to get this book out before Christmas." He held out the manuscript. "We're off to the printer! I'm not sure how long that will take. Don't wait on me for dinner."

Katherine sent him a tired smile. "All right, dear. I'll see you when you return."

Charles slipped on his overcoat and shifted his gaze to John. "Ready?"

John nodded, placed his own hat on his head, and followed Charles out the door. They hailed a passing cab and climbed aboard.

Charles's excited expression boosted John's spirit. If they

could get this book printed and out to bookstores in the next few days, it could bring in much needed funds for Charles and revive his reputation with readers.

He glanced out the cab window and noticed a young woman with glossy brown hair walking down the street. His heart leaped, and he leaned forward. Her face came into view, and his spirit sank. It was not Clara.

Charles sent him a concerned look. "What's wrong?"

John shook his head. "I thought I saw Clara."

"Are things still not going well?"

John grimaced. "I spoke to her father. But he didn't care that my parents were married. In his opinion I'm still *unacceptable.*" That last word tasted bitter on his tongue.

Charles scowled and huffed. "That's ridiculous! How can he be so unfeeling? The man reminds me of Scrooge—dismissing you for matters you have no power to change."

John sighed. Clara's father did reflect a bit of Scrooge's indifferent spirit.

"So, the decision is final? You're not allowed to call on her?"

"I'll see her at the Foundling Hospital Christmas party on the twentieth, but that will probably be the last time." He sighed and leaned back in the seat. That experience might be more painful than rewarding. How could he say goodbye and know he must never see her again?

"Well, don't give up. There may still be some way to make the old man change his mind."

John shook his head. If only that were true. He had asked God to intercede and done all he could. Was it time he let go of his hope to marry Clara, build a family with her, and share a warm and peaceful home? He closed his eyes against the pain throbbing at his temple.

Please, Lord, You see it all. Will You make a way?

CLARA GLANCED around the group of twenty-five young girls gathered in the classroom at the Foundling Hospital. Each girl fixed her gaze on Emily as she read the final chapter of *Oliver Twist*. Their eyes shone with the enjoyment of listening to a well-told story.

Emily turned the last page. "Mr. Brownlow adopted Oliver as his son. Removing with him and the old housekeeper to within a mile of the parsonage, where his dear friends resided, he gratified the only remaining wish of Oliver's warm and earnest heart, and thus linked together a little society, whose condition approached as nearly to one of perfect happiness as can ever be known in this changing world."

Mary Jane, a little blond released a happy sigh. "I'm so glad Oliver was adopted and taken in by Mr. Brownlow."

Sarah, seated beside her said, "Can you imagine how happy he must have been after all he'd been through?"

Mary Jane's gaze grew distant. "Yes, he finally had a home and someone to love and care for him."

It warmed Clara's heart to see how much the girls had enjoyed the story. Of course, they, more than many others, understood Oliver's plight. Each of these girls had suffered a similar loss and carried in her heart that same longing to be part of a loving family.

That brought John to mind, and Clara's heart clenched. Even though he had friends and a successful career, she sensed he longed for those same strong family ties.

With all her heart she wished she might be part of fulfilling those longings. But even if that was never possible, she prayed he would one day have a loving family of his own.

Her eyes stung at the thought of someone else becoming

his wife. But if she truly wanted what was best for John, then she must release him into God's care, and trust that He would bring about the best plan for John's future, even if it did not include her.

Emily closed the book and sent a smile around the room. "So, did you all enjoy *Oliver Twist?*"

The girls replied with joyful smiles and enthusiastic thanks for the story.

"I'm pleased to tell you Mr. Dickens has written a new story that will be available very soon."

A cheer rose from the girls, and several asked Emily to please bring a copy and read it to them the next time she came.

Clara recalled John had told her Charles was working hard to finish a novel in time for Christmas. With little more than a week until that holiday, would he meet his goal?

Clara turned to Emily. "How did you hear about it?"

"I saw the sign in Findley's Bookshop this morning. It's titled *A Christmas Carol* and should be out on the nineteenth."

Clara smiled. John had told her a little about the plot and characters, and knowing he had played a small role as an early reader made her even more eager to read it.

"We also have more good news." Emily grinned at Clara, then turned back to the girls. "We've planned a special Christmas party for all the children on Saturday, the twentieth, with games, sweets, and gifts for everyone."

Gasps and a happy chorus rose from the girls. "Oh, that's only three more days! Thank you, Miss Emily!"

Clara's spirit rose as she watched their response. She was glad they'd waited to announce the party until all the plans were confirmed and the gifts and refreshments had been purchased. On Saturday afternoon, the members of the committee and a few other volunteers would transform the dining hall into a festive chamber fit for the special celebration.

It might be the last time she would see John. Her throat tightened. Somehow, she must find the strength to remain cheerful for the children's sake and give them the joyful celebration they deserved. But it would be a bittersweet day.

A prayer rose from her heart. *Help me put aside my own heartache and focus on these dear little ones. I want to make it a special day for them—one that will give them hope and happy memories to carry into the New Year.*

CHAPTER EIGHT

*J*ohn strode down the hall of the Foundling Hospital carrying a large wicker hamper. The scent of freshly baked scones and currant cakes wafted through the linen cloth draped over the top, making his mouth water. The baker's wife had packed the treats carefully, layering each row with a strip of paper to keep them neat for the children's Christmas party. This delivery completed his list of duties in preparation for the day's special event. Now all he had to do was keep his focus on the children and off Clara Raymond.

He released a huff and shook his head. This might be his final opportunity to spend time with Clara, and he was determined not to do anything that would make it more painful for her. He adjusted his hold on the hamper and rounded the corner.

Voices carried down the hall. "Let's move these benches to the side." Wood scraped across the floorboards.

John entered the large dining hall and glanced around the room. Two men pushed a bench toward the west wall while two others lifted a table and moved it in the same direction, opening up the area in the center.

Across the room, Mrs. Worthington and Emily shook out a tablecloth and spread it over a table near the kitchen. He searched for Clara among the other women setting up for the party, but he didn't see her. His shoulders tensed. Had she stayed away to avoid seeing him?

He crossed toward Emily. "These are the baked goods from Haversham's. Where would you like me to put them?"

Emily met his gaze with a smile. "In the kitchen, please."

He nodded and continued through the doorway. Clara stood at the worktable in the center, arranging small cakes on a platter. His steps stalled, and he nearly dropped the hamper.

Clara looked up. Her eyes widened, then tenderness filled her expression. "John."

"Hello, Clara." His gaze traveled over her face taking in each feature. He should look away, but he couldn't.

She glanced at the hamper and then back at his face.

"These are the scones and current cakes from Haversham's." His voice came out rough, and he cleared his throat.

She sent him a trembling smile. "Thank you for bringing them." She pushed aside the platter. "You can put the hamper here."

He placed it on the table, untied the string, and lifted the linen cloth. "They were very generous. Don't they smell delicious?"

She pulled in a breath and nodded. "The children will be delighted." Her voice caught, and when she looked up at him, tears shimmered in her eyes.

His chest tightened, and he reached for her hand. "Clara." He wanted to say more, but seeing her tears made his words lodge in his throat.

"I'm so sorry, John." Her voice came out soft and shaky. "I've tried to make my father understand, but he . . ."

He pulled in a deep breath. "It's all right."

A flash of hope lit her eyes, and she tightened her hold on his hand. "I'm still praying."

He wanted to respond with something hopeful, but he'd resigned himself to the situation. A couple needed the blessing of their parents to build a strong and successful family. Mr. Raymond was firm in his decision, and John would not ask Clara to choose between him and her family.

He looked down at her hand, so small and soft in his, and longing swelled within him. Winning Clara's heart and building a family with her had been his deepest desire, but it was not to be. He had to accept it and let her go.

Mrs. Raymond walked into the kitchen, and her gaze darted from Clara to John. "Clara, your sister needs your help in the dining hall." Her firm tone and serious expression made it clear she was not happy to see them together.

John released Clara's hand and turned to face her mother. "Good day, Mrs. Raymond."

Her lips pursed. "Mr. Stafford."

Clara sent him a plaintive look. "I will speak to you later, John." She glanced at her mother once more, then walked out of the kitchen.

John turned and followed Clara, but he stopped when he reached Mrs. Raymond.

She met his gaze with a challenge in her eyes. "I hope you will abide by our decision and not make the day unpleasant for Clara or anyone else."

Her words stung, but John did not shift his gaze away. "I love your daughter. Her happiness and comfort are my greatest goal. I will respect Mr. Reynold's decision. I'll not seek her out after today."

Mrs. Raymond eyes widened for a split second, then her expression softened, and she gave a slight nod. "Thank you."

He held his head high as he walked past her, out the door.

~

CLARA BLINKED AWAY her tears and crossed the dining hall toward Emily. *Help me, Lord. I don't want to hold on to anger toward my parents, but this is so very hard. If only they would listen and trust John and me to make the right decision. Please, open their eyes. Change their hearts. Work in ways only You can.*

Emily looked up as Clara approached, and her smile faded. "What is it, dear?"

"John spoke to me in the kitchen, but Mother came in, ending our conversation."

Empathy filled her sister's eyes, and she reached for Clara's hand. "I'm sorry. I know this is hard. Try to focus on today and the time you have with him."

Clara's heart clenched, but she gave a slight nod. Her sister was right. She would not waste her last moments with John being self-absorbed and sorrowful. She wanted him to remember her with a caring smile, not tearful regret.

Mrs. Worthington walked to the center of the room and called all the volunteers together. Clara stepped forward and joined them. Movement to her right drew her attention, and she pulled in a sharp breath.

Her father entered the dining hall followed by Charles Dickens. She touched Emily's arm and nodded toward them. "Look!"

At breakfast, she had invited her father to attend the party, but he'd said he was too busy to make time for it. Why had he changed his mind?

Father stepped into the circle of volunteers next to Clara's mother, and Charles joined John on the opposite side.

"I never expected Father to come," Emily whispered.

"Neither did I." She was about to say more when Mrs. Worthington spoke again.

"What a pleasure to see you all." Mrs. Worthington's gaze traveled around the circle with a glowing smile. "Thank you for coming and for your work to plan and prepare for the party. The Christmas tree and decorations look lovely, and the kitchen is overflowing with treats the children will enjoy."

Mrs. Worthington smiled at Clara and Emily. "Our special thanks go to Mrs. Emily Wright, Miss Clara Raymond, and Mr. John Stafford, who took charge of the early planning when I was ill. They collected many of the contributions to fund the party and Clara and Emily arranged for the gifts to be made by the women in their churches." She clapped, and the other volunteers joined her.

Clara's cheeks warmed. She glanced across the circle and sent John a warm smile. The hours they'd spent together, preparing for the party, had given her a chance to get to know him, and his kindness and respectful actions had won her heart.

"Now," Mrs. Worthington continued, "we have only a few minutes until the children arrive. Would one of you like to lead us in prayer?" A moment of silence followed.

John straightened. "I will."

Mrs. Worthington's eyebrows lifted, but she nodded to him.

John's gaze traveled around the circle. "Let us bow our heads and ask God's blessing on the children and the party."

Her father studied John with a serious look then lowered his head.

John cleared his throat and closed his eyes. "Father, thank You for this opportunity to give these children a special Christmas celebration. We're grateful for all those who have contributed gifts and given donations to fund the party.

Please make this a happy day for the children—one that will bring them hope and remind them of Your birth, Your love, and Your care. Please be with us as we lead the games and activities and distribute the gifts. We ask all this in the Name of our Lord and Savior, Jesus Christ. Amen."

Amens rose around the circle, and many looked at John with approving smiles. Gratitude filled her heart. John's faith and willingness to lead in prayer showed his unique combination of humility and strength and deepened her love for him.

Mrs. Worthington looked down at her notes. "All right. Let's divide up and prepare to lead the games and crafts. Emily and Clara, will you take that table in the far corner for the Ball of Wool Game?"

Emily nodded and slipped her arm through Clara's. "This should be entertaining."

Clara glanced over her shoulder as Mrs. Worthington sent John to the opposite side of the room with Charles to lead in charades.

The sound of shuffling feet reached Clara, and she glanced toward the door.

The matron walked into the dining hall followed by a long line of solemn children. They quietly circled the room, their eyes darting from the Christmas tree in the north corner to the paper chains and evergreens hanging on the walls. There were no happy exclamations, only a few timid smiles.

Clara supposed someone had warned them to be on their best behavior and remain quiet and respectful. When the last child finally entered, the line came to a halt, and the matron stepped forward. Mrs. Worthington crossed to meet her, and they conversed briefly.

Clara and Emily exchanged questioning looks. Would the children be allowed to enjoy the party, or had they been told to remain silent? The point of the gathering was to give them a happy day. Surely, she and Emily could find a way to involve the children and lighten the mood.

The matron divided the children into groups and sent them to the different tables to play one of the games, cut out paper snowflakes, or string popcorn to decorate the tree.

Emily and Clara welcomed their group with warm smiles.

"Everyone, please take a seat," Emily began. "Have you played the Ball of Wool Game?"

Two of the children nodded, but the others shook their heads.

"Please feel free to speak up and enjoy our time together." Emily explained how to play, while Clara placed a ball of yarn in the center of the table.

Laughter erupted as the children puffed and blew to keep the ball away. Cheers and groans followed as the ball rolled off the table, and they began the next round. Relief flowed through Clara. The game was a success.

A few minutes later, the matron rang a bell, and the children moved to the next table. A new group of younger children arrived and took their places. Emily explained the game again and placed the ball in the center of the table.

Clara noticed one little girl, who looked about six, standing to the side. She cradled her arm across her middle and looked down at the floor. Her blond hair was pulled back under a white cap, and she wore a brown dress and white pinafore like the other girls.

Clara stepped next to her. "Would you like to join your friends?"

The girl shook her head and kept her gaze lowered.

"My name is Miss Clara." She softened her tone. "What is your name?"

A few seconds passed before she answered. "Jasmine." Her voice was so soft, Clara could barely hear her.

"That's a very pretty name. It's the same as a lovely white flower that has a sweet scent."

Jasmine slowly lifted her head. If eyes could tell a story, Jasmine's clearly revealed sorrow and pain.

Clara's heart clenched, and she bent closer. "I think you'd enjoy the game. Won't you come and try?"

Jasmine shook her head. "I can't play. My arm is hurt."

Clara glanced at the girl's arm cradled against her middle. Her long sleeve covered her arm, and Clara couldn't see anything different about it. "Did you fall and injure your arm?"

"No, it's always been this way."

Understanding filled Clara, and she gave a slow nod. "I see." She glanced at the children enjoying the game. "Do the others tease you about your arm?"

She gave a slight shrug. "Sometimes. Or they just leave me out of games."

Clara slipped her arm around the girl's shoulder. "I know what that's like. You see, I was born with one leg shorter than the other, and I have to wear a shoe with a thick sole to make up for the difference."

Jasmine glanced at Clara's feet.

Clara lifted the hem of her dress a few inches, revealing her shoe. "My left leg is not very strong, and that makes is difficult for me to do some things."

"What kind of things?"

"Going up and down stairs is a challenge, and dancing is out of the question, but I've learned to focus on what I *can* do and not let it stop me from helping others."

"Do people make fun of you?"

Memories rose, and Clara pressed her lips together. "Some have, and that was painful. But it made me want to always be kind to others and make certain that no one ever felt left out." She smiled at Jasmine. "Each one of us is designed by God in unique and special ways. He has a purpose in all He allows."

"Even my arm?"

Clara nodded. "Yes, even your arm."

Jasmine bit her lip and pondered that for a few seconds.

"Ask Him to help you, and He'll show you ways to do what needs to be done. That's a prayer I'm sure He'll be delighted to answer."

The little girl's gaze traveled to the table where the other children played. "I guess I could try to play."

Clara smiled. "That's the spirit. Come on. I'll find you a seat at the table."

Clara turned and she was surprised to see her father standing a few feet away. He studied her with a curious look and some other emotion in his eyes she couldn't quite read. She sent him a smile, then led Jasmine to the table and asked the children to scoot down and make room on the bench for her little friend.

An hour later, after many rounds of the game, Clara and Emily helped serve refreshments to the eager children. Their eyes rounded as platters of scones, current cakes, and ginger biscuits, were passed down the table. Then cups of cider were distributed. The children popped peppermint candies into their mouths, and a few more went into their pockets.

When all the treats had been distributed, Charles walked toward the center of the room. "Children, may I have your attention?" The children quickly quieted. "I'd like to read you the opening section of my new story. Since I know you'll want to see what happens after that, I'll be leaving two copies with the staff so they may read the rest aloud in the next few days."

He pulled a slim red volume from his jacket pocket and began reading. "*A Christmas Carol in Prose, A Ghost Story of Christmas* by Charles Dickens."

He lowered his eyebrows and took on a somber dramatic tone. "Marley was dead, to begin with. There was no doubt whatever about that. The register of his burial was signed by the clergyman, the clerk, the undertaker, and the chief mourner. Scrooge signed it. And Scrooge's name was good upon 'Change for anything he chose to put his hand to. Old Marley was as dead as a doornail."

The children's eyes widened, and several seemed to shiver with delight, for what child doesn't love a ghost story?

Charles's grin returned as he looked around the room, then continued the story.

Clara's gaze shifted to John. He stood by the far wall with arms crossed as he watched his friend. The look of connection on his face spoke of the bond he shared with Charles. Even though John had no living parents or siblings, he had learned the value of loyal friendship, and he experienced it with Charles.

Her heart melted a little more, and she released a soft sigh. She'd met no other man as selfless and loyal, or as committed and kind as John Stafford.

JOHN PICKED up one of the children's paper snowflakes and admired the intricate design. He set it aside to hang on the tree, then collected the leftover scraps of paper strewn across the table. Glancing around the dining hall, he recalled the many meals he had eaten here. Bittersweet memories tightened his throat. He'd lost touch with most of the boys he'd known during those years, but a few had contacted him after reading his articles or books. He'd been glad to hear how many had gone on and made successful lives for themselves.

The matron crossed the room toward him. "Thank you for

your help today, Mr. Stafford. If you're agreeable, I'd like to leave up the decorations and Christmas tree."

John nodded. "Of course."

She thanked him again, then turned and left the dining hall.

Charles joined John and clamped his hand on John's shoulder. "The party was certainly a great success. I've never seen so many happy children!"

John smiled and nodded. "Thank you for coming and reading to them."

"Glad to do it."

"They obviously loved your story, and they're not the only ones."

Charles cocked his head. "What do you mean?"

"I stopped by Weatherby's Bookshop on my way here, and the owner said they've sold all their copies of *A Christmas Carol*. He wants to know when more can be delivered."

Charles eyes rounded. "Why that's splendid! Let's make the rounds and visit some of the other bookstores in this part of town. There's nothing like a personal visit to strengthen bonds with shop owners."

John glanced toward the kitchen. He'd hoped for one more opportunity to speak to Clara. "I need a few more minutes."

Charles followed John's gaze. "Awe, yes. I believe Miss Raymond is still in the kitchen."

John's face warmed. "I have a gift for her."

"Well, what are you waiting for? Speak to her again. You never know, this may turn the tide."

He usually appreciated Charles's optimism, but today it struck a painful chord. The decision was final. He would not be courting Clara. Still, he wanted to give her a parting gift that would honor the season and their friendship.

Clara and Emily stepped out of the kitchen, and Clara's gaze darted to John.

"There's your chance." Charles grinned and gave him a slight shove.

John walked toward her, and she met him in the middle of the room. The tender and vulnerable look in her eyes hit him hard, and his chest contracted. "You brought a lot of happiness to the children today."

"*We* brought a lot of happiness." Her glowing eyes added depth of meaning to her words.

He smiled. "Yes, we make a good team."

"Thank you, John. I've never stepped out to do anything like this before. And seeing the children and how happy they were . . . well, it's been a wonderful experience. I'm very glad we could do it together."

He pulled in a deep breath and kept his focus on her dear face. "I have a gift for you."

"Oh . . . I didn't expect a gift." She bit her lip, and her cheeks turned a rosy pink. "I don't have one for you."

"That's all right." He took a copy of *A Christmas Carol* from his jacket pocket and held it out to her. "It's signed by Charles. I hope you'll enjoy reading the rest of the story."

Delight filled her expression as she ran her hand over the red leather and gold lettering. "Thank you. It's lovely." She looked up at him. "I'll treasure it, and not just because it's signed by the author, but because you are the giver."

He reached out and gently took her hand. "I want you to know you may always count on my friendship. If there is ever a time you need *anything*, please don't hesitate to contact me."

Tears shimmered in her eyes, and she nodded. "I will. Thank you, John." Her voice sounded soft and strained. "You will always have a place in my heart." She slipped her hand from his, then turned and hurried across the room to meet her sister. Emily placed her arm around Clara's back and guided her out the door.

CHAPTER NINE

*T*he afternoon, following the party, Clara nestled into the high-backed armchair and pulled the fringed wool blanket closer. The fire crackled and hissed on her bedroom hearth as she paused reading *A Christmas Carol* to sip her cup of tea. Outside her window, snow flurried softly against the windowpanes, muffling the sounds of the London streets beyond.

Images of the characters so clearly described in the story filled her mind: Bob Cratchit lifting Tiny Tim up on his shoulder as they walked through town, and Mr. and Mrs. Fezziwig dancing at their Christmas Party, and Bell, breaking her engagement to Scrooge because of his growing greed. Then there was old Ebenezer Scrooge himself—such a miserly, bitter man, yet even he was not beyond hope of redemption.

Her heart filled with anticipation as she returned to the story and read the final scene.

He became as good a friend, as good a master, as good a man, as the good old city ever knew . . . And it was always said of him that he knew how to keep Christmas well, if any man alive possessed the knowledge. May that be truly said of us, and all of us! And so, as Tiny Tim observed, God bless us, every one!

She sniffed and pressed the book to her heart. Lifting her gaze to the firelight dancing on the ceiling, she offered a prayer. "What a wonderful story! What a gift You've given to Mr. Dickens. Thank You that no one is beyond Your reach. Hearts can change. Lives can change. It's not too late for any of us to open ourselves up to your Spirit and become all we were meant to be."

A knock sounded at her door. She turned and called, "Come in."

The door opened, Mother entered, and concern filled her eyes. "Goodness, Clara, you've been crying."

Clara swiped her cheek. "Don't worry, Mother. These are happy tears. I've just finished Mr. Dicken's new story, the one he began reading to the children at the party. It's such a heartfelt tale. I'm sure you'll enjoy it."

Mother sent Clara a skeptical glance. "I'm not usually fond of ghost stories."

"This one is different, and it has a very happy and meaningful ending." Clara rose and held out the book. "Please, I'd like you and Father to read it."

Mother slowly reached out and accepted the novel. Her gaze traveled over the cover. "I can't promise your father will read it, but I'll do my best to convince him."

An idea struck, and Clara smiled. "Why don't we read it aloud with Father. It's not long, and it would be the perfect story to enjoy in the evening during the Christmas season."

Mother's expression softened. "I suppose we could read it aloud. Emily and Paul are coming for dinner. Perhaps after that, they would enjoy hearing it as well."

Clara's smile bloomed again. "That's an excellent idea."

Mother's expression became thoughtful as she studied Clara. "You put so much time and effort into hosting the children's Christmas party. I thought you might feel let down now that it's past. Yet, you seem quite happy this evening."

Clara pondered her mother's comments. The party had been a triumph, and seeing her plans come together to give the children such a wonderful Christmas celebration had been rewarding. But saying goodbye to John had pierced her heart.

Still, reading *A Christmas Carol*—the story John had helped Charles publish—had lifted her spirit and given her hope. God was in the business of changing hearts. And that truth would carry her through the days ahead.

After dinner that evening, Clara, her parents, and Emily and Paul gathered in the sitting room by the fire and took turns reading aloud *A Christmas Carol*. The story seemed to capture each one, and they eagerly read on by lantern light.

Clara enjoyed the story even more the second time as she watched her family members' reactions to each twist and turn of the plot. When Father read the passage with the Cratchit family mourning the loss of Tiny Tim, tears gathered in everyone's eyes. Father had to stop and clear his throat before he could finish reading the scene.

When Paul read the final page, with Scrooge waking up on Christmas morning, repentant and determined to change his ways, happy sighs and laughter filled the room. He closed the book and looked around the family circle with a broad smile. "What a splendid story! I've not enjoyed another so much in a long while."

Emily took her husband's hand. "I'm so relieved Scrooge repented and helped the Cratchit family." She grinned. "Wasn't that delightful to hear how he bought the prize turkey and sent it to the Cratchits on Christmas Day?"

Mother smiled. "It stirs up many fond memories of how we spent Christmas when I was young." Her gaze drifted toward the fire. "It was a wonderful family holiday with a joyful church service and then jolly feasting around the table." Her eyes glowed as she recounted the memories. "My mother made the best plum pudding!"

Clara had only known her grandmother on her father's side. The others had passed away before she was born. Was that why her family had made little of the Christmas holiday in the past?

Paul took his watch from his pocket. "It's late. Emily and I should be going." They rose from the settee.

Father stood. "Please take our carriage. Stevens can drive you home."

"Thank you, Father." Emily kissed his cheek. "Good night, Mother."

Clara rose and gave Emily a hug. "Good night, dear."

Her sister held her tight for a moment. "All will be well," she whispered. Then she and Paul collected their coats and hats. Mother walked out to the entrance hall with them.

Clara was about to follow when her father called her back.

"Come and sit with me, Clara." He lowered himself into the large, overstuffed chair near the fire.

His serious tone made her heart thump. "What is it, Father?" She settled on the footstool by his chair.

"I've been thinking about a few things, and . . . I wanted to tell you how impressed I was with all you did yesterday at the Foundling Hospital. It's no small undertaking to plan a party for two hundred children."

His words sent pleasant warmth flowing through her. "I didn't do it alone."

"No, but you played an important role and handled it well, very well." He looked down with a slight frown. "I'm afraid I sometimes forget you've grown up and are a competent young woman." He pulled in a deep breath. "Looking back, I realize I've been cautious and perhaps overprotective because of the physical challenges you face with your leg.

That has not been wise or helpful." Unusual tenderness filled his voice.

She reached up and took his hand. "It's all right, Father."

"I can see now that you're able to take on new challenges and make a difference in this world. I'm proud of you, Clara."

Her heart swelled. "Thank you, Father."

"And after this morning's sermon about not judging others because of their outward appearance or position in society . . . I believe I may have misjudged Mr. Stafford."

She stilled. Had she heard him correctly? "Father?"

"My experience at the party, the sermon, and that story . . ." he motioned to the copy of *A Christmas Carol* on the table beside them, "have made me question my decision. I believe we ought to become better acquainted with Mr. Stafford and see if he might be a worthy suitor."

Clara's heart surged, and she squeezed his hand. "Oh, Father, thank you!"

His eyes twinkled as he smiled down at her. "Why don't you invite him to dinner, and let's see how he handles himself."

She reached up and hugged him. "This makes me so very happy." She wanted to say more but her voice choked, and joyful tears flooded her eyes.

He patted her back. "There, there, my girl."

She pulled back. "I'll send a message tomorrow and invite him to dinner."

"He has no family in town. Why don't we make the invitation for Christmas Day?"

"Yes! That's a wonderful idea." She rose to leave, intent on writing the note as soon as she reached her room. But she turned back and kissed her father's cheek. "I'm grateful, Father. Thank you, for looking past the surface and seeing what is in my heart."

John followed Charles out of the printshop and into the snowy street. An icy wind whipped around the side of the building and flew down his neck. He tightened his scarf, but a chill raced through him. "That's good news Patterson can deliver more copies to the bookshops in the next day or two."

Charles grinned as he strode through the snow. "Yes, he's a fine fellow, a skilled printer, and an excellent friend!"

John couldn't agree more. Albert Patterson had taken him in at ten, treated him well, and continued to encourage him through the years. Now, he and his men had agreed to work extra hours to print additional copies of *A Christmas Carol* and restock the bookshops where it had sold out.

A poorly dressed young lad rounded the corner and walked toward them. He wore a ragged coat, and his nose and cheeks were red from the cold. He held up a newspaper with a hopeful look. "Read the latest *London Illustrated News.*"

"I'll take one." John reached into his pocket, took out a crown, and placed it in the boy's hand. The lad wore no gloves, and his fingers were chapped and cold. "Keep it all."

The boy's eyes rounded. "Thank you, sir." He quickly pulled a folded copy from the bag slung over his shoulder and held it out.

John tucked the newspaper under his arm. He preferred to read the *Times,* but the lad needed to sell his papers and get out of the cold.

"It's freezing." Charles scanned the line of shops. "Let's stop for coffee."

"There is a shop just down the street." They set off at a brisk pace while trying to avoid the piles of slush.

They soon reached the coffee shop and ducked inside. The welcome warmth and scent of coffee greeted John as he closed the door. They found a table and were soon warming their hands around mugs of hot coffee.

John opened the newspaper and scanned through the pages. His gaze lit on the literary review section and the first review of *A Christmas Carol*. He held his breath and silently read the opening paragraph. A smile tugged at his lips.

Lowering the paper, he met Charles's gaze. "They've included a review of *A Christmas Carol*."

Charles grimaced. "Is it written by Hillmont?"

John nodded, suppressing a smile.

Charles muttered and lifted his eyes to the ceiling. "Oh well, read on."

John cleared his throat. "This little book, which we predict will become the most successful, the most purchased, and the most read of all Mr. Dickens' Christmas productions, should be read by every fireside in the kingdom. It is written in a hearty, jovial style, and interspersed with some of the most touching scenes Mr. Dickens has ever penned. The moral is high and healthful—the sentiment pure and gentle—and the humor is rich and genuine."

A look of wonder filled Charles's face. "He liked it? Hillmont really liked it?"

John chuckled. "Yes, he did." He laid the paper on the table and turned it so Charles could see the article.

Charles's eyes widened as he continued reading. "If Mr. Dickens had done nothing else, this little Christmas book would have secured him an immortal place in literature. The tale is slight in construction, but great in purpose. It leaves the reader with a softened heart and a sense of hope. There is wisdom beneath its fanciful garb, and a moral that no Christian spirit can resist. Mr. Dickens strikes the chords of generosity and compassion with a master hand."

Charles looked up and shook his head. "Can you believe it?

"Yes! You've done it, Charles. You've won the hearts of your readers and made your mark with this story."

Charles leaned back, and his delighted gaze rested on John. "I could not have done it without your encouragement and help. No one else believed in me, but you stood with me through it all. Thank you."

John's throat tightened. To be acknowledged and appreciated by Charles meant more than he could say. "You've been a good friend to me all these years. I could do no less for you."

Charles gulped down the last of his coffee and lifted the newspaper. "May I take this? I must show Katherine."

"Of course."

"Oh, she is going to be so delighted! Reviews like this will boost the sales. Our financial troubles will be over, and we can glide into the New Year with great expectation!"

Charles folded the newspaper and placed a few coins on the table. "I hate to rush off, but I must take this good news home to my dear wife. This will make it a very happy Christmas."

John bid Charles goodbye and watched his friend stride out the door. The positive review and good sales of *A Christmas Carol* were a great blessing. Once again, God had answered his prayers, showing them his faithfulness and provision, and a prayer of thanks rose from his heart.

His thoughts turned to Clara and the gift he'd given her last Saturday at the children's party. Had she enjoyed reading the rest of the story? Had it lifted her spirit and given her hope? Would she have a happy Christmas?

The ache returned to his chest, and he breathed a deep sigh. Time to release his hopes for a life with Clara once again and entrust the future into the hands of the One who knew what was best.

CHAPTER TEN

*J*ohn slowly climbed the creaking wooden steps to his flat. He had an article to finish, but he couldn't seem to drum up any enthusiasm for the project. The dim light and musty scent of the stairwell reflected his dismal mood.

His pace slowed as he considered the empty hours ahead. What would he do after he finished the article? Charles had gone home with joyful news to share with Katherine and his children. No doubt a happy celebration would follow. But no one would welcome him home or be there to listen to the good news about the review or Charles's glad response.

He scoffed and tried to shake off his gloomy mood. He'd lived alone for years. Why did it hit him so hard that day? The image of Clara's tearful expression as they'd said goodbye at the Christmas party rose in his mind, and his spirit sank lower.

He removed his key from his coat pocket and inserted it in the lock. As he was about to turn the key, he noticed an envelope sticking out beneath the door. He bent and picked it up.

Swirling feminine script displayed his name across the front. His heartbeat picked up speed, and he tore it open.

Dear John,

My heart is bursting with joy! Our prayers have been answered! Father has had a change of heart and says you may call on me as a suitor. He suggested I invite you to join us on Christmas Day for dinner and our family celebration. We should be home from church by one o'clock. Please come as soon after that as you can.

I'm eager to see you and tell you more about the wonderful series of events that have happened since we last spoke. Father's change of heart is truly a miracle, and I am so very grateful.

Now that we can be together on Christmas, I know it will be a wonderful celebration. Please reply and confirm you're able to come. Until then, I wait with affection and hope in my heart.

Clara

Hot tears stung John's eyes. He blinked several times and scanned the letter again. He wasn't dreaming. Somehow, it was true. He would spend Christmas Day with Clara and her family. There was hope for the future. "Thank you, Lord!"

On Christmas morning, Clara and her parents exchanged small gifts after breakfast. They bundled up against the cold and attended the eleven o'clock worship service at St. John's with Emily and Paul.

Clara's stomach felt like it hosted a gathering of butterflies as she counted the hours until John's arrival. Even though Father had agreed John could call on her as a suitor, John still needed to gain Father's full approval before a formal courtship could begin. Much depended on how he handled himself and how the day progressed.

A tremor traveled through Clara. *Please, Lord, watch over us and help us.*

After a chilly carriage ride through London's snowy streets, they returned home from church. The scent of roasting goose and baking bread welcomed Clara as she crossed the entrance hall and handed her cloak to Simmons.

Emily slipped off her gloves and turned to Clara. "That was such a lovely service. Singing Christmas carols always warms my heart."

"And didn't the church look beautiful with all the candles and evergreens?" Clara said as she untied the ribbon of her bonnet.

The doorbell rang. Her heart leaped, and she flashed Emily a smile. "That must be John." She turned to the butler whose arms were filled with coats and hats. "I'll answer the door."

"Very good, Miss." As Simmons departed, Clara hurried across the entrance hall and opened the door.

John stood under the portico. He wore a black overcoat over a fine dark blue suit and brocade waistcoat with a creamy white cravat around his neck. He carried a large bouquet of red and white roses surrounded by soft evergreen fronds. Their gazes connected, and his smile spread wide. "Hello, Clara. Happy Christmas."

With her heart overflowing, she welcomed him inside. "Happy Christmas."

John greeted her father, then presented the bouquet to her mother. "Mrs. Raymond, thank you for your kind invitation and for including me in your family's Christmas celebration."

Mother blushed like a schoolgirl as she accepted the flowers. "We're glad you could join us, Mr. Stafford. Thank you. Thank you for the flowers."

"Please, call me John." He turned to Paul and offered him a firm handshake, then greeted Emily with a smile.

Clara's heart swelled as she watched him speak to each family member with such confidence and genuine kindness. Bringing her mother flowers had been a thoughtful gesture that was sure to endear him to her. How proud she was of him.

Simmons returned. "Luncheon is ready, Madam."

Mother thanked him and ushered them all into the dining room. She directed Paul to sit across from Emily, and John to sit opposite Clara. Simmons seated Mother at one end, and Father sat at the head of the table.

Simmons and Mrs. Trimble, their cook, entered with a procession of steaming dishes including a large goose roasted to a golden brown, chestnut stuffing, mashed potatoes, steamed carrots, red currant jelly, and fluffy white rolls.

Throughout the meal, John engaged in thoughtful conversation with Father and Paul, but he also included Mother, Emily, and Clara. His polite manners and wise responses seemed to impress them all, raising Clara's hopes.

When the last course had been cleared, John turned to Mother. "Mrs. Raymond, this was certainly a delicious meal, the finest I've had in a long while."

"I'm glad you enjoyed it. But we're not finished yet." Mother turned to the butler. "We're ready for the pudding."

Simmons stepped out, and when he returned, he carried a flaming plum pudding on a silver platter and topped with a bright sprig of holly. Happy gasps and exclamations rose around the table as he placed the platter next to Mother. The blue flames flickered and danced for a few seconds then died.

Clara clapped, and Emily, Paul, and John joined her.

"What a splendid finish to our Christmas dinner!" Father looked around the table with a pleased smile. "I daresay we'll remember this special meal all year long."

Mother sliced the pudding and topped each piece with a spoonful of custard then passed the plates around.

Clara took a bite and savored the rich, dense pudding packed with dried fruit and spices. The creamy custard on top was the perfect complement.

Father took a sip of cider and turned to John. "I recall the first time we spoke, I was critical of Mr. Dickens' choice of themes and characters. But I must say his latest book seems quite different. We read it aloud, at Clara's urging, and were quite moved by Mr. Scrooge's transformation."

John's eyes glowed. "I'm glad to hear you enjoyed it. It's been very well received. In fact, we've already had to arrange for a second printing."

Mother turned to John. "The descriptions of Fezziwig's family Christmas party reminded me of how we celebrated Christmas when I was a girl."

"There were so many touching scenes," Clara said. "The themes of generosity and caring for those in need give added meaning and can inspire our own celebrations of the Savior's birth."

"I quite agree," Emily said. "It's a wonderful story, and I can't wait to return to the Foundling Hospital and continue reading to the girls."

Clara turned to Emily. "When will you go next?"

"Wednesday afternoon at one o'clock."

Clara thought for a moment, then said, "I'll join you."

John met her gaze. "I wonder if they need volunteers to meet with the boys."

The thought of John joining them at the Foundling Hospital made volunteering even more appealing. "That's an excellent idea. Why don't you come with us on Wednesday?"

"Very well. I'll plan on it."

Mother placed her linen napkin on the table. "Why don't we adjourn to the sitting room?"

They all rose and followed her parents out. As they passed the open door to the library, John's steps slowed.

A thought struck, and Clara turned to him. "Would you like to see our library? We have an extensive collection, some dating back over two hundred years." She knew he might enjoy seeing the books, but it would also give them time for a private conversation.

Understanding flickered in his eyes. "Yes, I'd enjoy seeing your collection."

Mother looked their way with a slight frown and started to protest.

But Father touched her arm. "Mary, the door is open. There is no harm in allowing them a little time together."

Mother hesitated a moment more then gave a slight nod. "Very well."

Clara's hopes soared as she led John into the library. He crossed to the shelves, ran his hand across the leather spines of a few titles, then turned to her. "You have some very fine books here."

She nodded. "My grandfather began the collection, and my father continues adding to it. Each year, on my birthday, he gives me a new book." She smiled at the memory and the hours of pleasure those books had given her.

John took a step closer. "You are blessed, Clara, to have such a caring family and fine home. It's obvious your parents love you and want the best for you."

His words made her pause. "I'm afraid I haven't always appreciated them as much as I should. Thank you for the reminder."

He glanced at the open door and lowered his voice. "I must know. How did you convince your father to invite me today? What changed his mind?"

She motioned to the settee. "Let's sit." They settled in, close enough that they could keep their voices low and their conversation private. "The Lord used a series of things to soften Father's heart. He was pleased and surprised at my role in planning and carrying out the children's Christmas party. It made him see me in a new light—more as someone ready for adult responsibilities, not someone hindered by my differences. And I'm sure he was impressed by your prayer and interactions with the children at the party.

John shook his head and looked down, but she could tell he was pleased to hear her father's observations.

"On Sunday," Clara continued, "the reverend's sermon focused on not judging others by their outward appearance, rank, or social standing. It was quite a profound message. I could tell Father was moved.

"And finally, when we read *A Christmas Carol*, Father was very touched by Scrooge's change of heart. I think he might have even seen himself in the story. And isn't that the way of a good story? It has the power to reach into our hearts and help us see our faults and need for change."

John gave a thoughtful nod. "We prayed, and the Lord answered in ways we couldn't have imagined."

She pulled in a shaky breath. "Yes." She had stepped out in faith and asked for her heart's desire, and the answer had come in the most surprising way. A rush of gratitude filled her heart.

John leaned closer until his shoulder touched hers. "I could tell your father was still evaluating me today. Do you think I passed the test?"

She laughed softly. "I'd say you passed with flying colors. He wouldn't have agreed we could have time alone if you hadn't already won his approval."

His smile returned. "I'm very glad to hear it."

He grew more serious and reached for her hand. "Clara, I have admired you from the first day we met, and my feelings for you have only grown deeper as we've spent more time together. You have a kind and loving heart and a faith that challenges and inspires me. You are beautiful inside and have outward beauty to match." He tightened his hold on her hand. "I know my background makes me an unlikely choice, but if you're willing, I'd like to ask your father's permission to enter a courtship."

Her breath caught, and she lifted her hand to her heart. "Oh, yes, John. I'm more than willing."

Delight filled his eyes. "Then my heart is yours." He leaned forward and kissed her forehead. "Happy Christmas, darling. May this be just the first of many holidays we will celebrate together."

With her heart overflowing, she leaned into his embrace and rested her head against his solid chest. The warmth of his arms around her and the steady beat of his heart filled her with contentment and the promise of a life she'd once only dreamed of—now unfolding by God's kindness and grace.

Outside the library window, snowflakes drifted silently past in the lamp light, blanketing the garden in white. Yet inside, by the glow of the fire and the warmth of the words they had spoken, a new chapter of their lives had begun—a joyful tale with a very happy ending.

PART III
CHRISTMAS IN TETBURY
DECEMBER 2024

Emma looked out Mimi's kitchen window as snowflakes fluttered past, covering the rooftops and street below with a soft blanket of white. The peaceful scene added a hushed beauty to the story Mimi had just finished telling her.

Mimi dipped the next dinner plate into the soapy water and washed away the remains of the evening meal.

Emma replayed the story in her mind, wearing a wistful smile as she dried a serving bowl. "So, John won Clara's heart by giving her a copy of *A Christmas Carol*, the very copy you have downstairs."

"I'd say he won her heart long before that, but the Lord definitely used that book to help persuade her parents to agree to a courtship."

"And did they marry?"

"Oh, yes. Mr. Richards said Clara and John are his great, great, great grandparents."

Emma laughed. "That's amazing."

"They married in 1844," Mimi continued, "and had four

sons and two daughters, and enjoyed fifty-seven years together in London."

"Oh, I'm glad to know they had a long life together."

"Yes, we all enjoy happily-ever-after-endings. But what I find most intriguing is the way John and Clara were willing to pray and wait for God's direction, even when their situation seemed impossible. That took a lot of faith on both their parts."

Emma pondered Mimi's comment and thought of her own life. She had faith in Jesus and believed He was God's Son, but when things looked dark and uncertain, she usually worried more than she prayed. "I admire their faith. When I lost my job and broke up with Jason, I'm sorry to say it didn't occur to me to pray.

"Those were hard experiences." Mimi offered a compassionate look, but there was also the shadow of disappointment in her eyes.

Emma's throat tightened. When had her relationship with Jesus grown so distant? She hadn't given up her faith, but after moving to London, starting her new job, and dating Jason, she hadn't continued the daily habits that would have helped her stay close to the Lord. Then her world came crashing down, and she'd focused on her pain and panicked about her future. How could she have forgotten what was most important?

Mimi laid a warm hand on her arm. "God was right there with you even when you didn't call out to Him. Just like He is here now, inviting you back and offering His care and comfort."

Emma swallowed, knowing it was true. Even though she had ignored Him, He had not turned His back on her. And she needed Him now more than ever with her future so uncertain.

Would she be able to find a new job in London, or would

she have to move again? Would she ever meet someone who would truly love her and want to marry her, or would she stay single for the rest of her life?

"Prayer is a gift we give God and ourselves." Mimi handed her another plate to dry. "It connects us to Him so we can receive His peace. And when we combine it with reading His Word, He speaks to us, giving us insight and direction."

That was a comforting thought. She needed a guide, someone who knew what was best and would show her how to rebuild her life. "Thank you, Mimi. Those are good reminders. I want to get back to starting my day by reading my Bible and praying."

Mimi's expression warmed. "That makes me happy."

A smile tugged up the corner of Emma's mouth. Mimi was such a treasure.

"Let's attend church tomorrow." Mimi didn't wait for her reply. "The service is at 10:30, and then we can go out to lunch with a few of my friends. We have the best time together."

Emma nodded. "I'd like that." It was time for a change— time to reorder her priorities and renew her faith.

On Tuesday Morning, Emma settled into the chair at Findley's Teashop, opened her laptop, and scanned the incoming emails. All she found was a list of promotional messages, nothing else. Her shoulders sagged.

She'd sent her resumé to seven museums and hadn't received one response. Of course, it was December 21, and many people took time off to spend Christmas week with family. She probably wouldn't hear anything until after the New Year. Still, she couldn't help wishing someone might read her resumé and want to set up an interview.

Releasing a sigh, she closed her laptop and looked toward the window. A frosty blue sky peaked through the clouds sending rays of sunlight on the snowy village scene. Tetbury was a lovely place to spend the Christmas season.

Lord, forgive me for being impatient. I want to trust You with this job search and believe You have a plan and purpose for this time between what happened in London and what's coming next. I'm glad I can be here with Mimi. Please help me think of ways I can make Christmas special for her. Thank You for loving us and giving us this time together.

The young waitress approached. "Good morning. What can I get for you?"

Emma quickly scanned the chalkboard near the door. "May I have some peppermint tea and a cranberry scone?"

The waitress nodded. "I'll be back with those in just a minute."

Emma took her Bible from her purse and laid it on the table. She opened to the Book of Psalms and continued reading where she'd left off. She needed comfort, and the Book of Psalms was a good place to find it.

The waitress returned a few minutes later with the tea and scone. Emma thanked her, added sugar and milk to her cup, then took a sip of tea. The sweet, creamy mixture sent a wave of pleasure through her. Just right on a chilly December morning.

The door to the teashop opened, and a tall man with blond hair walked in. He wore a navy wool coat, jeans, and a green sweater. He glanced around the nearly vacant shop with an uncertain expression.

Their gazes met, and she offered a slight smile.

"Excuse me. I'm looking for Harrison's Rare Books and Antiques. You wouldn't happen to know where it is, would you?"

Emma straightened. "That's my grandmother's shop. It's just down the street, but she doesn't open until ten."

"Your grandmother is Alice Harrison?"

"Yes, that's right."

He stepped toward her, held out his hand, and offered a smile. "I'm Nathan Bridgeman."

"Emma Langley." She shook his hand, her curiosity rising. "How do you know my grandmother?"

"We haven't met, but I saw her website last night, and I was coming out this way to show a house, so I thought I'd stop by and look at one of the items she listed." He glanced at his watch. "I am a bit early." He hesitated a moment then looked her way. "Perhaps I could join you for a cup of coffee while I wait for the shop to open?"

Emma's cheeks warmed. His suggestion was surprising, but she tried not to make too much of it. "Be my guest." She motioned to the chair opposite her and studied him as he took off his coat. He appeared to be about thirty and had an athletic build and handsome face.

He settled in the chair. "Do you work with your grandmother?"

"No . . . I'm just here for a visit." She'd been about to say she worked at the British Museum, but that was no longer true. "But I love antiques, so I enjoy helping her when I'm here."

He nodded, a spark of interest in his eyes. "I'm looking for a Christmas gift for my mum. She's a fan of Beatrix Potter and her books." He sent her a questioning glance. "The author of Peter Rabbit."

"Yes, I love her books too." Emma thought of the Peter Rabbit tea tin and dishtowels at her flat in London.

"I saw a Squirrel Nutkin figurine on the shop's website. That's Mum's favorite character. I hope it's still available. I'm cutting it close with Christmas only four days away."

"I remember seeing Peter Rabbit, Lady Mouse, and Jemima Puddle Duck." Emma narrowed her eyes, picturing the display case in her mind. "And I believe she still has Squirrel Nutkin."

"Oh, that's good news."

The waitress returned, and he ordered coffee and an apple cinnamon muffin. While they waited for his food and drink to arrive, he told her about his work as an estate agent. He planned to show three homes to a couple later that day. "They're looking for a house in the Cotswolds with historic features, a good size garden, and a country view, but it must be near a village. That brought Tetbury to mind."

Emma smiled. "It's a lovely village, and there are a lot of beautiful historic homes in the area." That led to a discussion about her interest in history, her time at Cambridge, and her work at the British Museum. He was a good listener and seemed genuinely interested in what she had to say. He asked several follow-up questions that kept the conversation going.

Emma took a sip of tea, surprised to find it had cooled. She glanced at her watch. "Goodness, it's almost 10:30. I didn't realize we've been talking for almost an hour."

He grinned. "I've enjoyed it."

She returned a smile. So had she. In fact, she wished their conversation didn't have to end. "I'd be glad to show you the way to the shop."

His blue eyes lit up. "Thanks. I'd appreciate it."

They walked down Long Street together, and when they reached the shop, he opened the door and let Emma enter first. She thanked him, making note of the thoughtful gesture.

She scanned the shop and spotted Mimi speaking to two women at a display of jewelry in the corner. "It looks like my grandmother is busy. I can show you the figurines. They're over here."

She motioned to a glass case by the front window. Nathan

followed her across the shop. Sunlight shone through the window on the collection of porcelain figurines. She stepped behind the case, took out Squirrel Nutkin, and placed him on top. "Here you go."

Nathan bent closer to look at the little squirrel. He was painted brown with a white chest and black eyes. He wore a cheeky expression and stood upright with his bushy tail curled behind him. On his shoulder, perched a green apple.

"What a fine little fellow." He looked up and smiled. "My mum will love him."

The bell over the door jingled as the two women left the shop.

Mimi walked over to meet them. "Good morning." She offered Nathan a warm smile.

"Mimi, this is Nathan Bridgeman. He saw this Squirrel Nutkin figurine on your website and came here especially to see it."

Nathan held out his hand. "Mrs. Harrison, I'm glad to meet you. I've been searching for the perfect Christmas gift for my mother."

"And she is an admirer of Beatrix Potter?"

He nodded. "She has all her books and has been to see her home at Hill Top."

Mimi motioned to the display case. "Are you interested in the others? I was hoping to sell the collection together."

Nathan's eyebrows rose. "I hadn't thought of buying them all."

"Let me tell you about them. The woman who brought them in last month said her great aunt passed away. She was clearing out her house and thought these might be worth something." Mimi grinned. "She was right. These were designed by H. B. Allen at Beswick Pottery back in the early 1900s while Beatrix was still with us."

A flash of disappointment crossed his face. "So, that little guy is probably more valuable than I realized."

"Well, the value of an item is determined by the price someone is willing to pay." She showed him the price tag. "This is the asking price, but I'm open to a reasonable offer."

Nathan thought for a moment and made his offer.

Emma held her breath.

Mimi nodded. "I'm impressed by the effort you made to find a special gift for your mum. I'd be happy to sell him to you for that price." She took the figurine and wrapped it in tissue. "There's quite a story that goes with him. Do you have time to stay for a cup of tea?"

He glanced at his watch. "I'd like to, but I have to meet a couple and show a house at 11:30."

Emma released a soft sigh. He was leaving, and he hadn't asked for her number. She'd thought she'd sensed a connection when they talked at the teashop, but she'd been wrong before.

Mimi tipped her head. "I wish you could stay. I think you'd really enjoy hearing how Squirrel Nutkin helped bring a young couple together."

He glanced at Emma, then looked back at Mimi. "Perhaps I could take you ladies to dinner? That would give you time to tell the story."

A surge of happiness spiraled through Emma. An invitation to dinner was even better than being asked for her number. And including her grandmother was a sweet gesture.

Mimi glanced her way with a lift of her eyebrows, and she returned a quick nod. "That sounds like a delightful idea," Mimi continued. "We'd love to have dinner with you."

A TALE OF THE SEASON

By Marguerite Gray

"The secret of good writing is to have something to say--and write with an end in view." --Beatrix Potter, Over the Hills and Far Away by Matthew Dennison.

"For it is God which worketh in you both to will and to do of His good pleasure." Philippians 2:13 KJV

CHAPTER ONE

NEAR SAWREY, LAKE DISTRICT 1906

*G*lancing out the front window at the crystal blue sky and the front garden, Arabella Graham released a sigh. She was not here to stare at the hills and gardens, instead she crossed the drawing room to her grandmother's side. Nana sat in a chair surrounded by fluffy pillows with her leg in a cast propped on an ottoman. Arabella knelt by the chair and squeezed her grandmother's hand, still soft and smooth after sixty-five years.

How could Arabella think about wandering the green hills and exploring the village with her grandmother stuck inside? "Nana, are you sure you won't need me for a few hours?"

I don't mean to be selfish, but I don't want to be cooped up inside today.

Though confined to a chair and little activity, her paternal grandmother, Cora Graham, had reigned for decades as the competent matron of her estate with wisdom and purpose. Everyone loved her. If only Arabella had a bit of Nana's confidence.

The light tapping on her hand by her grandmother's long, elegant fingers, refocused Arabella's wanderings. Nana's chuckles and the twinkle in her grey eyes released Arabella from any guilt. "My dear girl, of course, you may go. I have my bell and a household of servants. I appreciate your companionship, but I don't expect your full attention."

After kissing her grandmother's smooth cheek, Arabella rose and grabbed her wide-brimmed hat from the sofa. Pausing in front of the foyer mirror, she saw that most of her unruly chestnut hair was in place. Hat adjusted, she tied the strings under her chin. It shouldn't matter on a country walk if a few strands were out of place. Thankfully, this was not London. Those shackles of society were gone for the summer.

On the front steps, Arabella stopped and raised her gaze to the sky, letting the sun's warm rays and the pure air bring her comfort. Even when it rained in the Lake District, she didn't feel the pull of the grey bleakness of London's gloomy rain. Either the environment really was different here or she was better able to shake off her troubles away from London society.

"Miss Arabella."

She turned toward the front gate of the manor house and saw her companion waiting for her. She waved and walked toward her new friend. "Oh, Lilly. I apologize. I hope you haven't been waiting long."

"Not long. Anyway, the day is perfect for our walk." As they strolled down the road, Lilly swung the basket that she often carried. Arabella guessed it contained a sample of treats for parishioners.

Lilly was Arabella's image of a village girl—twenty-four years old, only three years older than Arabella—with rosy cheeks and a warm smile. She wore a simple skirt and blouse, practical brown boots, and a straw hat. Arabella looked down at her own attire, the cut and fabric denoted finery not needed on a summer walk in the country. Perhaps Lilly could help Arabella find some simpler clothing.

Well, not today. Her black leather half-boots, long blue skirt, and billowing cream-colored blouse would have to do. At least this was how Lady Graham's granddaughter should dress, not that Arabella wanted anyone to attach that moniker to her. Could she ever simply be known as Arabella and not for her family connection?

Arabella placed her hand on Lilly's arm. "Ready. Where to now?"

Lilly nodded toward the village center. "I need to deliver this basket to a family outside of town. Not more than half an hour."

"Let's go." Arabella matched Lilly's easy gait.

For the past week, since Arabella had arrived at Graham Retreat to take care of Nana, Arabella and Lilly had taken daily walks in the village. Lilly always greeted her with a smile and listened to all of Arabella's ramblings. The perfect vicar's daughter—or anyone's daughter for that matter.

Many villagers milled about today. Lilly greeted them all, saying something personal to each one. The local grocer, setting out his fresh vegetables, waved to them.

Lilly stopped beside him. "Good day, Mr. Warren. How are you? Is your baby daughter feeling better?"

"Oh, she is so much better. Thank you, Miss Lilly. I'll be sure to tell my wife you asked."

In London, Arabella had mastered the non-committal nod, the brief acknowledgment of a person, the cold greetings, and the meaningless salutations. How did Lilly know what to ask these people? She called it heart talk. Arabella could learn a lot from Lilly. Could she find that place, like Lilly, where her words mattered? She'd try.

Arabella alternated between a lazy stride and long steps as they traversed the town to the gravel and dirt road east of the village. Green hills as far as she could see rolled on one side of the carriage path. She really did not know what to call the roads in the area. In London, most roads had been cobbled, paved, or packed, enabling heavy traffic to commute easily. Looking at this road, she would consider the comfort and ease to be better here.

Arabella tapped on Lilly's arm and gestured toward the pasture with a huge oak tree dominating the top of a hill. "How close are we to your parishioner?"

"The cottage is just a few yards around the bend. Why?" Lilly stopped and followed Arabella's gaze.

"I'd love to go sit under that big tree. Look, there's a stile and easy access." The breeze whipped around her skirt, and the grass waved in ripples, almost making a path for her.

Lilly pursed her lips. "I don't see a problem with that. I'll be less than an hour. Then I could join you. I have a few apples and pastries we could share."

Arabella licked her lips and grinned. "I'll be waiting right over there." She pointed at the big tree.

After waving goodbye to Lilly, Arabella climbed over the stile and into the field. She spread her arms and twirled around. Ah, fresh air and beauty in every direction. Her boots might not be the most appropriate, but she didn't mind. Perhaps they'd become her working boots. She had plenty of others.

Instead of stepping with the grace of a trained debutante, Arabella ran up the hill through the tall grass. With each exhale, she felt as though she released the dust and filth of London as well as memories of unsavory suitors, society rubbish, and her parents' expectations.

With each step, she shook off another layer of the heavy cloak of her unwanted destiny. She might have to pick up the pieces later. But here, on this hill, she could discard the trappings of her London life and embrace the simple country life. If only it was as easy as stepping over a stile.

I'd trade any day in London for the beauty of this day. How many do I have?

Looking up through the sprawling limbs of the old oak, Arabella imagined its occupants past and present—squirrels, birds, and insects. Possibly, at her feet in the long grass abided hedgehogs, grasshoppers, rabbits, mice. And at this moment—Arabella. For now, she was part of the scenery—a watercolor she wished to enter every day.

Sitting with her back against the trunk of the tree, she stretched out her legs. In her other life, the ground held puddles and rubbish. She could never plop down on the dirty city streets or even in the parks.

Smiling, she recalled having checked in this field for cow and sheep patties before getting comfortable. From this pose her view included acres of wildflowers—purple, blue, yellow, white, pink. The church steeple, rooftops, and fields dotted with sheep spread out before her. The peaceful beauty warmed her heart and eased her anxiety about the future.

Thoughts of what awaited her in London returned. She had only three months with her grandmother.

When Nana had asked for her assistance, Arabella had jumped at the opportunity with no qualms, knowing it would give her freedom from the agonizing season. Why did other young ladies thrive in those activities? She often chided herself for her outlook on her responsibility to her status.

I just want to choose my own path. Is that too much to ask? Yes, according to Mother, it is.

Laughing softly, Arabella thought of how she had escaped London halfway through the social season. It was difficult to be melancholy sitting under the shade of an oak tree in the soft wild grass.

I was happy to walk away from it all and avoided the result of a successful social season—and engagement to an earl, a lord, or a sir. No more invitations and courting opportunities for the summer.

Was God the author of her escape?

If so, thank You.

She closed her eyes as she thought of her heavenly Father caring about someone like her. Now, she had to determine her purpose and next steps. She desired the journey God had for her. It would certainly be nice if it included more of this peace and beauty.

SOMETHING FEATHERY WHISPERED against her cheek. She stretched and squinted through blurry eyes. Disoriented and startled, she swatted at the annoying sensation. The hairy snout of a monster sniffed her face. She yelped and sat upright against the tree. If only it would swallow her before the creature did. Rubbing her eyes, ridding herself of her dream state, she rolled to her knees. The monster and his nose backed away enough for Arabella to crawl a few inches and scramble to her feet.

Could she outrun a huge curly haired beast? She had to try. Her heart pounded at a triple pace as she ran. A guttural scream followed her.

Was that her voice? No chance of turning around to find the creature on her tail and her ultimate demise.

Run. Run. Never had she dreamed of a wild animal chasing her. The stile rested mere yards from her. The strings from her hat choked her as her hat flew behind her. Could she really be strangled by hat strings?

This is what I get for daydreaming.

A hazy figure emerged in front of her close to the road. A rescuer or another foe? Animal behind her and man in front. She could not choose the scary one behind her.

She hopped onto the top of the stile and lunged right into the arms of the stranger.

"Help! A wild animal is after me." She panted the words through her high-pitched voice.

The man's chest trembled and rumbled. Was he laughing? What was so funny about her near death?

She shifted in his arms, wondering if she should scramble to freedom and face her wooly pursuer or remain in place. At this moment, the man seemed the best option.

"You're safe now, miss." The man's hands loosened as her feet touched the ground. He was a good half foot taller than her five foot five. "I'm going to let go. I want you to turn around and face your fear."

The hairy monster?

Arabella pushed away from the broad, muscular chest. She'd take care of her first enemy before facing her second.

Slowly, she turned and saw a large, wooly sheep meandering toward her, though yards in the distance. He had not run after her, not with that slow, lazy stride.

"A sheep? That monster is a sheep?" Now, she understood the man's chuckles. Her hand covered her mouth as she giggled.

A soothing, calm voice answered her. "Yes, a harmless, though large, sheep. If I'm correct, his name is Fenwick."

The fiend had a name. Of course he did.

Heat crept from her neck to her cheeks. What a fool she'd been. She set her pride aside as she glanced at her companion.

Her jaw dropped for a second. Her rescuer appeared as a real-life country gentleman, complete with a tweed jacket and flat cap. Light brown curls touched his neck and the edge of his face. Blue eyes followed her inspection. Surely, she was in good company, although the situation was awkward. He probably considered her a ninny and a child. Who ran screaming through a field, frightened by a sheep? Obviously, she did. Weren't they a gentle animal? Shrugging off her embarrassment, she brushed grass and dirt from her skirt. She had to face her actions and audience.

He bowed his head to her. "I'm Thomas Randolph. And you've met Fenwick. His family and friends have now gathered to welcome you to Near Sawrey." He grinned and motioned to the half-circle of sheep who stared at her.

She felt like apologizing to them for her screams. "I hope I didn't scare them too much."

Mr. Randolph crossed his arms. "Perhaps you confused them. But they're used to people. Perhaps not a woman screaming though."

Arabella retrieved her hat and tried to fix her hair which now flowed down her back in disarray. It would just have to hang. "I'm Arabella Graham. I'm visiting my grandmother for the summer."

"Ah, Lady Graham who lives in the village. Welcome to Sawrey. I assume you're not often alone on these roads."

"Oh, no. Never. My friend is visiting at the next house around the bend. I thought I'd be perfectly fine. That is until I fell asleep, and you know the rest of the story." Arabella waved to Lilly as she came around the turn in the road. "There she is now. May I ask how you know the name of the sheep?" What kind of man called sheep by a name? It's not as if they could be pets like cats or dogs.

He picked up a leather bag at his feet. "I'm sort of a local animal husbandry volunteer—a bit of a veterinarian. I tend Miss Potter's sheep and other animals."

Arabella grabbed his arm and immediately released her grip. "Wait. You mean, Miss Beatrix Potter. I heard she lives around here."

"Yes, none other. Truth be told, she might know more about animals than anyone around these parts."

The Beatrix Potter. The creator of magical playgrounds for animals who seemed almost human. "I'm a huge admirer of her stories and artwork."

As Lilly approached, Mr. Randolph left Arabella's side and had a few words with Lilly. Of course, they would know each other. He probably went to Vicar Maxberry's church.

His grin stretched across his handsome face as he and Lilly returned. "Now, I'll be on my way, since you are in good company. I hope to see you soon, Miss Graham." He took her hand and nodded to her. "Good day."

She returned his nod, and her fingers trembled from his warm touch.

Mr. Thomas Randolph, I do hope we have more time to get acquainted.

As Arabella related her comical event with the sheep and Mr. Randolph to Lilly, the apple and pastry they shared tasted even sweeter.

CHAPTER TWO

*E*arly the next morning, Arabella sat on the edge of
her bed and stretched, eager to begin her day. Would
it be full of surprises as she cared for her grandmother?
Already she wondered when she would be able to roam the
hills again. She opened her window and took a deep breath of
fresh air.

As she splashed cool water on her face, she remembered
her dramatic introduction to Mr. Randolph. What would her
parents think? Would someone like him meet their expectations? He wasn't wealthy or of the peerage. So, probably not.

Would there be many more country gentlemen in church
today? Without Nana's presence, Arabella planned to plant
herself in a discreet section instead of up front where
everyone would see her. Could she be an ordinary *miss*
without connection? Not likely. But without being front and
center on her grandmother's arm, she could try, at least on
her first week attending services.

Arabella wanted to look her best, so she asked her grandmother's lady's maid, Marie, to help her with her coiffeur. On

other days, Arabella had sent Marie away and managed on her own. With her ventures out and about, her chestnut curls never stayed in place for long. A pin here and there kept her looking respectful enough for Nana and her time in Sawrey. But today, when she might make new acquaintances and perhaps see a certain local veterinarian, Marie proved a necessity.

Arabella squinted into the mirror against the pain of another pin.

"How is that, Miss Arabella?" The young woman smoothed the mass of hair once more.

With her hair pulled high and away from her face with a few ringlets at the side, the style gave Arabella a look of sophistication. "Thank you, Marie. You might need to come home with me to London."

"Oh, no, miss. I couldn't leave my family or Lady Graham."

Arabella patted Marie's hand. "I know. Don't fret. I wouldn't do that to my grandmother."

After receiving her grandmother's approval, Arabella checked her pink and white striped skirt and light-pink blouse in the mirror. This was one of her favorite outfits. The material was light and didn't weigh her down.

I'm not here to impress anyone. I'm going to church, not a London ball. If I can stay within Nana's acceptable sphere, I'll be happy.

The old Saxon church with its square tower occupied a central ground in Near Sawrey, complete with a graveyard on three sides. At the front of the property, a small section of green remained clear and inviting with a path leading to the entrance on the side. Could she sneak in unnoticed and find an inconspicuous seat?

Fortunately, she had shared her desire for being incognito with Lilly, who happened to be a greeter at the church door for any last-minute parishioners. Arabella squeezed her friend's hand. "It's good to see a familiar face."

She found a seat in the rear of the church close to the wall.

Perfect. I can be the peruser instead of the perused. At least for today. Nana will make sure I am known by those important in her eyes. But not today.

She scanned the sanctuary and saw a gentleman with curly brown hair in a fine black coat. Was that Mr. Randolph? He turned and their gazes met. Indeed, it was Mr. Randolph. He nodded and grinned, causing a flood of warmth to her cheeks.

Was he remembering her foolish race down the hill? She shrugged off her memory of that embarrassing moment and replaced it with a lesson learned. *Do not fall asleep in a pasture full of sheep.*

Once settled, Arabella set her concern aside and concentrated on the service and Vicar Maxberry's message. The minister encouraged his congregation to commit themselves to a season of fruitfulness. "'Herein is my Father glorified, that ye bear much fruit; so shall you be my disciples.' Take a look at the rest of chapter fifteen in John's gospel. Find your purpose in God's vineyard."

Arabella's throat quivered as she struggled to swallow. Was this message for her alone? How did the vicar know she longed to find purpose and be fruitful? Her gloved hand covered her neck as she stared at a stained-glass window, depicting Christ on His knees in the garden.

Father, You know I am concerned about what I should do now, next week, and next year. Today, You command me to bear fruit. Is that possible in my position? How much pruning do You need to do?

Now, with her head and heart occupied with new concerns, Arabella exited the church, hoping to disappear down the lane as she processed God's words.

"Miss Graham." Someone called her name, and the gravel crunched behind her.

She turned and met Mr. Randolph's blue-eyed gaze. "Good morning, sir. It's nice to see you." She grinned at the memory of their last encounter. "I imagined you might avoid the crazy woman from the pasture."

"Not likely. I will treasure that image." He gripped his hat in his hand. "I hoped you would attend this church. I know your grandmother is a parishioner. My parents have walked ahead, or I'd introduce you." His head bowed, covering his expression.

She viewed an elegantly dressed couple on the road walking toward a carriage. "Perhaps, another time."

He cleared his throat. "Yes. There is much I want to share at a later date. I'm expected at home soon." He looked around the churchyard. "I need to round up my brothers and join the family."

"Round up? Are they so young?" She envisioned a couple of eight-year-olds.

"Hardly. Thirteen and seventeen with the energy of youth."

She dipped her head. "Another time then. I don't think you'll have to rescue me from a sheep again."

He tipped his hat as he placed it on his head. "It was my pleasure. Good morn."

As she watched him depart, a nagging question rose in her mind. Why didn't he want her to meet his parents? Could there be unpleasant history between his parents and her grandmother?

Shaking loose of that thought, Arabella headed home and passed a field next to the church. Wildflowers swayed in the grass and formed a colorful blanket. She'd have to return later and sit among their beauty. Perhaps that would be just the thing to take her mind off of a certain handsome gentleman.

~

AFTER THOMAS FINISHED LOOKING in on Miss Potter's sheep and cattle at Hill Top, he found the caretaker on a ladder in the back yard. "Harold, do you need any help?"

The man descended a few steps. "Ah, sir, would you mind handing me that shutter. I had to fix the hinges."

Thomas passed the green shutter to Harold and waited as he screwed it in place. "What would Miss Potter do without you?"

Once safely on the ground, the caretaker wiped his brow on his sleeve. "I think the question is, what would my family do without Miss Potter? She was gracious enough to keep us on when she purchased the property. She's given us a place to live and honest work to do."

Thomas placed his hands on his hips and surveyed the property. This would be a fine working farm soon. Could Thomas turn his small farm into a prosperous business, proving to his father that he had the skills to manage the entire estate?

"When does Miss Potter return? I remember she said something about July." Thomas picked up a few tools and helped Harold carry things to the shed.

"I expect her anytime. She wanted to be here when the rest of the Herdwick sheep arrive."

If Thomas wanted to remain extra busy, he could spend each day at the Potter farm. But he had other obligations, including improvements on his own farm.

Thomas rode his bicycle through town. The villagers had not yet adopted bicycles as a viable form of transportation and exercise. But that didn't stop him. He enjoyed the speed and ease and thought it would soon catch on, even in the small villages.

Pausing for a brief rest, he peered over an old stone wall in Sawrey onto the gardens and rooftops of the quiet village. He had tired of Oxford and London after only a few months. This area was home, and once he made the decision to stay, he eagerly started investing his life among the people.

The church's square tower sparked memories of a pretty, little visitor. He felt guilty for sending his parents ahead on Sunday. He could have introduced them, but then he'd have a lot of explaining to do. He needed a little more time with Miss Graham before the inevitable truth spilled out. An afternoon? A week? A summer? No, he could not curtail the secret that long.

He got on his bike and rode toward a colorful field adjoining the churchyard. Shielding his eyes with his hand, Thomas caught sight of a blue ribbon blowing in the middle of a sea of wildflowers. Was that Miss Graham? He'd recognize that chestnut hair flowing down her back as Miss Graham's any day. *Miss Arabella.* He chuckled and realized she wouldn't expect any trespassers on her time in a vacant field.

Would she mind an interruption? All too soon she will guess my failure to divulge a piece of important information and want nothing to do with me. But not yet. We have a few minutes.

After parking his bicycle on the inside of the stone wall, Thomas adjusted his cap and pulled his brown jacket in place. Clearing his throat with a cough, he raised his voice and hand. "Pardon me, Miss Graham." What could be his excuse for stopping?

She twirled around and faced him. For a moment her beauty stopped him. The wide brimmed hat that shaded her eyes and white apron covering the front of her casual blue skirt and white blouse would spur any artist to paint her in this scenery.

"Mr. Randolph. How are you, sir?" She shifted her basket to her other hand.

He bowed and tipped his cap. "I was returning from a house call and saw you in this lovely setting. Do you mind if I join you? May I help with your basket?"

She looked at her display of flowers. "No, thank you. I'm still looking at the wildflowers. I have a hobby that requires samples of these beauties. When I see all of this color in God's handiwork, I want to capture a portion, preserve it, and pass it along." She raised her hazel eyes toward the rolling hills and sighed. "Of course, nothing compares to this masterpiece."

The wildflowers seemed to mean a lot to her. "What do you do with the flowers? Paint them on China or canvas?"

She shook her head, loosening another strand of hair ready to fly in the wind. "Oh, no. I'm not that talented. I press them and place them in frames, brooches, coasters, between glass, or arrange them in unique bouquets."

"Will you show me your art one day? My mother would enjoy seeing this beauty every day." He studied her, though he referenced the flowers. Could he manage acknowledging her beauty every day? So far, a resounding yes.

Miss Graham turned and focused on the hills and canopy of color. "Well, I think I have enough to keep me busy. I must return before Nana sends someone to find me."

The sun at their backs and the breeze rustling the grass and flowers beside the manicured path warmed his heart. A simple scene with Arabella in the center. Who needed elaborate dinners and parties? Some only desired a field of flowers and natural beauty.

Miss Graham walked toward the wall. "Oh, you have a

bicycle. Aren't you lucky." She ran her fingers across the red painted metal as if it was a piece of art.

He'd never seen anyone treat a bicycle with such respect. "Have you ever ridden one?"

She stepped back. "My parents have said no to my many requests. But I do so want to try." She drummed her finger on her lips. "I saw a bicycle in Nana's storage shed outside. I wonder..."

"I'd be happy to teach you if your grandmother would allow it. I'd enjoy that." If he had more time with Arabella, he'd have more opportunities to tell her the truth.

Her eyes twinkled as she faced the sun. A green and gold pool of hope and trust. "She might allow that, Mr. Randolph. Unless...I have a question. Do your parents have a good relationship with my grandmother?"

He blinked. What an odd question? "Well, yes. They have known each other for many years." All too soon, she'd ask the one question he didn't want to answer.

"Good. I'll ask her if I can learn to ride her bicycle." She laughed. "I can see me riding through town to do my calling."

He'd look forward to that sight. Arabella on wheels with her long hair—that should be neatly hidden under her hat— streaming behind her. A pleasant sight for sure.

CHAPTER THREE

*W*ith Lilly's help and Nana's approval, Arabella bought two ready-to-wear dresses of sturdy cotton fabric for walking in the fields or working in the gardens. That Wednesday morning, she wore a green skirt with a yellow blouse which reminded her of emerald fields in the sunshine.

Nana's garden held prize winning roses that could pose competition for any of Kensington Palace roses. Since her grandmother could not tend them herself, Arabella rolled her outside to the yard in her wheelchair where Arabella could receive instruction on how to pick, groom, and care for the variety of plants. She carried a small notebook and pencil in her apron pocket to jot down any tidbits from her grandmother.

After this summer, Arabella didn't know when or where she'd use the information. The only plot of any size near them in London was the large fenced in gated area in the center of a group of houses. Someone was paid to tend the plot of greenery. Roses weren't the London gardeners' specialty. Mother had a few potted plants in their tiny back garden, which was only large enough to host a table, four chairs, and an apple tree.

Nana's cheeks glowed with health once outdoors. "This is why I chose to remain in the family home." Her fingers clutched a pair of clippers that she used as a pointer. "But not your father. He favored the city, though I don't know why with all the crowds and heat."

"Mother prefers it too. I must have received my love for country life from you. Now that I think about it, Constance also enjoys life on her farm in the north."

"Oh, yes, your sister does love country life. Before my fall, I was looking forward to visiting her this summer along with my two great-grandchildren. The train I'd take runs close to their village." Nana stared at her extended leg hidden beneath her skirt. How quickly her sunny smile melted away.

"Nana, I'll go with you as soon as you're well." She would love to visit Constance and spend time with her and her family. Once she returned to the city, she'd grab any reason she could to venture into the countryside. She could travel by train with her grandmother, if her parents or future husband let her loose. But roaming was not a characteristic of her true life.

As Arabella pulled weeds, she learned the names of the green shoots piercing the ground. Her grandmother pointed out lavender, poppies, bellflowers, and carnations. Nana shared snippets about many people who lived in the village.

"Do you know everyone in town, even on the outskirts?"

Nana's grin returned. "I'd imagine so, especially if they go to the village church. I have many friends I normally invite to tea. Perhaps in a month, I'll be ready to entertain. Florence and James Rowe have a beautiful garden on their estate at the edge of town. Her boys keep her busy on their property. They have a grand estate ball and party in August. I'm sure you'll receive an invitation."

She didn't mention knowing the Randolphs. They probably weren't in her social circle. Arabella couldn't imagine her grandmother had anything against them. Thinking of Thomas reminded her of his offer to teach her to ride a bicycle. "Would you mind if I took the bicycle in the shed and fixed it up so I could learn how to ride?"

Nana laughed. Was she picturing Arabella on a bicycle or was it some funny memory? Had her grandmother tried riding a bicycle?

After her laughter dwindled to quiet breaths, Nana leaned forward. "A few years ago, a group of Sawrey ladies ordered bicycles and tried to form one of those women's riding groups that you see in all the magazines. It lasted for two months. I was one of them."

Arabella grinned. *Of course she was. This is where I need to be. I could enjoy all the pleasure of simple country living.*

"Father wouldn't let me ride in London. I don't think he'd object here, though." Would he? Riding a bicycle was not something she should probably mention in her weekly letter.

Nana waved away Arabella's words. "I'll handle Holman. He's a lot like his father. He always liked to say no."

Yes. Nana nailed that. Were all men like that? Well, Thomas seemed different. He said he'd teach me to ride.

"You'll have to take it to the hardware store where I ordered it and have someone check the tires and grease the gears and chain."

In the next hour, Arabella added more lines in her growing garden journal, then they went inside. As Arabella straightened Nana's pillows and blanket, she saw a row of small books in the glass cabinet behind the chair. "Are these Beatrix Potter books?"

Her grandmother twisted toward her. "Oh, yes. I have every one of them, and they're all signed."

Arabella slid the cabinet open and ran her fingers over the

spines before pulling out *The Tale of Squirrel Nutkin*. "This is my favorite. What a naughty squirrel."

Her grandmother smiled. "I enjoy them all, though I do feel silly having a collection of children's books. Yet, the lessons ring true for adults too."

"They certainly do." Arabella thumbed through the pages, stopping at a few incredible illustrations. "Have you met Miss Potter?" She sat on the sofa by Nana, mesmerized by the possibility of knowing someone so talented.

"Yes. She is a welcome addition to our village. She has her work cut out for her at Hill Top. You'll meet her soon. I'm sure I'll hear about her arrival."

I'll meet Beatrix Potter. What will I say? She is so accomplished. And here I am aimless and searching. I have education and training but nothing to recommend me to a talented author and artist like Miss Potter.

ARABELLA VENTURED out on her own for her mid-afternoon walk through the village—which included a main road and a few side streets. Her grandmother allowed her this bit of freedom within the familiar paths of Sawrey. Everyone knew everyone else. No harm in a little exercise outside of one's own garden.

She strolled past the Tower Bank Arms, an old tavern and inn that now served as a tea shop and pub. She'd love to stick her head inside and see what was going on, but she could wait until her grandmother recovered. Nana had planned to treat Arabella to afternoon tea. The beautiful arbor over the entrance doubled as a trellis for pink roses. The timeless round clock reminded her that all too quickly summer would leap into fall, leaving her right where she started.

As she glanced at the people in her path, she wondered if

each one knew his or her purpose. How did they find it? Did everyone know the purpose of their life except her?

I might have something important to do for the next few months. But what then? These people have jobs, families, homes, and meaning in their choices. I don't have a clue. All I have is London and someone else's plans for me.

She held her hands behind her back and determined to continue her walk, hopefully knocking some gray thoughts loose. Why let negative prospects of the future cloud a bright, cloudless day? If she truly enjoyed this way of life, then her demeanor needed to show it. Live in the moment with pleasure.

Her footsteps mellowed into an easy gait. The heady perfume of many gardens full of summer delights grounded her to the present. The sound of a tinny-like whine of a cat caught her attention. A few yards ahead by a slate wall, Arabella spotted a small black and white kitten. Its pitiful meow sounded like it was calling for someone to guide him home.

"Where do you live, little one?" She picked him up and stroked his head. "You aren't starving. Not with that round belly." Arabella took the stone steps by an open gate into a garden. After placing him on the ground, she watched him run across the yard toward a gray cat. The larger one began to lick his head and held the kitten still with a paw.

"Good. You found your home." Arabella glanced around the magical garden where trellises covered the wall and fruit trees dotted the yard.

Who lives here? Well, I'm not an invited guest. Still, this garden has such potential as if it's waiting to waken from years of neglect.

Arabella turned on the path, heading back to the road.

"Excuse me, may I help you?" A strong woman's voice caught Arabella mid-step.

She pivoted, embarrassed at being caught trespassing. "I'm so sorry. I found a kitten on the road and hoped to return it to the correct garden."

The rosy cheeked woman in a worn brown skirt and plain blouse smiled as she spied the kitten playing with his brothers and sisters under the trees. "That would be Tom." She laughed and her shoulders shook.

Arabella at once felt at home and forgiven. Her spontaneous instinct to rescue *Tom* proved positive. She walked toward the woman. "I'm Arabella Graham. I'm staying with my grandmother."

"Cora Graham. Yes, I've met her and enjoy her company. I'm Beatrix Potter, a part-time resident of Hill Top Farm."

Arabella's eyes widened and she lifted her hand to cover her mouth.

Stretching out her hand, Arabella said, "Oh, I am so glad to meet you. I usually don't enter gardens uninvited."

"Well, anyone who will rescue an animal is a welcome visitor anytime. If you have a few minutes, I'll show you a bit of my wilderness."

Time? I have all the time in the world for this brilliant artist. Somehow, I have to get control of my awe. The woman might have name recognition, but she dresses like any farm matron willing to muddy her boots and skirt for the perfect rose or an errant kitten.

Receiving her marching orders, Arabella fell in step with Miss Potter's long stride. "Oh, I'd love to see your garden. If it's anything like your books, it's bound to be marvelous."

Miss Potter picked up a basket by the gate opening into a walled enclosure. "You mean Mr. McGregor's Garden? I've not been here long enough to have the rows and rows of every vegetable for rabbits. But I have a start."

She hadn't expected Miss Potter to reference *The Tale of Peter Rabbit* in normal conversation. "How do you keep the rabbits and moles away?"

As they stood on the garden path, Arabella scanned the manicured plots of leafy green plants in neat rows. This could feed many little animals.

"I have the cats who roam the garden, a bit of wire mesh, and this wall. I think I'll be able to harvest a nice crop of vegetables even when a few disappear."

As she spoke, a little brown rabbit stuck his long ears and nose through a shrub. Arabella wouldn't tell on the wee creature. As far as she knew, Miss Potter might consider him a pet.

After checking the vines for beans and the potted tomato plants for new fruit, Miss Potter led Arabella through a green wrought-iron gate to the back of an old farmhouse. "I fell in love with this seventeenth century house and soon found living creatures had claimed the place first—mice and squirrels. Since then, they've had to find a different abode. A few of them found their way into my stories."

Arabella shivered. The way Miss Potter said mice conjured an image of a colony of the pesky rodents. "Oh, I wouldn't mind a squirrel."

Chuckling, the woman pointed to the attic window. "Not a squirrel but a family of them. That made it hard to sleep at night."

"True. I must admit I've never been around mice or squirrels in our house in London." The only animals in their London house were a cat and a small dog.

"Ah, London." Miss Potter motioned to a bench by the back steps of the house. The emphasized *London* caused a sigh. "I am from London too. I live here half the time and with my parents in London the other half."

This woman had to be at least forty. Arabella knew her to be unmarried. She assumed her independence was fully separate from her parents. But that was not so. Arabella's awe of

Miss Potter deflated a bit. A famous children's writer and illustrator living with her parents?

Can one never leave the bonds of parents? Marriage was probably the only way, but that led straight into the lead strings of another relationship. Arabella supposed six months out of the year was better than none.

With hands under her thighs, Arabella leaned forward. "I've never felt more at home than here for the past two weeks. London seems so far away. Yet, I must return. I have no idea what to do with my life. But I must do something."

Miss Potter lifted her face to the summer sky. "Only you can know what that something will be. Once I found myself alone in a sick bed, wondering the same thing. My parents wanted me to marry and be like everyone else. What must I do?" Silence allowed Arabella to absorb the question. "I had to draw. That was my earliest passport from my wondering what to do. Each day brings remarkable things for me to draw. Does that make any sense to you? You are so young. Possibly too young to have loved and lost." Arabella couldn't ask Miss Potter for details, but she'd heard the whisper of grief and darkness in her voice.

"You're right. I haven't been in love yet. My parents insist I take part in the season and make an appropriate match with a man I'll meet there. But I have so many questions about what's most important in life and love. I do so long for independence, especially from society's regulations and London's hectic pace."

Miss Potter reached into her pocket, pulling out a handful of seeds for the chirping occupants of the shrubs. "You sound like me twenty years ago. Independence comes with some strings too. Your family does not disappear. The financial gains aren't always guaranteed. And when love finds you, it can be fleeting."

A tear slipped down Miss Potter's cheek, but she didn't

bother wiping it away. Arabella had stumbled on a painful, private memory. "I lost my fiancé almost a year ago. I imagined a happily ever after that was not to be." She pushed herself off the bench. "But now I have Hill Top and all my animals. Regardless, I am happy in my dwelling, even with my forays to London to appease my parents."

Arabella's heart clenched. "I'm sorry. I hope one day I'll find that contentment."

Miss Potter raised her hand and pointed to the sky. "One last piece of advice. Make sure it is what God wants for you. His plans are best."

"Yes, I hope He tells me soon."

Arabella left with an open invitation to return at any time. One last glance at the fairy tale cottage with its own special magic spurred her forward, perhaps toward her own ever after. But would she have to wait until she was forty years old to find out?

CHAPTER FOUR

homas hadn't checked on Miss Potter and her animals since she'd returned to Hill Top, so he made time in his mid-week schedule to visit her. He didn't mind communicating with her caretaker, but something about the bright-eyed woman drew Thomas to her farm.

She loved all her animals—farm, domestic, or wild. He had found a kindred spirit, and they spent much time bouncing ideas and remedies off each other. Such as how to deter rabbits, moles, and squirrels from ruining a garden without causing the creature any harm. A little friendly redirection of habitats proved successful.

When he saw the green gate, Thomas commenced his usual shouting, not knowing if Miss Potter would be inside or out.

"Hello! Hello, Miss Potter, it's Thomas." He stood in the yard, anticipating an answer within seconds.

A moment later, a woman waved a handkerchief out of an upstairs window. "I'll be right down."

Thomas waved back. He wondered if the caretaker had gathered all the sheep into the pen until he heard bleating on the other side of the stone wall. Taking in all angles of the area behind the house, Thomas tried to visualize what this overgrown area could look like with a few seasons of care. If anyone could carry out a miracle, it was this creative, energetic newcomer.

"Thomas, how good to see you." The mistress of Hill Top reached out, took his hands, and drew him closer to touch her cheek.

Looking at her, no one would ever guess she hailed from London. She embraced the whole concept of independent farmer, unlike Miss Graham who probably could never truly shake off her London shell. Would he want her to disregard style and fashion? His mother had not, neither had Lady Graham.

"Miss Potter, I'm so glad you've returned."

She shook her finger at him. "I have asked you to call me Beatrix. We are partners in this world of nature far from societal parlors."

Perhaps he could relax a little. After all she wasn't so many years his senior, perhaps a dozen. "All right, Beatrix. I'm here to confirm the good health of your sheep and to clean out anything in their hooves and teeth. The local county veterinarian has treated them for diseases. This is a routine follow-up."

She patted his shoulder. "I still don't understand why you can't be the county's official veterinarian."

"How about because I have my own farm to run, and I have about half of the courses needed to qualify. And I don't need the job."

"Oh, right. I do forget. How is your *experimental* farm going? Is living in a cottage all you thought it would be?"

He chuckled. "I could ask you the same question. Same scenario—single, a farm, small living space."

"But different. I am adding on to this house. Anyway, you

will end up married and have a passel of children." She tsked and placed her finger on her lips in thought. "By the way, have you considered the vicar's daughter Lilly, or...oh, yes... or Lady Graham's granddaughter, Arabella?"

Thomas pulled in a deep breath. "About Miss Graham. She doesn't really know who I am. I introduced myself as Thomas Randolph, the local animal husbandry consultant. Nothing else."

Beatrix's wide eyes darkened. "This could be interesting. Why not tell her the truth?"

Why indeed? The result could close the door to a continuing friendship with Arabella, or anything more. He would share the truth, eventually. For now, he liked how they got along. "Will you play my game for another week or so?"

"Hmm. I can do that, but don't get too deep into sabotage. If feelings are involved, it could be unpleasant."

"It's nothing. A few bicycle lessons. I don't have time for a romance."

"If you say so." Beatrix walked toward the gate leading to the pasture. On the other side was a shed and pen. Her dozen heads of Hertford sheep congregated with their curly heads bobbing as they bleated.

With Beatrix's help, Thomas looked over one sheep at a time, finding nothing to warrant concern. He easily dislodged a few stones from hooves before taking a quick review of her two pigs, one goat, and her milk cow. The rest of the cattle would entail another visit.

Beatrix rinsed her hands in a rain barrel. "Now, let's go inside for tea."

He never refused the invitation even though he tried the first few times. The conversation was always stimulating and the biscuits and sweets tantalizing. His mouth watered at the prospect of a buttery concoction. He assumed she used fresh items from her garden in her meals.

Choosing his favorite chair next to the round serving table, Thomas relaxed into the worn cushions. No show or pretense here, although Beatrix could have an elegant place. She wasn't interested in the flamboyant. Neither was he. His abode, though comfortable, would never pass the strict London checklist. Sawrey would never be London, which made him thankful.

With a *tap tap* at the back door, Beatrix stopped pouring the tea. As she disappeared, he stole a cheese cracker.

"Arabella, come right in. You are just in time for tea." Beatrix's voice echoed in the foyer.

"Oh, I don't want to intrude. I brought you some fruit from the market." The soothing cadence from Arabella's polished dialect brought him to his feet.

When she saw Thomas, her grin widened. "Now, I really can't interrupt. You have company."

He admired Arabella in her summer frock of violet flowers on a cream background. Fresh as the fruit in her basket.

Beatrix took the gift and waved her hand in the air. "Pish, posh. It's only Thomas. And you're already friends."

True. A friend he would appreciate encountering more often. Arabella's blush and glance at him through her lashes encouraged his imagination to that of *close* friends.

"Thank you so much." Beatrix rummaged through her produce. "I can surely use the lemons and strawberries. I'll have to plant some strawberries next year."

Thomas pulled out his chair for her. "Why don't you take this seat?" He'd sit in another one.

She untied her hat, sat, and straightened her skirt. Her securely pinned hair remained in place while she adjusted it, very little escaping. His preference for long strands trailing about her creamy skin came to mind. He shook his head, discarding his errant musings.

Beatrix poured the tea into sturdy but beautiful teacups, sprinkled with butterflies in a pattern. She probably chose that so he wouldn't be stuck with a tiny, dainty cup which always proved awkward.

Arabella looked around the room. He followed her gaze to the collection of books and items relating to all of Beatrix's stories. He had done the same thing a few months ago.

Her face seemed as animated as Beatrix's characters. "Miss Potter, do you have plans for more tales?"

Setting her cup in its saucer, Beatrix narrowed her eyes. "Arabella, I have a request before I answer. Please call me Beatrix."

The younger lady blushed. "Very well, Beatrix."

Could he ask the same? He was tired of Mr. Randolph. "Miss Graham, would you call me Thomas? Especially since I'll soon be teaching you how to ride a bicycle."

"Why yes, Beatrix and Thomas. And please call me Arabella." She pulled her shoulders back and took a deep breath.

Beatrix grinned. "Back to your question. Yes, in the fall, I'll publish *The Story of a Fierce Bad Rabbit* and *The Story of Miss Moppet*."

Arabella clapped and tapped her boots on the floor. "I'm thrilled."

"You will really be pleased with the one I'm writing now." Beatrix paused and looked at Thomas. *"The Tale of Tom Kitten."*

Laughter bounced around Thomas as the ladies shared an inside joke. Hopefully, he was not the Tom kitten.

Holding her stomach in glee, Arabella calmed her breathing. "You mean Tom, the kitten I brought home to you?"

"The same one. He has continued to be very mischievous. And no, Thomas, he's not named after you."

He leaned into his chair. "Well, that wouldn't be so bad, although I try to stay out of mischief."

Beatrix nibbled on a sugar cookie before centering her gaze on Arabella. "Which book is your favorite?"

Tilting her head back and sighing, Arabella's cheeks crinkled with amusement. "I don't have to think about it. *The Tale of Squirrel Nutkin.*"

"Hmmm." Beatrix raised her eyebrows. "Why?"

Arabella fidgeted with the seam on her skirt and dipped her head before straightening in the chair. "Because I haven't always followed the crowd in London. I'd rather have different friends, attend different events, view different art. I don't enjoy being the same as everyone else. And here in Sawrey I can be myself." She chuckled. "But I don't want to have an owl chop off my tail."

Silence cloaked the room as Thomas tried to understand the bond between the women. Each from London and wanting a new start. With his attraction to Arabella, it could work out for him. Except for the one thing he hid from Arabella. If he didn't tell her soon, somebody else would.

Beatrix reached across the table, laid her hand on top of Arabella's, and patted it as one would a grieving soul. A touch of understanding. "We are the same, my friend. Each having to keep parents happy with a mask of obedience. Always returning or anticipating leaving."

Arabella placed her other hand on top of Beatrix's.

Did they even know he existed? Should he leave?

"I know I must return to London at the end of August, appeasing my parents' social obligations." Arabella's smile disappeared.

What could he do to help?

Beatrix tilted her head and chuckled. "And I leave for Lingholm House with my parents for part of the autumn. It doesn't matter that is my favorite time in the Lake District."

Thomas followed Beatrix's gaze. The farmhouse window framed the purple common violet and bluebell sprinkled fields, her Herdwick sheep dotting the land. Another thing to thank God for each day, which reminded him of his recent lapse in daily time with Him. Perhaps—no perhaps about it— he knew God cared about him and his estate plans. Yet, what about God's plans?

The ladies had already moved on to pressed flowers and sketches and something about children and pastimes. As if he suddenly reappeared in the room, Beatrix turned toward him, winking. What did that signify?

He grabbed one more ginger biscuit. "I must be on my way. My livestock needs a bit of attention." True enough. "The sheep market is in Hawkshead at the end of July if you want to attend, Beatrix."

Arabella gazed at him through her lashes. "Is it something I would like?"

He shrugged. "If you like sheep, pigs, cattle, food, and crafts. It is a village fair that keeps its emphasis on sheep."

Beatrix nodded. "I'm out to prove my hardy Herdwick sheep are perfect for the area. Let's attend, Arabella."

"Yes, please." Her amber eyes sparkled as if she were a child going to a fair.

Thomas adjusted his hat. "Are you ready for your first bicycle riding lesson, Arabella? Would tomorrow be too soon?"

"I've asked grandmother and had the bicycle prepared. I hope it doesn't take me long to learn." Arabella rose as Thomas backed toward the door.

Beatrix jumped to her feet. "I learned in two days. If I can ride a bicycle, you certainly can."

Thomas jerked his head toward Beatrix at the same moment as Arabella did. His jaw dropped. How many wonders did Beatrix hold close?

Beatrix crossed her arms. "Why the startled looks? It's not as if I'm ancient. One day you will see that forty isn't so terribly old."

His laughter joined Arabella's. Turning toward her, he bowed his head and caught her gaze. "Until tomorrow then."

As he rode his bicycle down the country road to his small house, Thomas thought of Tom the little kitten, Arabella, and Beatrix. They seemed to be made for village life. Would a farm just outside the village be too great a step? London to Sawrey might be the extent of how far Arabella would go. It was still a village with neighbors and shops. Even though his farm wasn't a far distance, it wasn't town. Could she handle that separation from activity?

Why did it matter to him? Beatrix had not yet made her move permanent, so why would Arabella after a mere month?

The fells and fields entertained his senses as the wind pushed him homeward. It was true—London was not for everyone, neither was Sawrey.

And someone like Arabella from a wealthy London family was not rural farm material in any scenario.

CHAPTER FIVE

*T*he July temperature mimicked June, yet the vibrant colors of the flowers, fruits, and vegetables brightened in the summer sun. Everything pushed upward for a chance of warm rays. Butterflies tapped the blossoms without warning. Arabella yearned to have a purpose like the insects who carried pollen from plant to plant, sniffing the fragrance, and spreading the fairy dust of life.

She'd never be a Beatrix Potter and pollinate the whole earth with beautiful sketches and fairytale words. But she could make her corner of the world brighter with gardens of flowers, sharing beauty with those who needed a little encouragement. Her time in Sawrey had also expanded her love of animals.

She'd hardly become independently wealthy like Miss Potter, but in four years, when she turned twenty-five, she'd receive her trust fund and be able to live comfortably. Perhaps in a place like this or with her grandmother.

Now, that's a thought. I can already see the brick wall of my parents' refusal.

It wasn't that she didn't want to marry. But her parents

wanted her to marry a titled gentleman who would bring prestige to their family. But that could never make her happy.

What would Squirrel Nutkin do?

He'd see life as an adventure and not follow the crowd, although that option almost ended in his demise. Well, she'd be careful and not stray too far.

In the foyer, Arabella secured her hat and laced her boots tight.

"Let me look at you." Nana's voice rang from the drawing room. "I'm glad you took my advice. You don't need extra strings or ribbons to get caught in the chains. Are your laces secure inside your boots? And do you have on long pantaloons?"

"Oh, Nana. I'm appropriately dressed and don't plan on spilling into the road in disgrace. Lilly will be with me until I am steady on the bicycle. With Thomas instructing and Lilly helping, I will be a professional in no time."

Her grandmother huffed. "I wish I could be with you. I'm missing so much." She knocked her knuckles against the shell over her leg.

"Soon, Nana." Arabella kissed her cheek.

Exiting the front door, Arabella found her blue bicycle right where she'd put it early this morning. Ready. Steady. Offering her an adventure.

Thomas and Lilly waited on the road. Their practice area was the circular drive leading to the house.

Lilly waved. "Hello, are you sure you want to do this? It looks wobbly to me."

For show, Arabella wobbled the bike back and forth, letting it teeter on falling. "Oh, I'm playing. I'll be fine. You'll learn next. This bicycle will be yours after August." *If only I could stay and find Lilly her own bicycle.*

Keeping both hands on the bicycle, she rolled it toward

Thomas. "Good morning. Are you ready? Any second thoughts?"

He quirked his eyebrows. "That is what I'm supposed to ask you."

She shook her head. "No way am I backing down."

He chuckled and placed his bicycle beside him after releasing the metal rod to hold it upright. "I need you to set the post and lean your bike in position. You shouldn't have to hold it. I'm going to show you the basics, then you'll practice with my help."

Arabella linked her arm with Lilly's, watched, and listened. She could do this and do it well.

Thomas demonstrated balance, handlebar usage, brakes, forward motion, and getting on and off the bicycle. She smiled as she watched all the motions. He was obviously fit and strong. Now, if she could separate his handsome form from the lesson she needed to master.

Put the good-looking Thomas aside and concentrate on the teacher Thomas.

She closed her eyes and then peeked. He was still there, but her focus changed to what she had to do in the present. She'd study his looks later.

His instructions halted. "Ready?"

"Of course." Arabella brought her bicycle beside her, with Thomas on one side and Lilly on the other. She straddled the devise, grabbed the handlebars, and pulled herself onto the seat. Lilly adjusted Arabella's skirt, tucking pieces of it into her boots.

Thomas held the handlebars. "Now, feet on the pedals, gain your balance, and when you're ready, start moving forward. I'll be holding on the rear of the bicycle as long as you don't decide to race away."

Lilly and Thomas nodded at each other. "Ready. Set. Go," echoed around Arabella.

After a few rocky attempts, she managed circles in the drive and successful stops and starts. Her companions clapped as her swaying and jiggling decreased. They backed away and allowed her to manage unassisted.

"Look at me. I'm flying." She wanted to put her arms out like she saw at the circus. But her hands remained glued to the handlebars as her head communicated with her legs.

I am free! I can travel all over the village by myself.

She stopped by her friends and leaned over the bars with arms outstretched, drawing them in for a hug. "Thank you. Won't my family be so—well, I was going to say proud. Shocked might be better, except for Nana. She's proud of me."

Thomas left the hug first and straightened his jacket. *Ah, too much closeness for him. Perhaps it wasn't the most appropriate public action.*

He retrieved his bicycle. "Now, for a genuine test. We are going to ride through the village and let the villagers gawk at us."

She shooed his words away. "*Tsk. Tsk.* They will just be envious."

Lilly picked up her basket. "I'll see you later. Next time, it is my turn."

Arabella waved. "I'll be your teacher." That was if she could make it through the village.

Thomas steadied her bicycle. "Let's go."

Her heart beat a cadence with her exuberance over her new vehicle of flight. "I'll race you."

Thomas's jaw dropped. He took hold of her chin and turned her face to meet his. "You will do no such thing. You, my little student, have not mastered the bicycle. Take care, so I can bring you back in one piece."

She batted her eyelashes and swatted his hand away from her chin. "I just wanted to see what you'd say. I'm not crazy. I can't believe I've conquered this metal wheeled creature after one try."

A sigh whistled through his lips as he wiped at his forehead. "You better not make me regret my generous offer to teach you."

Earlier, he had treated it as a neighborly lesson he might give a child. But as he moved in closer, Arabella wondered at his real motive. Why the extra attention? She had escaped the grand parade of suitors in London. Did this country farmer have an interest in her?

Shaking away shreds of summer nostalgia for a simpler life, she pedaled forward, leaving Thomas scrambling to catch up. If she fell now, it would be her own fault—just as falling in love would be her mistake alone, one of her own making.

Concentrate. No physical or emotional mishaps today.

The sky was too blue, the birds' songs too chirpy, the flowers too lovely—this was not the time or place for disaster. The shops and houses passed in a blur, as she concentrated on balance and forward motion. Even with Thomas following, she had to master this new contraption for herself, not to impress another soul, though she'd accept any praise if her grandmother, or Thomas, wanted to commend her for her accomplishment.

With her hands tight on the handlebars, she focused straight ahead. Using the town wall as a guide, she passed the orchard and Buckle Yeat Cottage next to the Tower Bank Arms.

She didn't begin with a destination in mind. It was as if her bicycle had control. The gate in front of Hill Top drew Arabella closer. Managing a topple free stop, she steadied herself for a prolonged view of wisteria creeping up the gray stone wall of the farmhouse. Poppies, irises, lavender, and a multitude of blooming plants held her attention.

Surely, they were meant to be praised for their beauty— God's creation.

Thomas parked beside her. "I should have known you'd end up here. I think you and Beatrix are fast friends."

Are we? I suppose sharing London, our escapes, and our parents' expectations bind us closer than others.

Arabella leaned on her handlebars. "How does she do it alone? The house itself is not large, but these gardens. Oh, my." Paths, walls, flower and vegetable gardens, an orchard, ponds. So much to explore and nurture.

Thomas peered around her, taking in her view. "She has a caretaker who has a wife and children. They help and live in part of the house. That's why she is adding on to it. She's even looking at buying another adjoining estate with a house. She needs only a small place."

True. I could be the same. As long as I had the gardens.

Thomas touched her elbow. "Shhh. Look."

Two brown rabbits ventured from the flowers onto the path. "Peter and Benjamin have come out to play or cause some mischief."

Thomas chuckled. "At least there is not an old Mr. McGregor to capture them."

She'd seen rabbits before on her former trips in the country. Though she'd been all over Europe seeing all the sights— Eiffel Tower, Colosseum, Venice, some châteaux—she had seen nothing as inspiring as English country lanes. She'd not share her extensive memories with Thomas, since the extent of his travels might only be Oxford and London. What else did anyone need to see?

Exploring and touring are wonderful pastimes if I could come home to this.

When the rabbits disappeared into the shrubbery, Thomas cleared his throat, bringing Arabella to the present again. "Would you like to go to the Tower Bank Arms for tea?"

Before saying "anywhere with you," Arabella faced him with heated cheeks. What was wrong with her? Pining for Thomas would not do. She'd not lose her heart on a few summer meetings. "Yes, tea sounds wonderful. Let's see if I can get back on my bicycle without help."

"Not far to go." He held one hand on her bicycle handlebars.

Arabella looked down the lane and could see the pub. *I can do it again.* Practice. With a forward push on the pedal, she wobbled forward and found her equilibrium. "I did it."

Flanking her right side, Thomas's grin buoyed her efforts. "You're a natural."

"Perhaps a natural, unstable, wobbly body. But I do love the experience. Thank you for teaching me."

He nodded in response.

They parked their bikes against the short stone wall and entered the old pub full of afternoon customers in for tea. She leaned into the slight touch on her arm as Thomas guided her.

THOMAS HAD second thoughts about this outing when he saw a few of his acquaintances at the bar. He had hoped no one he knew would be sharing a pint.

They greeted him with "Good day to you, sir." Perhaps Arabella would mistake their robust greeting as a joke.

A table in the back by a window would be perfect. He pulled out a chair for her, and he chose one with his back to the entrance. "We can see Hill Top from here. Is this all right?"

Arabella smiled as she bent toward the window. "Yes, I love the view. Are you certain you don't want to be closer to your friends?"

He hoped his voice sounded normal. "Believe me, this is exactly where I want to be. Here, with you."

A waitress appeared from behind him. "Good afternoon, Mr. Rowe. What would you like today? Our special tea sampler?"

Arabella raised her hand from the table and addressed the young woman. "I think you have mistaken him for someone else. This is Mr. Randolph."

The waitress looked at him, her lips clamped together, brow crinkled.

He gripped the edge of the table before waving the statement away. "No, it's fine. Yes, we'll have the tea for two. Thank you."

Would it all come to a head now? Had he waited too long? He never wanted to be forced into the admission.

Arabella sat back in her seat with her hands in her lap. She raised her head and studied his face as if searching for answers.

He knew this time would come. It wasn't as if he could hide his secret forever. Before she accused him of something, he would take the initiative. Perhaps forgiveness would come later. Surely good would come from the unveiling. But would it alter their friendship?

Truth pulled at his temples, his heart, his taunt stomach muscles. "Arabella, I need to tell you something."

She gave him a stony stare. "Really, Mr. *Rowe*, you have something to share?"

He deserved the piercing glare and so much more. "My name is Thomas Randolph Rowe. I am the oldest son of James and Florence Rowe." He tried to maintain eye contact, but he took a few seconds to watch his fingers crease the white tablecloth. He drew in a huge lungful of air, crossed his arms on the table, and claimed eye contact again. Her expression hadn't changed.

"My parents own Rowe Estates outside of Sawrey. Dad is a landowner and holds a seat in Parliament." Still no sign of emotion on her face. "I have two younger brothers— Edmund, seventeen and Steward, thirteen. They both live at home. I live in one of the farmhouses and try to make the land profitable with cattle and livestock. I really am a village veterinary assistant."

He scrunched his brow until it hurt and pursed his lips. Had he destroyed everything they could've had? He waited for her reply, but she remained silent. Even though he'd kept his true identity from her, that shouldn't change how they feel about each other.

Turning her gaze to the window, Arabella drummed her fingers on the table. When she faced him, she studied him, as if trying to see the real Thomas. Would he be able to convince her of who he truly was?

"I'm amazed I didn't see it." Her voice squeaked, and she cleared it with a cough. "Why didn't Lilly or Nana tell me? Or Beatrix? They all know who you are. Nana said she is good friends with your parents."

He lowered his head, wishing the others weren't involved. Squaring his shoulders, he confronted the prospect of losing Arabella's friendship. "Yes, she is. I haven't spoken to her, so perhaps Thomas Randolph sounded appropriate to her." He sighed. "As for Beatrix and Lilly, I asked them to not reveal my identity until I found an opportunity first. I never found that time."

The tea arrived in a yellow porcelain pot with blue and yellow flowered cups and saucers.

The silence bore a hole in his heart. *Think. What do I say? Why hadn't I thought far enough ahead?*

After Arabella poured the tea and stirred one sugar cube in her cup, she sat back again. "I thought I'd escaped the deception of London society, of men searching for a wealthy woman, and ladies seeking a title. It seems I landed right back into a masquerade. What I declined at home has found me in Sawrey. The ruse with the veterinarian bag and sheep market plans was quite good. What did you expect to gain from me?"

He pulled back from her stinging words. "I hoped you'd see me for myself. Not for my position or family. My parents shoving women at me is tiring. Setting up my own simple household and working as a small estate manager with a veterinary job on the side separates me from them. I didn't find purpose in my European tour or with the literature and philosophy sophisticates in Oxford. The earth and the animals helped me find my purpose."

A few tears slipped from Arabella's eyes. Tears for him? For her? Perhaps for the end of their friendship?

She wiped them away with her fingertips and picked up her cup. After a few sips, she held the cup in two hands at the table's edge.

The waitress interrupted again with the tiered cake and sandwich server. Fifteen minutes ago, he would have grabbed items immediately, covering his plate. Now, he stared around the layered dish at Arabella.

She flinched as if coming from a faraway stupor. "I'm sorry. The tears are silly. I've searched for my purpose and meaning and seemed to be moving closer to it. But it's evasive. You've found yours. I'm glad for you."

The *prim and proper Miss Arabella* now occupied the chair. Thomas cocked his head, amazed at the transformation. Had his deceit washed away the caring, fun-loving, adventurous girl? It appeared so as she nibbled on a cucumber sandwich.

His plate of colorful delights no longer held his attention. The next bite would probably sour in his stomach.

Somehow, he had to salvage something from their past

month together. "Can you forgive me? I'm an open book now."

Arabella replaced half of her sandwich on her plate. "You see, Mr. Randolph, I mean Mr. Rowe, I've been honest. You know all about me—the lady running from London to escape the greedy and titled ton. But the lure of the country clouded my view and draped me in a fairytale, allowing deceit to take hold."

Did she really see him in that light? He knew the revelation would be hurtful, but was he to be labeled a villain forever?

"Suppose I had told you at the beginning, in that pasture with the sheep, that I was the heir to a grand estate? Would we be having tea now, riding bicycles, and roaming Sawrey together? You weren't looking for an heir, and I wasn't wanting someone who saw only that. That part of my life is inevitable, yet for a moment I wanted a simple existence in order to be the best estate owner I can be."

She laughed and shrugged. "If I had known my rescuer was the heir to a great estate, I would have remained hidden for the rest of my stay."

Not Arabella. She might have hidden from him but not from everyone else.

"Well, then. I'm sorry I wasn't honest with you, but I'm not sorry about the time we've spent together. Perhaps someday you will forgive me."

They finished their tea in silence. She gazed out the window, while he studied her profile. Beautiful, even in her distress.

God, please intervene. I never meant to hurt her.

Her cup clinked against the saucer. "I'm more upset about the deceit than about your position in society. I will see myself home." A forced smile marred her face, while her fisted hands rested on the table.

He'd not give up easily. "I'm not like the others. Can't you see that? I should have known my family name and estate would cancel my efforts."

Arabella tilted her head, reached her hand toward him, then pulled it back. "We'll never know. You didn't give me a chance."

He stood as she turned her back to him. She skirted around the tables, leaving a faint hint of honeysuckle.

Their relationship was not a game. Love was not a trifling plaything. It worked for a month, but no longer. He'd broken the rules and would pay the price with a broken heart.

What am I doing? Love and a broken heart? I'm not that far into a relationship, am I? When did that happen?

He stayed at the table with a fresh cup of tea. Perhaps the strong brew would knock some sense into the situation. But it was only a temporary reprieve. His feelings could have changed at several points. Maybe in the field on their first encounter as she plowed through the field straight into his arms. Or when she picked wildflowers by the churchyard, when she showed her love of animals and willingness to get her hands dirty in the sheep shed or the garden. She trusted him with the bicycle lesson. And he failed her as he protected his secret.

All right, Lord. I turn this over to You. Heal Arabella's heart. And if it is Your plan, help us reconcile, even if only in friendship.

CHAPTER SIX

*A*ugust found Arabella berating her naïve trust in a certain country gentleman. What a poor choice she'd made. How had she let it happen? She should have known proximity to London had no hold on what men would do to trick a woman.

Stomping through her grandmother's garden jarred her senses. The birds didn't sound as chipper nor did the flowers smell as sweet. If only she was a better judge of people's character. She wasn't overly endowed with the gift of discernment. Thomas had held her hope in his hand. Perhaps he even had her heart. Well, not anymore. Her love life was hers again. How long would it take to give it away the next time?

A long time.

She had to forgive herself for falling for the first local she'd met after fleeing from the courting scene in London.

She had to forgive her grandmother who only failed to associate Thomas with a last name. Lilly knew and bent to the whim of a peer. She had shared with Arabella that she never felt comfortable with the ruse. Beatrix had gone along, hoping Thomas would confess sooner than later.

No one meant to hurt her.

Oh, but it hurt. Two weeks later, and my heart longs for him. For what could have been.

Arabella cancelled the outing to the Sheep Fair. Although she could have gone with Beatrix, she knew Thomas would be close. She refused to join in an exciting event in his presence. How had things turned so upside down? Why was she letting it create havoc with her time here? It was not as if there had been an understanding between them. But perhaps she wished it had turned into that.

The back door squeaked open. "Arabella, are you ready for church?"

"Yes, Nana. One moment." Arabella retraced her steps, making her gait light and graceful. Dragging her feet would never do.

Nana stood straight, no longer in a cast, with a cane in her hand for balance. Arabella knew being anxious about attending church was not an appropriate attitude. This week should be easier with her grandmother by her side. Last week, seeing Thomas from a distance had caused no disaster, so maybe this week would be easier.

Calmer now, she could almost smile as she watched the Rowe family enter and take their normal pew. She'd promised her grandmother that she'd entertain an introduction. Afterall, it wasn't the family who had deceived Arabella.

Thomas stood taller than his brothers and parents. The whole family had a polished, sophisticated appeal, though not showy as in a competition with the rest of the congregation. She closed her eyes for a second. Why did it matter now? Before, she hardly cared who wore what. Now, she scrutinized one family, wanting to find fault. Thomas wore a black jacket with gray trousers, toting a black top hat. Many others in the congregation wore the same. His might be a better cloth and cut but no more than a slight difference.

His mother wore a dress of a satin blend with few embell-ishments. Her equal in the old Saxon church was her grand-mother. There really was no hint of the parading of fashion as in London.

Why didn't Arabella put Beatrix in the same category as her grandmother and the Rowes? Why put any of these congregants in a category? Beatrix embraced the title of a country farmer mistress in garb, speech, and actions. She thrived in her uniqueness and identity. Arabella couldn't even do that. Not in London nor in Sawrey.

I thought I could find worth here. Have I given it enough time?

A jab to her ribs changed her focus to her grandmother. "Listen to the sermon, dear. Let God's word settle your heart."

Arabella patted Nana's hand. "You're right, Nana."

Within seconds, the minister faced the congregation and made eye contact with multiple people. How did he do that? Looking straight at her and everyone else at the same time.

"Today, I'll be broaching the subject of united in one body of one spirit. Do you ever feel as if society is segregated into different groups? It is not a phenomenon unique to our day. In his letter to the Ephesians, Paul writes in chapter two. 'But now in Christ Jesus ye who sometimes were far off are made nigh by the blood of Christ. For he is our peace, who hath made both one, and hath broken down the middle wall of partition between us.'"

Arabella's attention wrapped around those words. *Peace. Made one.* She'd heard these verses before, but now they made sense as she contemplated the lines drawn in class and soci-ety. She didn't have to live that way. Her marital options could be a duke, a gentleman farmer, or a pauper. Why did she have to let London decide who her friends would be? Why not a vicar's daughter or a farmer's wife?

Have I been too closed minded about Thomas? He hails from the group I'm trying to avoid, but look at his heart. Don't we all share the same spirit?

As she exited the church, Arabella walked beside her grandmother. Outside, the Rowes stood before them on the pathway. Thomas nodded to Arabella, causing heat to creep up her neck. She smiled at his gentle, questioning eyes. If she were to practice being in one spirit, she should forgive him.

I want to forgive him. Now how to do it and have it remain in place.

Her grandmother put her arm around Arabella and pulled her closer. "This is my granddaughter, Arabella. Mr. and Mrs. Rowe have an estate outside of town."

Arabella gave a slight curtsy. "Yes. I have heard my grandmother speak of you. It's nice to finally meet you." Knowing that Thomas had prevented their meeting earlier left a twinge of remorse on the edge of her forgiveness.

Mrs. Rowe nodded. "These are our sons, Edmund, Steward, and Thomas. I believe you already know Thomas, though."

What had he said about her?

He cleared his throat. "We have spent many pleasant hours together."

Arabella ducked her head. That could be interpreted in many different ways. She'd not explain for fear of stuttering through the explanation.

Mrs. Rowe's stare volleyed between them before landing on Nana. "Cora, I am so glad you accepted our invitation to the Harvest Ball. Miss Graham, I do hope you will attend."

"I plan to. I believe I return to London the next day."

The dark-haired woman reached for Arabella's hand and held it. "I hope your time here has been pleasant, and that you'll come again soon."

Somehow, Arabella managed to maintain eye contact with

Mrs. Rowe, though she longed to see Thomas's reaction to her words. "I love this part of the country. I will be back soon."

Nana leaned forward. "I hope she'll spend Christmas with me."

Christmas? That's a new request.

Before departing, Thomas leaned closer and whispered, "I hope this means you're on the verge of forgiving me."

She squeezed her gloved hands together in front of her. "Perhaps, Mr. Rowe. We'll see."

How could part of her say she forgave him while the other still held on to the past?

ARABELLA RELEGATED thoughts of Thomas to the corner of her mind. She would not let him spoil the adventures she could enjoy in the last few weeks of summer.

On this beautiful, clear August morning, a rose-perfumed breeze greeted her at Hill Top's gate. She carried her flower basket and a small hamper of sweets from the bakery. Arabella had assured Beatrix that the red squirrel hunt could wait for another time. But her friend convinced her that "a promise is a promise." She wouldn't let Arabella leave without seeing where Squirrel Nutkin lived.

Beatrix always blended in with the greens and browns of the garden, permitting the flowers to showcase their natural colors.

Today, Arabella wore yellow and picked a pink poppy for her hair. Not camouflaged at all.

"Beatrix, are you ready?" Arabella looked in all directions, knowing her friend could be anywhere on the farm.

"Here I am." Beatrix stepped through the green gate and latched it closed. "Let me get our sandwiches and my sketch pad."

Soon they headed away from the village along a path through the sheep and cattle pasture. Arabella was no longer skittish around the larger animals, although seeing them would forever remind her of Thomas's gallant rescue.

Thinking about the natural world had opened a whole new realm for Arabella. Any excursion out of doors added baby steps in her education. "Do you really think we'll see Squirrel Nutkin and his family?" On this occasion, the line between fiction and reality seemed to blur in her mind.

Beatrix shrugged and grinned, leading the way down the hill to the edge of a stream. "Well, I studied him here for quite a while before he made it into his book. They really do have individual personalities. If he's not here, he is off on one of his wild adventures."

Matching her stride with Beatrix's, Arabella felt as eager as a child to see something new. Beatrix halted and placed her arm out to prevent Arabella's forward pace. "Shhh. Do you see that big old oak tree? Look closely, between the branches and in the knots on the trunk."

At first, all Arabella saw was the tree's brown bark and green leaves. Then two brown heads peered out of the hole—one on top of the other. In the branches, a few squirrels ran toward a nest high above. The squirrels spotted Arabella and Beatrix and began chattering as they fixed their dark beady eyes on them.

"They're the red squirrels that became the characters in my books. Their dens are the nests you see among the branches, and some found homes in hollow knots."

Mesmerized by the squirrels' nearness, Arabella sat in the cushiony grass, crossed her legs under her skirt, and settled for a spell. One squirrel stood out, and she imagined him to be naughty Squirrel Nutkin. He raced one way, while the rest chose a different path, chattering their disappointment at Nutkin.

They're a lot like my parents. I can imagine them reacting in a similar way when they discuss me. Why can't I just follow the rules, marry a wealthy London lord, and be done with it? Because I can't. I want love and wide-open fields. I want this life, but with a husband and family to love.

As the squirrels played near the babbling creek, Arabella and Beatrix turned their laps into plates. Her friend's ham and cheese rolls paired nicely with Arabella's apples and cream-filled pastries. Tin cups with fresh brook water washed everything down with an extra jolt of summer freshness.

Arabella picked a stem of grass and rubbed it between her fingers. "May I ask you something?"

Leaning against a small tree, Beatrix relaxed in the sun's warmth. "Of course." She opened one eye and smiled at Arabella.

"Do you like living alone at Hill Top? I guess what I'm wanting to know is, are you fulfilled in your role here?" Arabella didn't want to pry, but she wanted to understand if life could be worthwhile outside of London society, and without a husband.

Beatrix turned toward Arabella. "Let me tell you a story that might answer both questions. I had resigned myself to being a spinster, a dedicated daughter, and living with my parents for the rest of my life. But I yearned for independence and my own livelihood.

"A few years ago, my books and illustrations provided that to a certain degree. At my age I never expected to fall in love, but I hadn't counted on Norman Warne sweeping in and capturing my heart."

Beatrix focused far across the hills. "Our engagement was not lovingly accepted by our families. Perhaps they would have come around in time. But after two months of planning and drawing closer, he died."

She stopped for a moment and looked down. "I didn't

know how to go on. How could I go back to how things were before I fell in love? I had long discussions with my parents about what to do. Since I've always loved the Lake District, I found this place and have made it my own. I fulfill my familial duties part of the time while still enjoying a certain amount of freedom here at Hill Top."

Beatrix sighed and met her gaze once more. "So yes, I'm content with a purpose and people to love. How can I be lonely with all my creatures and my imagination?"

Arabella dipped her head and let tears trickle into her lap. This story belonged to Beatrix, yet Arabella's own path was similar. Would she ever love and suffer a loss like her friend? When she turned twenty-five, she'd have enough money from her trust fund to live in a cottage somewhere. But as for a mission or purpose, that proved elusive. Why didn't God spell it out for her?

Beatrix secured Arabella's hand in hers. "My dear girl, have you thought about sharing your feelings with your parents? Perhaps they differ from mine, although it sounds as though they think a wealthy London gentleman is the answer. Marriage of that kind is not for everyone. Also, I believe marriage in general is not for every woman."

Arabella nodded then shook her head. "Oh, I do want to get married but not to someone of my parents' choosing." She raised her sight to the squirrel family, chasing after each other's tails in the trees. "For a moment, I pictured myself here with . . . well, here with my grandmother." *And perhaps Thomas?*

"Hmph." Did Beatrix wink at her? "I believe you meant to say Thomas. I'm not blind. You've shared you don't know how to forgive him. Can't you find a way?"

By now, he had probably set her aside as a silly debutante. "Why did he put up a farce? He knew my background."

Beatrix shrugged. "Ah, perhaps that is why. Thomas has

had his share of eligible young ladies from titled, wealthy, and even impoverished families knocking at his door." Putting her finger to her chin, Beatrix blinked in the sunlight. "He enjoyed the idea of your liking him for his modest dwelling, common attire, and humble ambition. He wasn't the heir to the vast estate. He was just Thomas."

Arabella lowered her voice to a whisper. "And Thomas was enough for me. I don't want an heir or a vast estate." As far as she knew, life in a cottage would be fine. Her role would be to care for her own small kingdom in a humble abode with an honest and simple living instead of the constant state of competition and pretense.

Leaning forward, Beatrix furrowed her brow. "Let me understand. You don't want the role of lady of the manor because of your experience in London society? What if God has created you to be a mistress in the country as a helpmate to a wealthy gentleman? Could that be your purpose?"

Could it? Arabella lifted her head and straightened her shoulders. The sermon's inspiration collided with Beatrix's story and wisdom, forming a coherency Arabella had missed. It all started to make sense. Had she looked at this all wrong, putting all prestigious men, women, and families in one big category? Why did all of them have to be the same? In a way, she was doing exactly what her parents did. She had to stop labeling everyone and judging with an imperfect standard.

She raised her eyes toward the perfect heavens. *Thank you, Lord!*

Springing to her feet, Arabella grabbed Beatrix's hands and pulled her into a circle dance. "You are a genius, Beatrix. You and the reverend had to knock some sense into me. I don't have to spurn my upbringing, my parents, or society. There are good seeds at all levels—you, my grandmother, my sister, and…and Thomas. I don't have to be the exact copy of anyone else. Thank you!"

When Arabella stopped twirling, Beatrix placed her hand over her heart. "Well, I think you have figured out some things. Now, I'd advise you to talk to God about *His* plans."

So true. I'll try not to mess up everything again. I'll follow Your will, God, and pay attention to all the lessons. You lead, I'll follow whether here or in London with or without Thomas.

Her steps guided her toward Hill Top, stopping occasionally to pick wildflowers. She'd make a bouquet to remember today. A turning point. She had no notion of what to expect. Only that she would concentrate on implementing God's will as her foundation.

CHAPTER SEVEN

*T*he end of summer loomed as a pivoting point. The green hills with their patchwork of multi-colored wildflowers suggested evidence of days of sweet perfume and lazy afternoons. Arabella had only a few more days to enjoy fresh clover fields and grazing sheep.

Only three days remained until the harvest ball at the Rowe estate. After that, her parents would whisk Arabella back to London into a cloudy world with tiny glimpses of greenery in the miniscule gardens.

I will miss the earthy aroma of tilled earth with the promise of fall crops waving in the breeze. It will be months before I hear a sheep or a cow. They will carry on their morning conversations oblivious to my absence. Will anyone notice when I leave?

Arabella's afternoon was free. Grabbing her notebook and pencil, she put them in a small bag with an apple and a black-berry tart. Knowing her way around the fields now, she headed to a favorite spot.

The old oak standing tall and alone in Beatrix's field opened its branches to her, offering shade and a sturdy post for her back. The view across the hills had not changed in two months. But her heart had, making her inevitable departure a gloomy prospect in contrast to the sun rays dancing through the wavy pastures. When had country life collected all the sunlight, leaving any other life dull?

She took out her notebook, scanned the area, and wrote what drew her here. Peace, the vastness, green hills, squirrel chatter, sheep, cattle, and steeples. Pulling in a deep breath tickled her nose. The mixture of the perfume of fresh grass and flowers overpowered the earthy scent of sheep and cattle.

Her palm skimmed over the blades of grass, and she appreciated the cushion of greenery beneath her.

Father in heaven, how can I return home if I leave my heart behind? My memories and my desire to return one day will suffice. That has to be enough.

Closing her eyes, Arabella leaned against the tree trunk again. A few effortless breaths calmed her all the way to her toes.

God has me, and He has a plan.

Whistling interrupted the nattering of the birds and squirrels. Arabella peeked from under her hat and smiled. Thomas sauntered toward her with his hands in his pockets, producing a good rendition of "A Bird in a Gilded Cage." She tried to whistle along but broke into laughter, adding applause at his attempt.

"Such talent, Thomas. Even the birds stopped to listen."

He bowed as if a maestro on the stage. "I aim to please. Am I interrupting?"

"Hardly. You're welcome in Beatrix's field any time." She brushed her skirt, releasing debris and wrinkles. "I won't bother asking who told you of my whereabouts. Nana and Lilly would be the first to share."

Thomas sat cross-legged in front of her. "Not today. I saw you from the road. A green canvas with a bright yellow center gave you away."

Was she glad to see him? She'd forgiven him for deceiving her, but she didn't seem able to step back into their former easy friendship. A friendship she had imagined leading to something more, perhaps even love. She wasn't certain, but she might be inching closer.

Thomas twisted a blade of grass between his fingers as he stared at his hands. After a minute, he set it aside and wiped his hands on his pants. Finally, his blue eyes sought hers. "Have you forgiven me, Arabella? I'm truly sorry for my lack of courage at the beginning."

Courage? What was so courageous about admitting one's true identity? Had he been that concerned about her taking advantage of his social position? Or perhaps, like her, he wanted to discard the façade of being prim, proper, and perfect.

"Oh, Thomas, I forgive you. I'm just confused about what to do next." Was there a next move? On whose part?

He reached into his jacket pocket and handed her an item wrapped in brown paper. "I'm not giving this to you because you forgave me. It was yours the moment I saw it at the market in Hawkshead."

Her fingers trembled as his hand touched hers. Hawkshead—the sheep fair she had avoided in her angst. The package fit in her palm, weighing a few ounces. "What is it?" She flitted her gaze to his handsome face with an elfish grin. She offered a quick silent prayer, forgiving him in her heart as well as in word.

"Open it." He clasped his hands in his lap. Was he as excited as she? Wasn't that the way with gifts?

With her finger, she loosened the paper and discovered a small porcelain figurine. She stared at a four-inch squirrel with a bushy tail holding a green apple. "It's Squirrel Nutkin! You remembered." She ran her fingers over the top of the squirrel's head.

Thomas shrugged and grinned. "A local shop carries some of Beatrix's books and gifts."

She gently laid the gift on her lap, wishing her free hand could touch Thomas's cheek in thanks. It was sweet of him to think of her. Touching his sleeve and squeezing his arm, she melted into his smile. "Thank you. I'll treasure it."

Before she let her teary state descend into a watery mess, Arabella shook her head and resolved to be cautious of their relationship. She had to be careful and not assume the gift meant more than Thomas intended.

Friendship and a summer diversion? That wouldn't be so bad. A friendship that survived a deception wouldn't be hard to imagine. She might be able to save heartache by delegating Thomas to the role of friend.

She shared her pastry as they chatted about the upcoming ball and her imminent departure. Dwelling on that made her anxious. Besides leaving these pleasant hills, she'd step back into the existence she'd escaped. What was the point of talking of freedom and this paradise, when her normal life awaited her?

Beatrix spoke of both her lives. Yet the lady always knew she'd return to Hill Top. Arabella didn't have that promise. This sojourn stood as a onetime venture. There was no buying a house and living alone.

She gathered her items, wrapping the Squirrel Nutkin figurine in a cloth from her basket. It had already secured a place in her heart, and she wanted it safe for the journey. Well, if she were honest, the place in her heart was for Thomas, not just his gift.

At the stile leading to Beatrix's backyard, Thomas helped her over. "Would you allow me to walk you home?"

She debated spending more time with him, but her new determination to treat him as a friend still landed very close to wanting it to be more. She shook her head. "No, thank you,

Thomas. I have some things to do. And for some reason, I cannot think very clearly with you around." She dipped her chin in embarrassment. Flirting was not the way to rid her of his attention. "Thank you again for Nutkin."

He tipped his hat and paused with his foot on the stile, his arm on his knee. "I'll see you at the ball in a few days."

"Yes. We'll be there."

It would be her goodbye to Thomas and the dear people of Sawrey. Why would God lead her here, only to deposit her back in the darkness?

Why? Because I've changed and perhaps what was dark and dismal before will shine with His purpose now. I can pray that is the case.

THE EVENING OF THE BALL, Thomas stood in front of the foyer mirror, struggling to fix his cravat. His mother's reflection stepped into view, and his eyes met hers.

"You have gone above the usual, Mother, with all the preparations. Did we really need all the indoor flowers and plants? And the new China? What was wrong with the old settings?" He let his cravat hang as the contraption refused to adjust like he wanted.

She shrugged, removed her gloves and, with easy expertise, tied the cravat just right. "If only your brothers would stay in proper attire all evening. I've persuaded your father to remain in place instead of showing the neighbors the new equipment in the barns."

Thomas chuckled. She had avoided her answer for the additional table settings. She could control the decorations but not her young sons and husband. "Good luck with that one. You know Father enjoys sharing estate improvements with the county."

That was one reason his father allowed Thomas his own farm—to have an arena to experiment with crops and animals. So far, Thomas's advice and trials had led to an increase in products and profits.

His mother patted the front of his jacket. "You look especially handsome tonight. It wouldn't be for a visiting Londoner, would it?"

He wouldn't be pulled into her prying right now. "Mother, dear, don't play matchmaker tonight. You've invited a parish full of ladies, and I will not be proposing to any of them."

She pouted before relinquishing him. "I guess I'll have to depend on your younger brothers to marry."

Thomas smiled at the thought of Edmund or Steward as husbands or fathers. Would he find someone to partner in his life? He thought, perhaps, he had. But now, doubts shadowed his optimism. Tomorrow, she would be on the train back to her old life—a life he'd have a hard time sharing, even if she wanted him there. But she seemed determined to return to her world and do her parents' bidding.

Before the guests arrived, Thomas stepped out the front door and onto the gravel. Gas lanterns marked the drive, bringing a warm glow to the stately yellow-stone residence. Rowe Hall was not a royal residence but elegant and spacious enough to impress the upper echelon. His parents kept it in good repair for a one hundred and fifty-year-old building. Somewhere in the last hundred years, his ancestors had turned the property into a working estate. He would continue in that vein in order to keep the house and acreage intact.

Would he do it alone? Without heirs?

He sighed. His brothers would not disappoint his mother or their deceased ancestors.

Checking on the stables, Thomas found everything in order for the additional carriages and horses. Locals would walk or be delivered. Others from neighboring counties would find ample space and accommodations. Some of his parents' guests would spend a few days in their house.

Thomas glanced at the distant hill where his house waited for him. One evening of guests would prove sufficient for him. He looked forward to the comfort of his quiet abode.

At the eighth hour, the drive and house exploded with light from candles, gas, and electric fixtures. Thomas stood as a sentinel next to his mother and father with his brothers in starched attire. For one evening, the Rowes polished their country ways for the spectacle.

Townspeople, merchants, farmhands, magistrates, parliament members, and debutantes filed by Thomas. The one he sought failed to be one of the first guests. Had he disappointed her so much she'd fail to come? Surely, her grandmother would stress the importance of the Harvest Ball—a Sawrey tradition.

Through the open double doors, Thomas spied a vision in royal blue. *Arabella*. Chestnut curls cascaded over her shoulders, with strings of tiny pearls tucked in the tresses of her high coiffure. She gazed at him with shining eyes reflecting the light around her. He held his breath, afraid she might disappear.

His lack of attention to the guests in front of him earned his mother's elbow to his ribs. Managing the pleasantries, he watched as Arabella and her grandmother entered the foyer.

His father greeted Cora Graham as the old friend that she was. Arabella dipped and offered her hand to him like a true lady.

When it was his turn, Thomas kissed her gloved fingers and studied her openly. *Beautiful*. He had hoped to find her on the dance floor or in an alcove, not a reception line.

He calmed his voice. "Miss Arabella, I'm so glad you're

here. I hope you'll allow me to show you around and will save a few dances for me."

"Why, Thomas, of course. You are, after all, the only gentleman I know here."

Was that the only reason she'd spend time with him? It wouldn't take the others long to gravitate toward her beauty and uniqueness.

ARABELLA STOOD with her grandmother in the elegant ballroom. She hoped this evening would be a happy farewell. A bookend for her adventure, a diversion from her normal routine. Her grandmother knew Arabella did not want to step back into the parlors and ballrooms of London. Beatrix also understood Arabella's reluctance to depart.

But what did Thomas think about her leaving? Was it too late for either of them to change the future? No one could halt her departure. They had made the decision by not taking their relationship to another level. A friend would not demand she stay. Would a fiancé? Since that was not in the cards, why waste any time thinking of Thomas as a potential marriage partner?

Still, she longed to stay with her grandmother and had considered refusing to get on the train or hiding in Beatrix's barn. Yet, she had a life to lead, and God would guide her. For now, that life was taking her back to London.

But in this moment, at this ball, all she could think about was Thomas.

"May I have this dance?" Thomas bent closer, his breath tickling her neck. "The music might not be to your standards, but it shows the talent of the local people."

Did she come across as an elitist snob? "Thomas, I have

been very impressed with the cultural climate here. The musicians are inspiring. Let's dance and forget our differences."

The lively steps and twirls allowed her touch to linger on Thomas's arms and hands. Could she bottle this tingle? Would she find it again in another parlor? With another man?

She shivered at the prospect. "I think I'm ready for refreshments."

Thomas's hand rested on her back as he guided her to the elaborate tables laden with scrumptious sugary treats and hardy savory bites.

After choosing a blackberry scone, she accepted a cup of raspberry lemonade from Thomas. "Thank you. As long as there is music and food like this, Sawrey outranks any social event I've been to in London." She knew for sure that the fare was extremely fresh here. From garden to table in a few steps.

He chuckled. "I agree, although it's been a few years since I've participated in a society ball. I much prefer the pace and company here."

"I'm surprised that the mixing of classes works so well."

Thomas chose a strawberry tart from the colorful fruit options. "These people are the backbone of country life. We all work together."

"Hmm. And you include yourself in that mixture?"

He nodded. "Most definitely. I'm out in the fields with the crops, the harvest, and the livestock. If my farm succeeds, so do all the workers."

Working together, one in purpose. That's what I'm searching for. I cannot think of one organization in London where all levels of society work together like this.

Perhaps her frustration was with the fragmented community of home. Here she knew the vegetable seller, vicar's daughter, and the heir to an estate. And it worked just fine. No one cared how it looked.

And I cannot forget having a friend who is an independent female author.

"You are correct, Thomas." She lifted her punch cup and touched his. "To finding a project or niche where the purpose is for the good of everyone."

Thomas stared at her with a half-smile. He opened his mouth and closed it before any words escaped. Why wouldn't he speak?

She clucked her tongue and waved her hand in front of him. "Thomas?"

He shuddered free of his daze. "Hear, hear." He nodded. "To purpose."

She had no idea what her future held. No wonder he might be skeptical about adding few words to her toast. If she didn't understand what awaited her in London, why would Thomas?

He discarded their empty dishes on the table and touched her elbow, guiding her to a bench facing the dance floor.

While adjusting her satin skirt, Arabella wondered at his seriousness. Had she said something to trigger his melancholy?

As she waited for him to speak, she studied the ballroom —his world and childhood home. It was hard to take it all in with one sweep—the high ceilings with ornate chandeliers, the polished wood floors and paneling, marble-topped tables, elaborate staircase in the foyer, and family portraits throughout the rooms. Everything glistened as a place for him to cherish.

She bit her bottom lip when she realized she'd leave tomorrow without seeing his farmhouse and the choices he purposely made to help him embrace his future as heir.

For a moment, she forgot his nearness until he reached for her hand and clasped it in his. "Arabella, how I wish you didn't have to leave. There is so much I've yet to share with you. When will you return?"

She hesitated. "Perhaps at Christmastime. Nana has invited me, but that doesn't mean my parents will allow it. My presence will be needed at our annual Christmas party."

He squeezed her hand then released it. "I see."

Did he? How could he understand the grip her parents had over her? She was not at leisure to come and go as she pleased. The strings might stretch a little, but they were still very much attached.

He sighed, crinkling his brow. Did he know his eyes played against her determination to walk away unscathed? His lips missed the mark of a smile. "I want you to stay. Yet you have convinced me that you must return to London. A few more dances, and then you'll disappear."

"Thomas, it has always been this way." Was she in the wrong? She never made a promise. "A summer. A vacation. I cannot stay." What if they had two or three more months?

"If you could stay, if we just had a little more time, things might be different for us."

But I have no more time. Not even one day.

Thomas belonged to her dream world. The place without rigid standards and obligations. A realm where she could find a home in the country to share with a husband and family. A vision that now had familiar faces. A loving, handsome one in particular.

He held out his hand. "Let's dance and save the goodbyes for the midnight hour. Perhaps it is only for a season."

CHAPTER EIGHT

OCTOBER 1906 LONDON

*A*s Arabella had done once or twice a week following her arrival in London, she combed the small green garden squares searching for woodland creatures. If only she could find a rabbit, a mole, or a hedgehog—something to bring her closer to the Lake District.

After doing some shopping, Arabella asked the driver to leave her at Hyde Park for half an hour. She'd walk through and meet him on the other side. The small lake was nothing like Esthwaite Water or Lake Windermere, but she could admire the waddling ducks and the chattering, playful squirrels in the trees.

Sounds of the city—carriages, trams, street vendors, people—meshed as a mixture of unharmonious noises. Why hadn't it bothered her before? Where could she capture the peace of Sawrey—the birds, insects, sheep, dogs, and cows? She couldn't, not miles from the Lake District.

Returning home with her packages, Arabella set them in the foyer by the staircase. Her mother had sent her on a mission to pick up shoes and a hat for a Sunday afternoon gala. Another box contained Arabella's new gown for a banquet in a few weeks.

Quick to fall back into a routine, Arabella relegated her summer experience to a place of fond memories, like one of Beatrix Potter's fairytales, making her question if it had really happened.

"Arabella, is that you?" Her mother called from the drawing room.

"Yes. I'll be right there." Discarding her hat and gloves, Arabella brushed her hand down her skirt, hoping the grime of London wasn't evident on her hem or shoes. She never cared about the bits and pieces of the green hills she'd carried around after her country hikes. Yet, her mother had not been there to scold her.

She found her mother ensconced in a high-backed cushioned chair with a letter opened on her lap.

"I received a letter from your Grandmother Graham." Her mother handed Arabella an envelope from the table next to her chair. "And here is one for you."

Hopefully, it contained good news. Perhaps Nana had shared the same with her mother. "She is well, I pray. I left her in excellent health."

Tapping her letter with her fingers, her mother chuckled. "She always bounces back. I hope you have that Graham constitution."

Arabella flicked her finger under the seal and drew out the letter. She paced as she read, drawing near to the large paned window.

Dearest Arabella,

I hope you have adjusted to your life in London again. At least the pace is slower in the off season. I'm sure many will soon be preparing for the Christmas festivities.

That is the main reason for this letter. The other is to share how much I miss you. If I read the signs correctly, I think you found your place here in Sawrey. I wrote to your mother regarding Christmas. This year I want to have a grand celebration here at Graham Retreat instead of coming to London. I asked your mother if you could join me in the planning and implementation of the details.

Would you consider coming in mid-November? The party will be held in mid-December, giving families an opportunity to travel after for Christmas if they have plans.

Arabella looked at her mother, hoping and praying for an affirmative answer. "Mother, what did your letter say?"

Her mother straightened, elegant hands resting in her lap. Arabella couldn't read her mother's suppressed emotions.

Setting her letter on the table, her mother rose from her chair. "I assume your letter contains the same request from your grandmother. I've an inkling to refuse, but I don't know if I could live with the hurt feelings."

Cupping Arabella's cheek in her palm, her mother smiled, releasing her stern mask of propriety. "You are a lot like her. Your father couldn't wait to get away, and all you want to do is return. It will make her happy and you too."

Arabella gave her mother's neck a big hug. "Thank you. I promise to be a huge help to Nana."

"Hmm. I've been watching you. I think you left a piece of your heart in Sawrey. If it means that much to you, I'm sure your father will approve too. We can all be back here in time for Christmas."

A smidgen of remorse threatened to dampen her joy. Why did she think her parents would miss Christmas in London? But Christmas in Sawrey with Nana would be beautiful. She knew why. Her parents' friends and business associates expected them at all the events. They lived for the hustle of the Christmas season.

Yet, Arabella yearned for a fresh experience like Christmas in the Lake District with her friends and family, sitting in her pew in the small church.

Forgive me, God, for being greedy. Thank you for the month I will have there. Oh, and please let it snow. I want to see the rolling hills covered in white clouds of pure magic.

"I'll write Nana, and we can start planning."

Her mother sat at her escritoire and folded the letter, setting it aside, probably for Arabella's father to read. "You must have your father's approval before you commit."

That wouldn't be a problem. She'd butter him up with familial love for his own mother. He couldn't tell both of them no, could he?

~

November 1906

Sawrey

ARABELLA STOOD at the gate of Graham Retreat gazing at the road in front of her. Her fingers caressed the wrought-iron frame as if it would disappear from her memory if she let go. Her awe wasn't for the mansion behind her, but more for the villagers, horses and carriages, and children with their dogs on leads.

I'm home. How can that be? I only just left all my familiar possessions, books, and parents in London. Yet, this place feels like home. It's more than a place. It's, Oh, I don't know. It's part of me.

It was a Friday afternoon, her first day back in Sawrey. Nana had regained all her health and then some. She could probably beat Arabella in a foot race.

After greeting Arabella earlier at the train station, Nana had regaled her granddaughter on the status of the house as they rode in the carriage. The woman had commandeered help for her Christmas ball like a general in the army. Every room would be overhauled, not allowing one single spider to keep house in the corner of any room. All scraps and scars on floors and walls would receive expert care.

"I've been meaning to do this for years. A few renovations will bring the house up to date."

Arabella linked her arm with her grandmother's and pulled her closer. "It sounds like you've left nothing for me to do."

Nana's gray eyes squinted before laughter lines joined her exuberance. "No, my dear. All the makeovers had to be complete before the decorating begins. You are my partner in that scheme as well as being a hostess. I will keep you busy, but not so busy you can't enjoy your friends."

Arabella was taking her grandmother's advice as she headed toward Lilly's to catch up on the comings and goings of the villagers the past few months. Although still familiar, she noticed the altered scenery—bare trees, few flowering shrubs, and a crisp, windy chill on her cheeks. Winter in the Lake District promised snow.

Since Nana always came to London for Christmas, Arabella had never spent the season here. Would she love it as much as the summer of green hills?

Beatrix said fall was her favorite season in the area. Had she returned? Arabella had forgotten to ask Nana.

Arabella studied the people going about their day. A part of her hoped to run into Thomas. No, it felt more like her whole being desired to see him. How many letters had she started to him? All ended in the trash. Whatever they could have had ended before it really started. That was a shame. Her parents might have approved of him.

Arabella knocked on Lilly's door, and her friend greeted her with a hug and a kiss on the cheek.

"You really are back. Lady Graham told me you were coming, but I imagined London stealing you away for good."

"Sweet Lilly. The pull is to Sawrey, not London."

Hands on hips, Lilly dropped her jaw and feigned unbelief. "This is what you want?"

Arabella twirled around. "Yes, all of it." And if Thomas could be her—her what?—her love interest, then there would be no place comparable.

That's a big if. Will I see him in the village? Will he be at the party, which is still a month away?

If she were daring, she would show up at his farmhouse. But she wasn't daring today. She might be out of her element in London, but her manners and upbringing held firm. If Thomas wanted a relationship, he'd have to step forward. Nothing clandestine would come from her. Unless...no, she couldn't involve Beatrix or Lilly, could she?

Lilly told her housekeeper goodbye and stepped onto the village road with Arabella. "I have so much to share, things I couldn't tell you in a letter."

Arabella nudged her friend's arm with her elbow. "Why not? I could have used some village tattle."

"It wouldn't have been gossip," Lilly whispered as if she had a secret to keep from the birds and the trees. "A young gentleman has asked to court me, and father said yes."

Arabella halted and faced Lilly. "Oh, I'm so excited for you! Do I know him?" It only took half a second for her imagination to picture two couples enjoying an evening walk through the village. Only one problem. Thomas didn't know of his participation in her dream.

"His name is Samuel Martin. He's from the next town of Far Sawrey. I met him at a parish social. His family owns a dairy." Her friend swung her basket from side to side. "Oh, Arabella, he's clever and attentive, and ever so handsome and interesting. He wants to have a bookshop in town. I think you'll like him."

The cool breeze nipped at her cheeks as Arabella watched

Lilly's face blush from the mere mention of Samuel. "If you like him, then I will too."

Giddy chatter swirled around them as they walked through Sawrey, depositing them at Hill Top. Arabella glanced past the gate. Was Beatrix back? She wished for the camaraderie they'd shared in the blossoming summer days. Beatrix, her animals, gardens, and . . .

Arabella's hand halted Lilly. "Do you hear that? Has Beatrix returned?"

Lilly shook her head as they entered the front garden and stalked toward the whistling beyond the house.

Her friend's voice quivered. "Aren't you afraid, Arabella? Let's not walk up on someone on our own. What if . . ."

"Don't be silly. The person is whistling." Arabella let the tune filter through her memory. "It's 'Bicycle Built for Two.' You know, 'Daisy, Daisy, give me your answer, do!'"

They approached the green gate and continued to the barn. Lilly fell a few steps behind Arabella as the whistling volume increased, and a cow mooed.

Arabella stopped, causing Lilly to run into her and yelp.

A man popped up from behind an enormous cow. "Arabella? Well, well. I didn't expect to see you here. And Lilly too."

With her hand over her heart, Arabella released the air caught in her lungs. Perhaps she *had* been afraid. "Oh, Thomas. I'm so glad it's you. I don't know what I would have done if a stranger was trying to steal Beatrix's cow."

He leaned his arms on the cow's back and grinned. That same smile had dominated her dreams in London.

Oh, how I've missed him.

"Let me finish with Gertie, and I'll meet you at the bench behind the house."

Exiting through the winterized vegetable garden, Arabella willed her heart to steady.

Lilly chuckled and planted herself in front of Arabella. "Do you know what I see?" Her friend's eyebrows rose. "I think you and Thomas have some talking to do. You are as skittish and smitten as any couple I've seen."

"But we're not. We're friends. Nothing else."

"Perhaps. I'll step into the front garden and wait for you there."

"You sound like an old matron, Lilly." Arabella sat on the bench and crossed her arms. Smitten? On her part, that was true. Possibly more like in love. Or in love with the idea of love. No, it was more than that.

Arabella could not just sit and wait. Beatrix's gardens always had something to explore.

QUESTIONS FILLED Thomas's mind as he finished tending Gertie. *When had Arabella returned?* He knew about the Christmas party planned at Graham's Retreat, but he had not been sure she would commit. How many times had he determined to jump on a train and race to London? Time had slipped away. The harvest and mending of fences and stalls consumed any pining for what might have been.

Who am I fooling? I could have made time to take that trip to London. But without knowing how she would respond, I didn't want to take the risk.

Now that she's here, God has given me another chance to win her heart. I have nothing to hide this time. My deep love won't be a secret for long.

Thomas dusted off his coat and pants then washed his hands in the rain barrel. He opened the green gate, expecting Arabella to be waiting.

He looked around, but he didn't see her.

A familiar tune carried through the apple grove. He

released his breath and replaced his puckered frown with a huge grin.

"Daisy, Daisy, give me your answer, do." His voice joined her notes. He wanted to lift her and swing her around and give her a "I really missed you" kiss. But his dream wasn't necessarily hers.

She twirled her green skirt around her form, welcoming him with luminous eyes and a cheerful lilt in a sing-song cadence. "It seems I enjoyed your tune from earlier."

He pushed his hands into his coat pockets. "It is catching."

She drifted toward him. "Have you ever ridden a bicycle built for two?"

He matched her steps until they halted a few feet apart— arm's length—but his hands were tucked away. "I haven't. Maybe we should try."

Smiling her response, Arabella clapped. "Yes. Wouldn't we start tongues wagging?"

He conjured up other things to fuel the gossip, such as walking through town holding her hand or kissing under the oak tree or . . .

Instead, he bowed his head for a second, gaining strength from what . . . his mud-caked boots? Better focus on her face where he could deduce her true feelings. "I've missed you, Arabella. I'm glad you are back. Will you be here through Christmas? I'd love to take you sledding when it snows or share some hot chocolate or apple cider by a roaring fire."

That last one sounded romantic and out of place for now.

She swayed without breaking his gaze. "That sounds heavenly. A white Christmas. Here. With Nana, Lilly . . . and you. You will come to our Christmas party, won't you? It will be the village event of the season."

"Of course. Your grandmother has talked of nothing else. My whole family plans to attend. Speaking of my family, we want you and your grandmother to dine with us soon. I'll pin down the details now that you're here."

Tilting her head, Arabella's features softened. There was no storm cloud darkening her brow. A miracle for sure. It seemed time had softened her heart toward him. He would do all he could to prove he was worthy.

He picked up his bag he'd left at the back door. "Let me walk you home."

"Thank you. But I have Lilly with me."

He reached for her hand and kissed her gloved fingers. "Until later."

CHAPTER NINE

$\mathcal{T}$he next morning, Arabella moved another box of decorations to the sofa. She laid out some golden balls and found a length of yellow rope. Perhaps she'd make garland.

What was Thomas doing now? Their conversation yesterday stirred new hopes. Did he really want to spend time with her, giving her a special Sawrey Christmas?

There was no time for hot chocolate in front of a fire with Thomas right now. Arabella intended to make herself indispensable to her grandmother. Their decoration preparations for the party had begun in earnest. The calendar said three weeks, but their lists shouted *now*.

Her grandmother rummaged through another box of decorations. "I know I have a spool of wide red ribbon."

"Nana, we have some here." Arabella held up two large rolls of the red satin material.

"Yes, but that is not enough." Nana dove into the abyss once again. "Here it is. Enough for five more large bows."

How many did they need? Oh, the details. No wonder

mother hired someone to decorate their house. But this was much more fun.

"Would you like some music, Nana?" Arabella edged toward the gramophone on a table in a corner. The polished brass horn faced the center of the room. "What will it be? Beethoven's classics or Hayden's repertoire?"

Nana hugged the ribbon to her chest. "There is a new one of the London Symphony."

Fingering the records in their protective sleeves, Arabella found the requested one. After several rotations of the handle, the music filled the spacious drawing room.

Placing a folded cloth on Arabella's arm, Nana pointed to the fireplace. "Why don't you drape that over the mantel and add candlesticks and whatever you find to spruce it up."

Arabella enjoyed working with the colors of Christmas—various shades of red and green, sprinkled with gold and silver. Even if no one else appreciated the decorations, Arabella did. She anticipated many nights curled up in the oversized chair with a book and cider. And . . . *Thomas*.

She paused, bringing a gold cord to her chest. When would Thomas spend an evening with her in front of a fire? Daydreaming was silly. Those were wistful scenarios that might not happen. Better to finish this task and use her mind and hands to complete a few more Christmas gifts.

Marie entered carrying a silver tray with the daily correspondence. Nana took one letter, then Marie walked toward Arabella. "A letter for you, Miss."

"Thank you." Arrabella turned it over and furrowed her brow at the unknown handwriting and stationery.

She opened the envelope and scanned the sheet. "Oh. How surprising! Nana, this is an invitation to dine at Rowe Hall."

Nana put her letter on the table. "Yes, we are expected

next Thursday evening." She winked at Arabella before rummaging in another box.

Hands on hips, Arabella raised her eyebrows at her grandmother. "Did you have anything to do with this?"

Her grandmother's hand fluttered over her heart. "No, not I, my dear. But if you think really hard, you might know who did."

Thomas.

ARABELLA LOOKED out her upstairs window at a blanket of snow covering the countryside. The white world sparkled with pinpricks of sunlight. The only activity she could imagine was a sleigh ride, something she had never done.

Beatrix had returned earlier in the week, making Sawrey more perfect with her friend close at hand. Arabella would love to traipse through her friend's garden and admire the beautiful snowy landscapes. Would the sheep be present or take shelter elsewhere?

As much as she'd love to wander the hills and visit her friend, Arabella had a full day of decorating ahead. Her parents would arrive in a week. All had to be completed so their attention could be on Christmas festivities and time with family.

The hours passed quickly. Arabella had to leave enough time to prepare for the dinner that night. Arabella's mind jumped to scenarios all involving Thomas. Would they have time to speak alone?

Could their relationship mean more? That would explain her errant heartbeat and short attention span.

More greenery on the staircase rail or less? A few more baubles on the door wreath. What had Nana suggested?

Oh, bother. I might as well forgo any more decorating for today.

She grabbed a sugar cookie from the tea tray. "Nana, I'm going to rest before I get dressed for dinner."

Turning her head, Nana held up a bell ready for the Christmas tree. "All right. Thomas will arrive at five o'clock."

Another piece to ponder. Nana had a perfectly splendid carriage and driver. It wasn't as if Thomas or the Rowes had sent a carriage for everyone. This courtesy had Thomas written all over it. And Arabella desired it to mean more than dinner with his parents or a Christmas meal with a neighbor.

She believed a miracle could happen in one evening.

THOMAS BLINKED AGAIN at the exceptional decorations. The old hall with the original dark oak paneling, shone with the luster of hours of polishing. The inspiration from the outdoors graced the front hall with greenery hanging and draping everywhere possible. If he didn't know better, he'd think the massive cedar tree burst from the floorboards with yards of white lace woven in the braids mimicking snow.

Why did this Christmas season shine brighter than others? His immediate answer—*Arabella*. She stood beside the tree observing a crystal bird ornament. The candlelight rays splayed as starlight in her hair.

Thomas shook himself. His task was simple as he remembered the two cups of cranberry juice in his hands. He couldn't lose his senses. He had an entire dinner to manage with small talk and pleasantries before his surprise. A soft smile played on his lips. The intimate gathering with just Lady Graham and Arabella as guests played into his plans.

"Arabella." He slipped close to her side and handed her a crystal cup. "You look beautiful tonight." Adorned in a green gown with gold threads, Arabella sparkled next to the ornate tree. Her smile assured him of a pleasant evening. His impatient imagination moved them beyond these walls and these extra people. If there was any hope for later, he had to pay attention now.

She deserved more than his stares. "What do you think of the snow?"

"I've never seen so much for miles and miles." She leaned toward him and whispered, "I wanted to go for a long walk today and see what the sheep see. But I'm afraid I would have sunk into its depths with no one to rescue me."

He let out a light laugh. "It can be dangerous. My advice is to stick to the roads and have someone with you." *Like me.* "I have a surprise for you after dinner."

Rising on her toes, she looked through her lashes at him. Her grin gave away her enthusiasm. "A surprise? Can you give me a hint?"

"Maybe one. It's white."

She searched up and down and all around the room. "That will never suffice. I guess I'll have to wait."

He'd take her away right now if his parents and her grandmother wouldn't stop him. No, he'd bide his time and be a good example to his brothers. For all anyone knew, Arabella was the granddaughter of a neighbor. Nothing more.

As much as he didn't wish it so, that might be all she remained.

AFTER AN ENTERTAINING MEAL with Thomas's brothers filling in any lulls of conversation with stories of their school escapades, Arabella waited with the Rowes and Nana in the foyer.

Thomas had disappeared with his brothers the second after they consumed the last crumb of their seed cake. She enjoyed the scrumptious dinner of lentil soup, new potatoes in cream, and roast chicken. The hosts had not served a rich, elaborate meal to impress them, making Arabella love this lifestyle more.

Why did everyone stand around her now? Did they know about the surprise? Their quirky smiles and slanted gazes gave away any pretense of innocence.

She refused to engage in twenty questions, so she invented scenarios. Perhaps he planned to give her a potted plant from the greenhouse or a cuddly bunny. More greenery or another wreath?

Steward and Edward stumbled through the front door, righting themselves seconds later.

Edward bowed with his hat in hand. "Miss Arabella, your chariot awaits. Or should I say your sleigh?"

She clasped her gloved hands. "A sleigh ride? I've never been on one before."

Mrs. Rowe handed her a fur mitt and a fur-lined hooded cloak. "You will need these. Thomas has some hot bricks for your feet and blankets."

At the mention of his name, Thomas appeared, red-cheeked and winded. "Are you ready, Arabella? A winter wonderland is ready to explore. We have a full moon and lanterns to guide us."

This special surprise was for her alone. Everyone knew about it, and their smiles said they approved.

"Yes, I'm ready." She latched on to his arm. Was this a dream?

Mr. Rowe stepped toward Thomas. "Stick to the road. I don't want to have to dig you out."

Thomas sighed. "Yes, sir. I'll be careful."

Steward held the horse, a massive black shire. Arabella had seen one in a magazine. "What's his name?"

"Oakley. He's made for the snow and enjoys pulling a sleigh—or any conveyance." Steward patted the horse's neck.

Thomas placed the step close to the sleigh and guided Arabella to the bench. He placed a few bricks close to her feet and draped a wool blanket over her lap. "You should be warm enough without the wind blowing. It shouldn't snow this evening."

And I'll have you next to me.

Whoa, Arabella. This gift doesn't necessarily come with a warm embrace and handholding. At least, I don't think so.

For now, I have Thomas, a sleigh ride, a full moon, and a white world of possibilities.

CHAPTER TEN

o go on a sleigh ride in the Lake District a few weeks before Christmas with a handsome man at her side had never been on her wish list. But it should have been.

Thomas settled next to Arabella before taking the reins from Steward. "Ready?" He winked at her and clicked at Oakley. "Onward, boy."

As the sleigh jerked into motion, Arabella slipped her arm through Thomas's and scooted closer. She told herself it was for balance and security. Truthfully—for his warmth, strength, and well, wasn't that what a sleigh ride should be? He patted her hand and leaned his body toward hers.

Perfect.

She could close her eyes, absorb Thomas's presence, and create a romantic synopsis of what might happen. Or she could open her eyes and experience all the magic shining around her, in brilliant white, black, and midnight blue.

The only romantic scenario I want is this one.

Thomas whistled and Oakley trotted at an even pace as the sleigh glided over the snow. "The last time I went on a sleigh ride was with my grandfather before he passed away. Now, you've given me a reason to polish the old sleigh and put it to good use."

She tugged on his arm, bringing his gaze to hers. "Thank you, Thomas. You've made today very special. I've had many new experiences in Sawrey, but I didn't expect the place and people to become such an intricate part of my life."

The sleigh's lanterns swayed, sending streams of light dancing across the fields, scattering them into crystal patterns and mosaics. Silence masked the serene landscape, the place Arabella marked as full of promise and possibility.

Thomas's whisper joined the silence as if a part of the scenery. "Arabella, who are you becoming? What do you want?"

I want you.

"That's easy. This is what I want." She waved her hand in a half circle, encompassing the entire vista. All of Sawrey. Every pasture and sheep. The cottages, the woods, the creatures.

His sigh morphed into a chuckle. "You would give up London and all it offers? I thought when you returned there, you'd embrace society again."

"That was the plan—at least my parents' plan. But my heart is here. This feels more like home than London ever will. I love the sheep, the pigs, rabbits, squirrels. They hold my attention more than any fancy ballroom."

The silence, more pronounced than before, drowned out the horse's snorts and her pounding heart. Did he believe her? Voicing this truth propelled her into a course of action that her parents would reject. Yet, what if they saw how she melded into this society? Would they embrace her request? Could she stay?

Somewhere in her dreamy state, they had turned onto a narrow road off the main byway. With each smooth glide across the snow, Arabella saw the details of a house emerge, a multitude of lanterns outlining the drive. A multi-level home sprawled before them with yellow light flowing from the windows, beckoning them to come in and stay a while.

Thomas halted within the front gate. "This is my home. Nothing grand but ever so comfortable and more than meets my needs."

The oddest thing came to mind. She could see him here, fitting in much better than at the big house. A crackling fire, good books, hot cider.

"It is beautiful, Thomas." A perfect image, one seared in her mind forever.

He tied the reins over the handrail, turned in his seat, and faced her. Taking her gloved hands in his, he gazed at their linked fingers. Her hands were warm and comfortable in his. With the snow and cold wind whipping through the trees, she expected a constant chill. Not so, sitting here with Thomas so close.

His eyes, sparkling in the lantern's glow, shone as ebony with pinpricks of light against the white background. Never had a black and white world appealed to her. Usually, she was drawn to the vibrant splashes of color in her daily existence.

"Arabella." He squeezed her hands, pulling her closer. "You are so beautiful in the moonlight. I've wanted to show you my home and farm for months. But the right moment never came. I have envisioned you as part of my life, but it seemed like a dream."

The same dream had kept her awake many nights.

"I wonder if there is any hope of you sharing all of this with me." He cupped her cheek in his hand, caressing it with his fingers.

Nothing could stop her from moving nearer. He tilted her chin up and met her lips with his in the warmest touch, filling the evening with sparks of amazing, beautiful energy. She had no idea what to do with the closeness, the heat, the unspoken words. The cascading flames of fire blurred lines between dream and reality.

The pressure deepened against her lips, causing her breath to hitch and possibly fail her. But she regained her stability and marveled she could stay upright. Thomas's arms offset her weakness as she returned his kiss with equal fervor.

The minutes, or mere seconds, of the kiss ceased as Thomas touched her upper arms and released her lips. He rested his forehead on hers. "I know I should apologize, but I'm not sorry. I've wanted to kiss you for a long time."

The air filling her lungs centered her in the present. "Oh really. And how long would that be?"

"If not during the sheep drama, then in the field of wild-flowers soon after."

Oh, that was a long time. "Well, I'm glad you brought me here. The sleigh ride guaranteed you'd get your kiss."

"Arabella, there's so much I want to ask you. Before we go any farther . . ." He hesitated with a deep sigh. ". . . do you think you could live here?"

She adjusted her position and glanced around, noting the magical aura with the mixture of God's stars and moon and manmade light. "Here? In Sawrey?" What was he asking?

"At the moment, I would take a positive response for anywhere close in the Lake District so we could have every opportunity for our relationship to grow."

No promise of marriage or ever-after love? Was she relieved or disappointed? Could she be both?

"Yes, Thomas. I could stay. I've hinted at becoming an extended companion to my grandmother. She insists she doesn't need a constant companion worrying over her. A permanent live-in granddaughter, she'd take in a minute. But I have one enormous obstacle—my parents."

Thomas settled beside her with his arm around her, and she rested her head on his shoulder. "That's a tough one. I annoyed mine enough that they gave me a chance to prove myself. Maybe yours will too."

Prove what? That I can thrive outside of London and my parents' social parameters. That I can be happy outdoors, in a community with hardworking villagers and farm animals, with limited social engagements.

After untying the reins, Thomas glanced at her with his wide starlit eyes. "I want to ask you to be open to what the season can offer. I believe in miracles and God's plans." He winked. "I think you'll be surprised."

The physical distance between them on the snowy journey to Rowe Hall had diminished, resounding in a newfound warmth. Arabella refused to name the change, allowing time to dictate whether this was a snow mirage or a white wonderful miracle.

CHAPTER ELEVEN

*Q*uestions lingered after the sleigh ride. Over the next few days, Arabella's thoughts danced with different scenarios involving Thomas. The one question she desired, and dreaded to hear, resonated deep within her. Dare she let it out to germinate? No one needed to know her off-limits question.

Will you marry me?

The air in the parlor dissipated as she released the thought. She sat and hugged her knees, catching a cedar-scent. Now that it was out of her system, perhaps she could go about her chores.

Her parents had arrived yesterday. At least the decorations and Christmas party plans impressed them. Yet, her mother laced her comments with woes about Arabella's future.

Standing at the sound of the approaching footsteps, Arabella pressed her fist over her stomach. How simple life was with only her grandmother. Now, her parents could appear anywhere in the house.

"Arabella, there you are." Her mother wore a lacy day

dress that surpassed Arabella's everyday wear in the country. "Oh, you look like one of the servants. What if someone comes to call?"

Arabella's hands pressed down her white apron covering her blue and green checkered skirt. "Not to fear. I would remove my apron."

Sitting prim and proper in a high-backed armchair, her mother spread her skirt in elegant perfection. "What has happened to you? I can't believe you enjoy this . . . this country-lady existence. But I can see by your rosy cheeks and bright eyes that something about it appeals to you. Help me understand."

Her mother gestured for Arabella to sit on the sofa. Really? Since when had the socialite Virginia Graham wanted to know Arabella's opinion? Perhaps just this once, the season had worked a miracle.

"Mother, there are so many things." Arabella's imagination took hold, ready to express her love for this place and its people. "This village and this house are only the outward shell of what really exists here. The people make life blissful and purposeful. They bring the beauty that you see. I have found my place to flourish, not just for this season."

She reached for her mother's hand but pulled back. Not too much too soon. Nothing Arabella shared would appeal to her mother, but she continued. "The animals are amazing with their antics. Yes, the farms smell of livestock, but the flowers drape their unique aroma over the other. The walks, the hills, the vibrant colors, even the cloudy skies offer fresh air and comfort. Can't you, for a moment, admit the charm is compelling?"

Her mother relaxed into the chair and studied Arabella in silence. Where were the words of contradiction? Arabella searched and found her mother's lips curved into a smile, eyes glowing with softness.

"I don't know what it is, Arabella, but something is different about you in this place. You are not sulking or frowning. Instead, my dear girl, you are healthy and happy. I do wonder if something else has awakened your senses."

Yes, Thomas.

Seconds later her mother reached for Arabella, stood, and brought Arabella with her. "When you have time, I'd like to go on one of these walks you've mentioned."

Could it be that her mother was willing to accept Arabella and her dreams?

BETWEEN HER PARENTS' arrival and the final details for the festivities, Arabella only saw Thomas in church and once at the pub where she introduced him to her parents. Politeness all around. Even her father let some of his social polish blend into a nicer, less abrasive version.

But at the same time, Thomas poured on a smidgen of his Oxford shine which he had discarded ever since they'd met.

I guess we all have a bit of social whitewash at the ready.

The long-awaited gathering would unfold in a few hours. Arabella had time to talk to the kitchen help and servers, check the greenery and decorations, and tend to her appearance.

Breathe. This will be nothing like the London season. It's friends and family.

Marie helped her slip into her silver gown with a sheer overlay, the silver threads catching every ray of light. Arabella twirled in front of the cheval mirror. She fingered a silver butterfly on a thin silver chain. Her mother might drip in diamonds and jewels, but this was enough for Arabella.

She patted her hair, hoping the pins held the high chignon in place. The only person she desired to impress was Thomas.

Would he step into her dream and ask the only question she desired to hear? Her answer was ready. The obstacles had not moved, except, perhaps, a layer of doubt about her mother's reaction had shifted.

She released a solitary groan. It could all be for nothing. The big, "what if," hung beside the mistletoe. Would he step forward? Or would she? Or would they both take a wide berth around the subject?

Oh, Thomas.

THOMAS ARRIVED at Graham Retreat and left his hat and gloves with the butler. His perusal of the rooms—with the glittering lights and the rich greenery sprinkled with bows and ribbons—would not have occupied his thoughts except this was what Arabella had poured her time into for two weeks.

He had barely spoken to her, much less carried her off to dinner or a moonlight carriage ride. The last moments he'd had alone with her included the *kiss. The* unbelievable kiss. Why had he not asked her the all-important question that night? If he had, would the answer have been 'yes'?

Thomas's fine attire matched his father's, Mr. Graham, and a few other gentlemen with gray pants and black jackets. The rest of the men wore their brown, green, and comfortable best suits.

He searched and found Arabella standing with Lady Graham by the mantle. A perfect vision he wished he could capture with his camera. Perhaps one day soon. Her rosy cheeks and luminous eyes gave her an ethereal glow. The dress of silver filaments contributed to the angelic image.

His Arabella. *Almost.*

His parents preceded him in line. When Arabella placed

her hand in his, the warmth seeped through her gloves into his fingers. "Happy Christmas, Arabella." He bowed and kissed her hand. "You look beautiful."

"I'm glad you're here." She pulled him closer and whispered, "What do you think? Isn't it beautiful?" She gazed around the room.

"Yes. Gorgeous." His glance never left her face. "Do you think we can talk later? Preferably under the mistletoe."

Arabella blushed and tapped his arm with gloved fingers. "Thomas, behave. Go mingle. I have a job to do."

He returned her wide grin. "Later, then."

When had he ever felt so cocooned in the season? It was not only the decorations and light shining from every corner and wall. Christmas had seeped into his soul. It lodged into his being, too special to put into words.

He gravitated toward a small table covered with lacy material, sprinkled with thin red and gold ribbons. The creche displayed on pieces of golden hay reminded him that Mary, Joseph, the shepherds, and the angels knew the true meaning, and it had nothing to do with decorations and gifts. There, in the middle of wooly animals, smelly remains from a stable, and earthly objects of a common life Jesus, his Savior, had been born.

Covering his heart with his hand, Thomas remembered it all. The truth was as simple as one of Beatrix's stories. Except this was life changing.

The celebration of the birth of Jesus wrapped around his heart. Filled with awe and thankfulness, Thomas embraced His ultimate sacrifice and purpose. He had a lifelong commitment to Jesus, and it wasn't tied up with ribbons and sparkles.

Thomas breathed with renewed hope. *The tale of the season is permanently right here inside me.*

CHAPTER TWELVE

*A*rabella left her grandmother's side and mingled as a hostess should. Stretching on tiptoes, she yearned to spot Thomas. She didn't see him, but she found Beatrix by the Christmas tree. She had missed her friend while in London, although Beatrix had left the area too.

"Beatrix, thank you for coming."

The woman's attire aligned with her social status, one she'd wear for events in London. The hunter green satin skirt and lacy cream-colored blouse with a seed pearl trim elevated Beatrix in Arabella's mind. It proved one of Arabella's notions. One could dress the part without being glued to the role.

"My dear Arabella. I've been awaiting this time since I received your invitation. Everything is beautiful. You and your grandmother are a truly inspiring duo."

Beatrix bent and retrieved a package from under the tree. "I have a little something for you."

Arabella accepted the rectangular gift. "For me?" Beatrix nodded, and Arabella kissed her cheek. "I have one for you too." She reached for a red paper wrapped package and held it out. "Happy Christmas."

They shared the wonder of opening gifts like school children—with sighs and wide-eyed amazement.

Soft laughter accompanied Arabella's excitement as she gazed at the watercolor painting of the Sawrey hills with yellows and greens meeting the blue and white sky. "Oh, you gave me an original painting." A signature piece. "Thank you, Beatrix." The image blurred through tears.

Beatrix unwrapped her gift. "Ah, finally, one of your creations." She held up a silver broach with wildflowers from Hill Top pressed beneath the glass. "I will always have a bit of home with me."

Arabella had carefully picked, pressed, and designed a colorful creation unique to the Lake District.

They hugged through tears before returning their gifts to a hideaway spot behind the tree.

Beatrix glanced around the room and nodded to someone behind Arabella. "One piece of advice if you care to listen to someone who knows." Arabella fixed her attention on Beatrix. "Don't miss your chance."

"My chance? For what?" What was she missing?

"For love." Beatrix patted Arabella's arm and stepped around her into the celebratory crowd.

Love? What did Beatrix know?

Arabella turned toward the guests. The first person in view was Thomas, leaning against the door frame by the parlor. Was that who Beatrix meant? Loving him would not be a problem. That was a given. But love needed to go two ways.

Thomas's black jacket fit his broad shoulders and muscular arms, making him extremely handsome tonight. His curly brown hair, without his customary hat, touched his collar. He looked so sure and confident. Why shouldn't he be?

He straightened and gestured her forward before he tilted his head slightly toward the parlor.

She pointed to herself and mouthed, "me?"

He nodded then left his post.

This is my chance.

The perfect Christmas miracle of Christ's birth was more than enough on any day. But tonight, could she hope for an additional miracle designed especially for her purpose and life in this world.

Arabella knew that happily-ever-afters belonged in fairy-tales. What if this place, this time, and these people were *her* story? Her imagination could stop its wondering and searching. Especially if her fairytale included a happy ever after for her and Thomas.

She followed him past people and through the rooms, not stopping when she heard her name or when someone touched her sleeve. For all she knew, she might have ignored her parents and Lilly and numerous others. Thomas determined her steps and attention.

Finally, the circles of guests disappeared as she entered her grandmother's sunroom, a modern addition to the back of the house. He took her hand and drew her toward a table with a small Christmas tree.

"Thomas." The candlelight danced in his eyes as the tug, like puppet strings, continued to pull her toward him. "What are we doing here?"

"Hmm." He took the last step between them and ran his fingers along her cheek. "We are enjoying a quiet moment away from everyone."

She pressed her cheek into his palm. "I know that. But why?"

He released her for a second and drew something out of his pocket. "Will this help remind you?" He held up a sprig of mistletoe, dangling it in front of her before raising it above their heads.

Heat warmed her cheeks and neck. "Mistletoe. You remembered."

He placed his arm around her waist and peered down at her upturned face. "I've thought of little else. Your kisses hold so much promise. Why would I chance missing anymore? May I?"

"Yes, perhaps one." *Or two or three.*

His hand holding the sprig relaxed and rested on her neck, guiding her into the perfect position for his promised kiss. The warmth of his lips against hers sent a tingling all the way to her toes. She wanted to bolt and continue at the same time. Curiosity . . . and the promise of love held her firmly within his arms.

Love for a country farmer and local veterinarian. She would deal with the heirdom and estate later.

He pulled away, dropping kisses on her nose and forehead. "There is more."

"More kisses?" She rose on her toes and pulled him closer.

"Perhaps later, Arabella. There are some things you need to know."

How could a smile look so serious? She'd have to curtail her kissing fantasy for now. Was he leaving? Was someone ill?

"All right." She dropped her hands to her sides. "I guess it is sort of difficult to kiss and talk at the same time. Is it bad news?" What if she burst out with, "I love you?" Would that make everything better or worse?

He ran his fingers through his hair before placing his hands in his pockets. "Arabella, I love you."

She struggled to catch her breath and swayed. He reached for her, steadying her with his gentle touch. "You love me? You really love me?"

"Oh, my dear. Why is that so difficult to understand? I love you and have for a long time."

She shook under his hold and pushed out a deep breath. "I love you too. My fear prevented me from acting on it. It's an impossible situation. I live in—"

"I know. You live in London, and I live here. Could you choose Sawrey over London, a simple life over a social one, me over all others? Arabella, will you marry me?"

She nodded, and her heart screamed yes. But how could she let love be enough with so many questions? "Thomas, what about my parents and yours?"

He placed both his hands on her upper arms, as he bent to be even with her eyes. "Are they enough to stand in our way? Will you marry me even if no one supports us?"

Her doubts flew away. She had prayed for God's plan and purpose and received His answer at this moment.

"Yes, yes. I will marry you. Now, soon. I choose you, the hills, and your farmhouse. I choose love."

She bounced on her toes, hugged him tightly, and kissed him with a forceful seal of more to come.

When Thomas caught his breath, he reached into his pocket again, withdrew a tiny box, and opened it. A silver band with pearls and rubies caught the candlelight. "I had this made for you in Oxford. Thank you for promising to roam these hills and fields with me for a lifetime."

He slipped the ring on her finger. A perfect fit. Its brilliance didn't compare to the light rising in her heart. Nothing else mattered. They had each other and would forge into the future together.

"One other thing." He held her hand close to his heart. "On the night of the sleigh ride, your parents gave me their permission and blessing."

The wall crumbled, and the debris flew away. "Truly? That's a miracle indeed."

He nodded. "Arabella, they love you and want you to be loved. They see this is the journey meant for you. Perhaps it's a bit off the path they desired, but it's the right one for you and for us. I love you."

"And I love you."

She smiled as the pieces of her life's puzzle moved into place. In Beatrix's story, *The Tale of Squirrel Nutkin*, the mischievous animal followed his own schemes and survived, but with his tail cut off. Arabella had strayed from her parents' plan for her life, sometimes using methods that seemed wayward, but Beatrix's advice along the way and God's plan brought her to this place with her life and her tail intact.

Arabella and Thomas wandered back to the Christmas celebration hand-in-hand into the loving, congratulatory arms of family and friends.

Beatrix winked at them as if she had spun the tale herself.

Arabella knew it was more than a tale. God's best workmanship created love beyond measure. This life had God's design all over it.

PART IV
CHRISTMAS IN TETBURY
DECEMBER 2024

After a cozy dinner at the Priory Inn, Nathan offered to escort Emma and Mimi back to Harrison's Rare Books and Antiques. As they strolled down the street, Emma tucked her hands into her pockets and glanced up at the star-studded sky and then at Nathan.

Their conversation over dinner had flowed easily. He asked her about her family, and she told him her parents had retired to Italy, and her brother was married and lived in Glasgow. The conversation shifted to what they liked to do in their free time, and she told him about visiting several National Trust estates. He mentioned hiking and volunteering as an ESL teacher at his church each Thursday evening. Hearing him speak openly about his faith and involvement in his church community had touched her heart.

Emma released a wistful sigh. He had so many good qualities. If only they lived closer to one another.

Her thoughts returned to the story Mimi had shared at dinner. "Thanks for telling us about Arabella and Thomas.

I'm glad they finally found their way past the issues that separated them."

Nathan nodded. "I'll be sure to tell my mum the story behind her gift."

Emma smiled, imagining him repeating the tale to his family. "I've always admired Beatrix Potter's storytelling gifts. It's good to know she was a faithful friend as well as a talented artist."

Mimi tucked her arm through Emma's. "I believe Beatrix's example of balancing family expectations with finding purpose in life were a great help to Arabella."

Emma pondered Arabella's longing to escape London and enjoy life in the country. It stirred thoughts about the direction of her own life. Now that the door had closed at the British Museum, did she really want to return to London? She had no job, no income, and few friends there. The last two weeks in Tetbury had reminded her of a different kind of life —one where family, faith, and community made each day meaningful.

Their steps slowed as they approached the front door to the shop.

Mimi took her keys from her pocket and turned to Nathan. "Thank you for walking us home. That was very thoughtful."

He nodded. "My pleasure." He reached into his jacket, took out two business cards, and handed one to Mimi and the other to Emma. "If you ever need an estate agent, I hope you'll text or call."

Mimi smiled as she scanned the card. "I'm not planning to move, but thank you, Nathan. I'll hold on to this." Her gaze shifted from Emma to Nathan. "Good night." She stepped inside and closed the door, leaving them standing outside.

Emma's face heated, and she looked down at the card.

Mimi couldn't have been more obvious. Would Nathan take the hint and suggest they get together again?

"Well . . . it's been a great evening." He shifted his weight to the other foot. "I'm glad I had a chance to get to know you . . . and your grandmother."

She looked up and met his gaze. "Yes. I enjoyed tonight. Thank you for dinner."

He pulled in a deep breath. "I should go. It's a bit of a drive back to my place."

She forced a smile, pushing away her disappointment and wishing for more. "Good night, Nathan."

He hesitated, looking as though he wanted to say more, but then he nodded and walked toward his car.

She watched him climb in and start the engine. She should go inside. It was silly to stand on the doorstep and wave goodbye to a man she'd only met that morning. She did it anyway, and her heart sank as his car disappeared around the corner.

After breakfast the next morning, Mimi asked her to watch the shop while she went to the dentist for her annual checkup. Emma happily agreed and kept busy updating the shop's website and greeting customers who came in looking for last-minute Christmas gifts.

She turned on instrumental Christmas carols and rearranged a few displays. Her gaze caught the Beatrix Potter figurines, and her thoughts returned to Nathan. Slipping her hand in her skirt pocket, she felt the smooth texture of his business card.

He'd said she could call or text. She shook her head. Maybe she was old-fashioned, but she didn't want to be the one to reach out first. If he was interested, he would have to make the next move. She bit her lip and fingered the card, questioning her stance.

How likely was she to meet someone else like Nathan? She replayed their conversation in the teashop and then over dinner, considering what she'd learned. He was hardworking and successful at his job, and he cared about his family. He seemed sincere about his faith and was thoughtful and well spoken. She sensed a definite connection and attraction. Not just physical—it was something deeper.

Did he feel it too?

She closed her eyes. *Lord, You know what's in my heart and in Nathan's. If there's something more for us, please make it obvious to us both.*

Mimi returned at eleven carrying a pretty Christmas tin. She popped off the lid and the scent of ginger and cinnamon filled the air. Mimi held out the tin filled with ginger biscuits.

"Mmm, those look delicious." Emma selected one and took a bite, savoring the sweet chewy treat.

"I stopped in to see my friend Nancy at Creswell's Bakery. She sent these for us to enjoy."

"That was thoughtful."

Mimi slipped off her coat and hung it in the closet. "I had a call from Arleta while I was there."

"The woman who works here with you?"

"Yes. Her daughter had a baby boy three days ago."

Emma smiled. "That's wonderful." A new life was always good news.

"Yes, it is. Arleta is smitten. Her daughter wants her to stay, and she agreed."

Emma's eyes widened. "You mean she's not coming back to work with you?"

"That's right. She resigned." Rather than looking upset, Mimi's eyes shone. "I have an idea."

"What is it?"

"You have all the skills needed to run this shop and make it even more successful. Would you consider staying?'

Emma stared at her grandmother. "You want me to stay and work here?"

"Yes. I've loved having you with me. And I'm not getting any younger. I'd like more free time. If you were here, we could share the load, and then one day, when the time is right, I could pass on the shop to you."

Emma's gaze darted around the shop. Could she stay? Was this the next step she should take? She turned to Mimi. "I love the idea, but are you sure you want to pass it on to me? You've invested more than thirty years into this business."

Mimi nodded. "I've been thinking and praying about this for some time. Your visit and Arleta's decision seem like confirmations."

Emma's thoughts spun. The events of the last few weeks had freed her from most of her commitments in London. The lease on her flat was a month-to-month agreement and could be easily canceled. Moving to Tetbury and working with Mimi would give her a new focus and the fresh start she needed.

She reached for Mimi's hand. "This would be a big step for both of us."

Mimi's eyes glowed with confidence. "Yes, it would. But if you're willing to stay, I'd be delighted to have you as my partner, and then one day the shop will be yours. We'll put it in writing and do everything properly."

Emma pulled her grandmother in for a hug. "This is amazing. Thanks so much."

Mimi stepped back. "I don't want you to feel you must live with me. If you'd like to find your own place, I'm perfectly fine with that."

Emma's heart lifted, and she couldn't hold back a grin. "A new home in Tetbury sounds wonderful."

"Of course, you're welcome to stay with me as long as you like." Mimi's eyes twinkled. "But I happen to know an estate agent who could help you find the ideal place."

Emma's cheeks warmed. What would Nathan say when he heard she was staying? Should she call him and let him know? It gave her the perfect opportunity to reconnect. But she wasn't in a position to buy a house. She had some savings, yet even renting a flat might be out of reach for a time.

Emma pulled in a deep breath. "I'd eventually like to have my own place in Tetbury, but for now, I'd like to stay with you." And when she was ready, she knew someone who would be glad to help.

Christmas Eve finally arrived. Emma and Mimi closed the shop early, had dinner with three of Mimi's friends, and attended the candlelight Christmas Eve service. As they returned home, a soft snowfall dusted the village, making it look like someone had sprinkled powdered sugar on plum pudding.

Emma slept peacefully that night, relieved and thankful for answered prayers.

On Christmas morning, she and Mimi exchanged gifts and enjoyed a leisurely brunch. Still in their pajamas and robes, they watched their favorite Christmas movie, *While You Were Sleeping,*

As the credits rolled, the shop cell phone rang. Mimi waved her hand. "Just let it go. No one should be calling on Christmas day."

Emma sensed a stirring in her spirit and rose from her

chair. "Maybe it's important. I'll get it." She crossed the room and lifted the phone. "Hello?"

"Emma? This is Nathan Bridgman. I'm calling to wish you a Happy Christmas."

Her heart swelled, and her smile spread wide. "Hi, Nathan. Thank you, and Happy Christmas to you."

Mimi's eyes lit up, and she lifted her hand to cover her delighted grin.

Emma crossed to stand by the Christmas tree and looked out the bay window. "I hope your mum enjoyed her gift."

"Oh, she did. You should've seen her face. She was so happy. Thank you for helping me."

"You're welcome. I'm glad we had what you were looking for."

A few beats of silence followed. "So . . . I'm not working tomorrow on Boxing Day, and I wondered if you'd like to go with me to visit a historic estate near Bristol. It's a beautiful place called Tyntesfield. Have you heard of it?"

"No, I haven't."

"They decorate for Christmas, and the reviews online say it's well worth a visit."

She suppressed a squeal. He was asking her out on a date! "That sounds wonderful. I'd love to go with you. Thanks."

"Great. I'll pick you up at 1:00." She could hear the relief in his voice. "It's about an hour's drive. We can take our time touring the house, and then have an early dinner. How does that sound?"

"It sounds perfect" She laughed softly.

"What's so funny?" There was a smile in his voice as he asked.

"I'm just glad you called." She pulled in a deep breath. "It feels like a very special Christmas gift."

He chuckled. "Well, that's good to hear. I wasn't sure how

long you were staying in Tetbury, and I wanted to see you again, so I thought I'd better call today."

Her smile spread wider. "Well . . . I have some news. I've decided to stay."

"Really?"

"Yes. Mimi invited me to help manage the shop, so Tetbury will be my new home."

"Oh, wow. That's great . . . I'd say you've just given me a special Christmas gift."

Her heart did a little dance. He'd called. He'd made plans to spend time with her and chosen something he knew she would enjoy. Tomorrow couldn't come soon enough. And she had a feeling this was just the first of many days they would enjoy together.

Emma said goodbye to Nathan and clicked off the call. With her heart full of anticipation, she reached out and touched the Christmas tree ornament featuring a grandmother reading to a little girl. She'd given it to Mimi that morning as a reminder of the special bond she shared—a love for stories that touched hearts and changed lives.

Mimi crossed the room and joined her by the Christmas tree. "What did Nathan say?"

"He asked me to go with him tomorrow to tour an estate and then have dinner."

Mimi's eyes rounded. "Oh, that makes me so happy!"

Emma grinned, and Mimi pulled her in for a hug. Closing her eyes, Emma soaked in the warmth of her grandmother's love and offered a grateful prayer of thanks for Mimi, for Nathan, and for all that was to come.

Christmas in Tetbury had turned out even better than she'd dreamed. It was the perfect place to enjoy a very English Christmas with family and faith to treasure and hope that would carry her into the new year.

If you Enjoyed this book, We hope you'll leave a review on Amazon, GoodReads, or BookBub.
Thank You!

Your Next Great Read Awaits at Our Websites!
Carole Lehr Johnson : https://carolelehrjohnson.com/
Carrie Turansky: https://carrieturansky.com/
Marguerite Gray: https://margueritemartingray.com/

AUTHORS' NOTES

Dear Readers, thank you for traveling with us to England and stepping into the lives of three literary figures we admire —Jane Austen, Charles Dickens, and Beatrix Potter.

We enjoyed researching their lives and learning more about their writing. We hope these stories help you to imagine what their daily lives and friendship might have been like. Their influence continues today through their writing and commitment to create characters and stories that reflect life, love, and lessons for the heart.

From Carole:

Jane Austen holds the hearts of millions of women around the world. I've had the good fortune to visit her homes in Chawton, Bath, and Steventon—some more than once. Her writing has captured the attention of readers since 1811, although she published her first work, Sense and Sensibility, anonymously as By a Lady. Stepping where she walked so long ago, in the rooms where she lived, and the countryside she loved so dearly, brought me closer to this beloved author.

Her works encompass romance, wit, and the social customs of the day, as well as the moral conduct woven through her well-documented faith. Only three of Jane's prayers survive, thankfully available in the public domain.

Such a remarkable woman left us with much to consider about life, love, and relationships. Researching the era in which she lived has been a joy, and I apologize if I have included any historical information inaccurately. Learn more about my books at my website: https://carolelehrjohnson.com/

From Carrie:

Charles Dickens is such an interesting man! I enjoyed learning more about him and creating fictional characters to weave into his life around the time he was writing A Christmas Carol. He did have a good friend who acted as his first reader and encourager, but I have changed his name and fictionalized their interactions. *A Christmas Carol* is a timeless story that has themes and lessons that are still relevant today. I recently listened to it on audio and encourage you to listen or read it this Christmas season! Please visit my website to learn more about my novels and novellas: Learn more about my books at my website: https://carrieturansky.com/

From Marguerite:

As a preteen I visited Hill Top in the Lake District, the land of Beatrix Potter where I fell in love with her adventurous characters, especially Squirrel Nutkin. The year 1906 is a pivotal time for Beatrix as she gained her independence with the purchase of Hill Top. Arabella, my fictional character, learns how to navigate life's choices through her friendship with Beatrix. I hope you enjoy the whimsical journey with new friends. Please visit my website to learn more about my books: https://margueritemartingray.com/

MORE BOOKS TO ENJOY

Books By Carrie Turansky

Free Short Story at Carrie's Website
Keeper of Her Heart

Stand Alone English Historical Novels
Shine Like the Dawn
Across the Blue
The Legacy of Longdale Manor
A Token of Love

The McAlister Family Series
No Ocean Too Wide
No Journey Too Far

The Edwardian Brides Series
The Governess of Highland Hall
The Daughter of Highland Hall
A Refuge at Highland Hall

The Bayside Treasures Series
Seeking His Love
A Man to Trust
Snowflake Sweethearts

Stand Alone Contemporary Novels
Along Came Love
Surrendered Hearts

Novellas and Novella Collections
Where Two Hearts Meet
Christmas Mail-Order Brides
Waiting for His Return
Moonlight Over Manhattan
A Very English Christmas

∾

Books By Marguerite Gray

Revolutionary Faith Series
Hold Me Close, Book One
Surround Me, Book Two
Bring Me Near, Book Three

Elements of Hope Series
Flames of Faith

Novellas
Crystal Clear, A Christmas Novella
Promise Me Christmas
A Very English Christmas

Nonfiction
Spanish for the Short-term Missionary

∾

Books By Carole Lehr Johnson
Permelia Cottage
A Place in Time
The Burning Sands
Of the Past and Eternity
Christmas at Permelia Cottage
Seasons of the Past
Woven in the Mist
A Very English Christmas

DO YOU LOVE READING OR WRITING NOVELS SET IN THE UK & IRELAND?

Join us at Inspirational UK & Ireland - Books, Readers, and More Facebook Group!

Each week we discuss books we've enjoyed along with travel photos, and fun facts about the UK & Ireland. We invite authors whose books are set in those countries to sign up for a Take Over Tuesday and share about their books, research, and themselves. It's a lively and supportive group of readers and authors.

You'll find Carole, Marguerite, and Carrie there, and we'd love to connect with you! Visit the group: https://www.face book.com/groups/285183069885837